A Charter For The Commonwealth

by

RICHARD F. WEYAND

RICHARD F. WEYAND

ISBN 978-1-7321280-2-6
Printed in the United States of America

Cover Credits
Planet Image by: Nastco
Spaceship Room by: Natalia_80
Standing Woman by: miya227
Seated Man by: Romax Productions
Composition by: Romax Productions
Model: Nelson Shaffer
Back Cover Photo: Oleg Volk

Published by Weyand Associates, Inc.
Bloomington, Indiana, USA
June, 2018

CONTENTS

A Charter For The Commonwealth

Most of the names of the characters in this book are the names of Facebook friends who volunteered their names for that use. However, this book is a work of fiction. All of the characters, institutions, and activities described in this book are fictitious, and any resemblance to actual people, institutions, or activities are completely coincidental.

As just one example, Arlan Andrews, the major villain in the book, is also the name of a great guy and a really nice person.

Thank you to all those who volunteered their names.

R.F.W.

RICHARD F. WEYAND

The Invitation

The Honorable James Allen Westlake VI looked south out of the picture window of the Planetary Governor's office of the Earth colony on the planet Jablonka. His capital city of Jezgra spread out before him, both south and east. To the west was the great sea, the Voda Ocean.

The decision point had finally come, and he hesitated on the cusp.

His father, patriarch of one of the great families of Earth, had arranged this appointment for him ten years before. Then only twenty-eight years old, he was given administrative control of the entire planet, indeed the entire system. His charter was to maximize the profits Earth might make from the colony – from its asteroid mining operations, from its exports, and from tariffs on the imports the colony needed to expand, or even to survive.

He and his wife, Suzette Westlake nee Fournier, herself the progeny of another of the great families, had moved here with their two small children. And, over the years, a curious thing had happened. They had fallen in love.

With the planet. With its people. With their spirit.

They had come to believe the path they were on was not the best one, for Jablonka, for Earth's other colonies, for humanity – even, long term, for Earth itself. Managing Earth's colonies for the benefit of a hundred or so wealthy families on Earth, they knew, did not lead down the path to humanity's best and brightest future.

Westlake had thought long and hard on it, but now his time was running out. There were ten years remaining on his charter as planetary governor, at which point he would be expected to return to Earth and assume control of his father's holdings for the benefit of his children, siblings and cousins. He had set the ten-year anniversary of assuming the governorship as his decision point, and it was now here.

He went over to his desk and, on a piece of his engraved stationery, wrote a brief note. He sealed it in a matching envelope, wrote two names on the envelope, and rang for his driver.

1

Professor Gerald Ansen and his wife, Professor Mineko Kusunoki, were both at home today, it being between terms at the University of Jablonka. Ansen, at 68 years old, was retired from the university's history department, while Kusunoki, age 39, was a professor of sociology.

Ansen had been one of the fledgling university's first graduates almost fifty years before, and had moved back to Jablonka after receiving his doctorate on Earth, from Oxford University. Kusunoki was Earth born, and had accepted a position with the University of Jablonka after receiving her doctoral degree from the University of Tokyo. Their fields of study overlapped, and they had fallen in love despite the difference in their ages.

For all that, their marriage was a curious one. Ansen had tremendous appetites – for food, for drink, for tobacco, and for female companionship. He was a notorious roue, and had not slacked off once married. Kusunoki, by contrast, was a homebody, most comfortable curled up in the big armchair in her office, reading, writing, and studying. The part of their relationship most important to both of them was on the intellectual level, and their discussions of politics, history, and social organization would often run long into the night.

They were both at home when the large unmarked ground car pulled up in front of their home in Jezgra just after lunch.

"I'll get it," Ansen called to Kusunoki when the doorbell rang. He got up from his desk and walked out of his office, across the hall from hers, and down the hallway to the front door.

When he opened the door, he was a little nonplussed to see a man in a plain black uniform there, with the big black ground car at the curb behind him. He half expected to be arrested, on the grounds his writings were subversive or treasonous, but the uniformed man merely handed him a small envelope.

"I was instructed to wait for any response, sir."

"Well, come in, come in," Ansen said.

"I'll wait here, sir. Take your time."

"Very well."

Ansen closed the door, leaving the uniformed man on the stoop, and looked at the envelope. Kusunoki had joined him in the entry to see who their visitor was.

"It's addressed to both of us."

Ansen pulled a small penknife from his pocket and slit the envelope open. He extracted a single-folded piece of stationery with the planetary governor's seal. The note was personally written in a precise and decorative hand:

> *Profs. Ansen & Kusunoki,*
> *I would appreciate the courtesy of a visit*
> *at your earliest opportunity.*
> *James Allen Westlake*

"I'll be damned," Ansen said, and handed the note to Kusunoki.

"That goes without saying," she said as she accepted it.

Kusunoki read the note and handed it back.

"It's not an arrest warrant, unless it's a camouflaged one," she said.

"I half expected one by this time. I have been pretty blunt in my writings the last ten years or so. 'Life in prison' just doesn't have the sting it once did."

Kusunoki chuckled. "So are we going to meet with him?"

"Oh, certainly. My curiosity is killing me. What would the scion of one of Earth's most powerful autocratic families want with a classical liberal rabble-rouser like myself other than to see me hanged?"

"Convince you to see the error of your ways?"

"Unlikely. Well, I suppose there's only one way to find out. Are you available right now if the driver says now's a good time?"

"Sure. Just let me grab a wrap."

Ansen opened the door. The driver was still waiting on the stoop.

"Would now be a good time to visit his Excellency?" Ansen asked.

"Yes, sir. I was told now would be a good time if you were free."

Kusunoki came back with a shawl around her shoulders.

"All right, then," Ansen said. "Let's go see Mr. Westlake."

The Proposal

"Ah, Professors. Come in, come in."

The young, handsome, and impeccably dressed Westlake came around his desk to greet his professorially rumpled visitors, and shook their hands in turn, beginning with Kusunoki.

"Pleased to meet you, Professor Kusunoki. And you as well, Professor Ansen. Please, be seated."

Westlake waved them to the side seating arrangement in his office, and Ansen and Kusunoki took seats on the large sofa. Westlake sat in a chair opposite.

"Can I offer you some refreshment? Tea, perhaps?" Westlake said to Kusunoki.

"Tea would be lovely. Thank you, Excellency."

"And you, Professor Ansen? I have a very good bourbon you might enjoy."

Ansen was surprised at Westlake's due diligence, but replied evenly. "A large bourbon, with just a touch of ice, would be welcome, Excellency."

"Excellent." Westlake turned to the butler who had shown them in. "And a coffee for me, Henson."

"Very good, sir."

There was a finely crafted cigar humidor, with ashtray, cutter, and lighter, on the coffee table. Westlake turned the humidor toward Ansen and pushed it in his direction on the coffee table.

"Please, Professor Ansen, feel free."

Ansen raised an eyebrow, and Westlake nodded. Ansen opened the humidor and selected a cigar, an Earth import, which made it deliriously expensive. He unwrapped it, cut the end off, and lighted it. Westlake was content to sit back and wait while he did so.

Only when Ansen was settled with his cigar, did Westlake begin.

"First, thank you for coming to see me."

Ansen waved his cigar in a dismissive gesture, and Kusunoki nodded.

"I want to ask you some questions, which pertain directly to your academic specialties. I believe I already know the answers, but I want to confirm them with you. Then I might have a small proposal to make to you.

"First, are the Earth's current political and economic arrangements with the colony planets sustainable, oh, say, on the medium term?"

Ansen and Kusunoki looked at each other and back to Westlake.

"This is not some sort of trap," Westlake said. "First, for my own safety, this conversation is not being recorded. Second, as I said, I believe I already know the answers to these questions, so I will just tell you I do not believe they are sustainable on the medium term. Am I right in that?"

"Yes, that's right," Ansen answered, and Kusunoki nodded.

There was an interruption as the butler returned with a tray, which he set on a side table. He had a small pot of tea for Kusunoki, a small pot of coffee for Westlake, and a small tray with cream, sugar, and lemon wedges, which he set between them. Cups, saucers, and spoons followed. He then put a large rocks glass of bourbon with a single ice cube in front of Ansen. He also set the bourbon decanter and a small bowl of ice cubes, with tongs, on the coffee table and followed them with a small plate of cookies in the center of the table.

"Thank you, Henson," Westlake said.

"Certainly, sir."

After the butler had left and closed the door behind him, Westlake resumed his questioning.

"When the current situation changes, how does it change? What is the most likely scenario?"

"The pressure continues to build," Kusunoki said, "until the colonies rebel against Earth's rule and seek, and ultimately win, their independence."

"This is because the distances are so great. Is that right, Professor Kusunoki?"

"That's correct, Excellency. The physical division, combined with the unequal relationship, results in growing pressure until the political division occurs."

Westlake nodded. "And when the colonies split off, do they do so one at a time, or in groups?"

"If the split is earlier, it has to be in groups. Strength in numbers. The longer it is until the split happens, the more the pressure builds and the more likely it is the split is piecemeal."

"And how violent is the split?"

"The violence will be proportional to the force disparity between Earth and the splitting colony or colonies."

"So the stronger the splitting group is, the less violence there will be?"

"That's right. It's counterintuitive, but small rebellions get put down much more viciously than large ones. There is less possibility of reprisal against the parent country, so there is less restraint in the response."

"And what sort of government do the splitting colonies end up with?"

Until this point, Ansen had been content to sip his bourbon and smoke his cigar, but at this question he stirred and took the floor.

"Historically, it could be just about anything, Excellency. Representative republic, loose commonwealth, strongman autarchy, plutocracy, fascism, communism, it runs the gamut. It depends."

"On what does it most depend, Professor Ansen?"

"On the structures already in place."

"So whatever is in place at the time of the split, remains in place?"

"Usually. By the time the split is *fait accompli*, everyone is tired of the destruction and disruption, and they work with the existing structure. The alternative is to go through another period of disruption to change it, and people are weary of the whole process by that point. Change won't come for at least another generation, usually two."

"All right. Good," Westlake said. "I appreciate your honest answers. I had gotten this far on my own, and I'm glad I was right.

"So let's review. The current situation is not sustainable on the medium term. The colonies will split off from Earth and pursue their own goals as one or more independent nations. The amount of violence associated with that will be held to a minimum if the colonies stick together. And the ultimate structure of the resulting colony government will be a reflection of the structure under which the split occurs."

Kusunoki and Ansen both nodded.

"That's a good summary of the most likely outcomes, yes," Ansen said.

"And, if the colony government that results is, for example, a

6

representative government, with broad individual freedoms along classical liberal lines, what happens next?"

Ansen raised an eyebrow, and Westlake chuckled.

"Over the last five years, I have read everything you have ever written on the subject, Professor Ansen. I know your politics like the back of my hand. Let's say your dream government emerges from the split. What happens next?"

"Historically speaking, Earth and the colonies fight another war, at Earth's instigation, to finally settle the issue."

"And?"

"Earth loses. The current structure can't compete with an open society."

"And?"

"The Earth government falls."

"And is replaced by what?"

"Sooner or later, an open society. It has to be, to compete. Either that or it falls into backwardness and, ultimately, irrelevance."

"And what would the relationship between the colonies and the Earth government be then, Professor Ansen?"

"Friends, Excellency. Plenty of historical precedent there. Britain and India. Britain and the United States of America. France and Vietnam. France and Algeria."

"Yes, that's right," Kusunoki said. "With the political pressures resolved, the cultural ties draw the colonies back into a relationship with the colonial power, but now in a friendship of equals."

Westlake nodded, and sat back in his chair smiling.

"You see," Westlake said, "you two are professionals, students of this area with decades of experience. You have thought through all these issues, studied them, written about them. How things have unfolded in the past –" with a nod to Ansen "– and why they unfold that way –" with a nod to Kusunoki. "I have had to work my way through your writings, and give quite a bit of thought to it, to replicate that understanding. But, now that we are all agreed on the situation and its likely prospects, the question is, What do we do about it?"

Westlake leaned forward, elbows on knees, hands clasped.

"And so I would make you a little proposal. I would like the two of you to design a government for the colonies. A classical liberal, open society type of government. When the split happens, that is the structure that must be in place. Let it be seared in place by the flames of war, so it prevails when the smoke clears. Make it the very best government you can, using all your combined knowledge of history and sociology. Design the future, and make it the best future you can."

Ansen and Kusunoki just stared at Westlake. Was the scion of one of Earth's most powerful families, and likely the richest individual off Earth itself, authorizing them to foment revolution against himself?

"Excellency, I – I don't understand," Kusunoki said.

"We are all agreed, correct, Professor? Over the medium term, the colonies split away. The best possible outcome is for the colonies at that point to adopt – or, rather, to have already adopted, and retain – a classical liberal government. An open society. And ultimately, if we are lucky and we've done our homework, that classical liberal government will prevail against Earth, and Earth itself will ultimately become a classical liberal government, an open society, and be on friendly terms with the colonies.

"Why would I not seek such an end, knowing the current situation is not stable on the medium term, and knowing it is the best way to minimize the violence of the transition?"

"But you're privileged within the current system. Why would you wish to change it?" Kusunoki asked.

Westlake turned to Ansen. "Professor Ansen?"

Ansen had been staring off into the distance, eyes unfocused. Now he stirred. He turned to Kusunoki.

"Revolutions most often arise out of the upper classes. Sure, they have to be supported and carried out by the lower classes if they're going to succeed, but the instigation comes from within the upper classes, especially from among wealthy professionals. Russia. France. The United States of America. China. Vietnam. Very common."

"Indeed, Professor Ansen. That is what stood out to me as well, in my studies. And if not me, then who? As a little further explication, Suzette and I have enjoyed our time here, and we have fallen very much in love with Jablonka and its people. You both made the personal decision to be here – you, Professor Ansen, when you returned from Oxford, and you, Professor Kusunoki, when you out-migrated from Earth – so you must be able to relate to that.

"A caution, however. The Westlake family's charter on Jablonka expires in ten years. Which family will succeed us here I cannot predict. For the next ten years, however, you have carte blanche – in your writings, in your organizational activities, in your preparations. After that, I will no longer be able to shield you and your friends.

"As for my public statements and actions, I will, of course, be very much opposed to your goals and your activities. Make no mistake. I will not abandon my duty. I will oppose you. But I will not oversee a regime of oppression and violence in what we all know is a losing battle against historical forces.

"My opposition will take place in the sphere of ideas, without the use of police or military forces. Until Earth itself responds, of course, at which point it is out of my control. But I *will* respond with editorials and public statements. You will be forced in the court of public opinion to defend your ideas and your actions."

"Which will only make them more popular, of course," Ansen said.

"Of course," Westlake replied. "Responding to my criticism will also force you to publicly work through your ideas. I will keep you honest, Professor Ansen."

"Good luck with that, Excellency," Kusunoki said, and Ansen and Westlake both chuckled.

"I can also affect to a certain degree the actions of other planetary governors. Urge them to wage a war of ideas rather than of police suppression. I can reasonably argue that police suppression will aggravate rather than solve the problem, and recommend that, as long as it remains in the realm of ideas, it is a useful safety valve. I will be helped in convincing them of that if your side refrains from violence against the current regime until the break actually occurs. Most of them will heed me, which will make your task easier. A few will not, which will also make your task easier."

"As examples of the problem," Ansen said.

"Of course. And as rallying cries. You need a few of those, but not too many. Widespread police suppression won't avert the sociological inevitability of the breakup –" Westlake nodded to Kusunoki "– but it will make it harder to steer outcomes and to limit the violence."

Ansen and Kusunoki nodded.

"There is one more person you need to talk to. Georgy Orlov."

"The mining magnate?" Ansen asked.

"Yes. He has asteroid mining rights on many of the larger colony planets. He's here on Jablonka. Georgy and I went to school together, and he is of like mind on what is coming, and what needs to be done. If you are going to be able to fend off Earth, he has the closest thing there is to a navy. He will be in touch with you.

"As for us, my dear Professors, we have never met. This meeting never happened. We will likely not meet again."

Ansen pulled Westlake's handwritten invitation out of his jacket pocket and set it on the coffee table.

"There is no record of any meeting having occurred, Excellency."

Westlake nodded. "You have ten years. Good luck."

The driver returned them to their home in Jezgra in the large unmarked ground car. He handed Kusunoki out of the car first, and then Ansen. Once Ansen was out of the car, the driver reached into the driver's compartment and retrieved a plain grocer's bag, and handed it to Ansen.

"With his Excellency's compliments. For your private stock, sir."

There was a slight emphasis on the word 'private.'

"Ah. Thank you."

"Yes, sir. Good day, sir."

And with that the driver got back into the car and drove off.

Once in the house, Ansen looked into the bag to find a bottle of that wonderful bourbon and an entire box of the Earth-import cigars. There was also a large tin of a rare Earth-import Japanese tea.

Now What?

Ansen and Kusunoki were sitting in the comfy armchairs in their living room, the front room with the big picture window looking out onto their street in the faculty district of the university. Life outside went on as normal, for as much as life inside had changed.

"I must say, His Excellency the Planetary Governor has excellent taste in gifts," Ansen said, and drew on his Earth-import cigar.

"It pays to have friends in high places," Kusunoki said, before taking a sip of the excellent tea that had been a gift from Mr. Westlake.

"Not friends. Well-behaved enemies, more like. We are structural antagonists, adversaries by virtue of our positions. We have no choice but to oppose each other. It's too bad, in a way. In another life, we might have been friends in fact."

"Point taken. So what do we do now? It's one thing to speculate and write academic articles, another thing entirely to actually make it happen."

"Indeed, indeed," Ansen said. "Well, we need some sort of founding document, a constitution or charter, for the new colonial government. We need a way to defeat any Earth forces that come calling. We need to get public opinion on our side. And we need to do all those things across multiple colony planets."

"A tall order."

"Yes, but, like every large task, it is made up of many small steps. The first thing to do, then – and the hardest to do properly – is to draw up a list of those small steps."

"One of those steps, surely, is to get more people involved," Kusunoki said.

"And in multiple areas."

"Which areas?"

"The areas of the other steps, of course," Ansen said. "We need more people writing pieces to move public opinion, on multiple planets. We need people working on a charter, designing a government. We need spacers – current spacers, retired spacers – to

11

man ships."

"You need ships first!"

"Actually, no. I think we need spacers first, to steal the ships."

"Steal the ships?" Kusunoki asked.

"Of course. Otherwise we have to build them. We can steal them faster than we can build them."

"What ships are you going to steal?"

"All of them," Ansen said. "Warships, freighters, passenger liners, anything, everything."

"How do you steal a ship?"

"Easy. When they arrive at a planet, they rotate their crews for planet leave. When the shuttles go back up, they go back up with our pilots, and our people as passengers, and they take over the ship."

Ansen took another drag on the cigar, and stared at the ceiling.

"Thinking about it, there's probably an even easier way," he continued. "When they arrive at a planet, they need restocking. Food, in particular, as well as water for reaction mass for the engines. So when they get here, you simply don't restock them. Without water, they can't go anywhere else, and without food, they're going to have to surrender sooner or later. They don't carry much extra."

"Won't Earth notice their ships are disappearing?" Kusunoki asked.

"Eventually. It's a one- to two-month crossing from one planet to another even at .8 gravity through hyperspace. Most ships go out for six months or a year at a time, making multiple stops. It will be months before Earth even notices, more months before a pattern becomes apparent. And what will their reaction be?"

"Send out more ships to see what's going on."

"Exactly. But once they get here, they're stuck in flypaper as well. And it will be more months before Earth realizes those ships aren't coming back, either," Ansen said.

"Can't they shoot at us?"

"Yes, but it takes a considerable effort to do much damage to a planet. Kinetic bombardment is probably the most effective. But they would have to be armed for that, and Earth doesn't really have any large warships. There's been no need. And there's a pesky problem with bombing the planet."

"Which is?" Kusunoki asked.

"You've just destroyed the only supplies available. Now you're never getting home."

"There must be a way around that. How would you fight a space war?"

"No one knows," Ansen said. "It's never been done. All the colonies are Earth colonies so we're all one big happy family. The Earth has no real navy, because there's been no one to fight with. All they have are a few armed frigates to enforce the commerce regulations, and those are mostly in the colonies, so we'll capture many of those. They're no more prepared for this than we are.

"But if you're going to fight a war, you have to bring your supplies with you so you're not dependent on being locally supplied. Their ships don't do that now. They're calling on a friendly port, after all."

"I never thought of a spaceship as being so helpless. It seems, well, wrong somehow," Kusunoki said.

"Spaceships are very dependent on infrastructure, and if you can't depend on the infrastructure already in the system, you have to bring it with you. They haven't thought that through yet. But they will."

"But they have no warships anyway."

"We have to figure they'll jury-rig some sort of offensive capability, just as we will," Ansen said.

"So we end up with warships and navies and such. That's kind of sad, actually."

"As soon as you have two political entities rather than one, you have the potential for war. You of all people know that."

"Yes, I know it. It doesn't mean I like it," Kusunoki said.

"Actually, the police forces on planet are probably the bigger issue. Mr. Westlake has said he won't use them here, but that won't apply across all the colonies."

"Which could get ugly."

"Perhaps," Ansen said. "Most of the police forces are recruited locally, though, and moving large additional forces from Earth will not be possible."

"Because we control the ships, through control of their refuel and resupply."

"Exactly. Once they get here, they're captured."

"So, we come to the one big question, Mr. Revolutionary. How do we win?" Kusunoki asked.

"The Earth's major families run the colonies as a profit center. Many of the colonies would be quite wealthy without Earth's constant draining of resources, through import and export taxes, income taxes, sales taxes, and restrictive commerce regulations. To win, all we need to do is cost them money. If we turn their profit center into a loss center, and they see costs mounting into the future, they'll want to be done with us. There should be a lot of small ways we can disrupt their profits. Throw sand in the gears. I'll have to do some research into how all that actually works behind the scenes."

"Which means a major round of parties and dalliances."

"Very likely."

"As long as I know where your heart is, Love."

Ansen took her hand from the arm of her chair, lifted it to his lips, and kissed it softly.

"You locked it away years ago, my dear."

The Admiral

It was three days after the meeting with Westlake that Ansen answered the front door about 11:00 in the morning to find a man on their stoop in the work uniform of the Orlov Group, the mining concern that worked Jablonka's asteroid belt. He held out a card to Ansen without a word. On the blank side was scrawled a note.

Might I call on you to discuss history at 2:00 today?

The front of the business card was printed. Together with the logo of the Orlov Group, it announced:

Vice Admiral Jarl Sigurdsen (ESN, retired)
Vice President of Mining Operations
The Orlov Group
One Orlov Center
Jezgra, Jablonka

Ansen pocketed the card.

"You may tell the Admiral that 2:00 would be fine."

"Very good, sir."

He turned and walked back down the walk to his car and drove away.

Ansen went back in the house and considered the card again. A retired vice admiral of the Earth Space Navy.

Now that was interesting.

At precisely 2:00, the doorbell rang. Kusunoki answered it, and showed the admiral into the living room where Ansen sat smoking a locally manufactured cigar. Ansen stood to greet him.

"Welcome, Admiral. Come in, come in. Have a seat. May I offer you a refreshment of some sort?"

They shook hands in the middle of the room. The tall, slim, crisply dressed Sigurdsen contrasted with the shorter, bulkier, more casually dressed Ansen.

"Water would be fine, Professor Ansen."

"Very well."

Kusunoki left the room to return moments later with a pitcher of ice water and a glass for the admiral.

"Thank you, Professor."

They all settled into the big armchairs in the living room.

"My wife will be joining us, if you don't mind, Admiral. She has an interest in matters of history as well," Ansen said.

"Of course, Professor Ansen. I hoped she would."

Sigurdsen nodded to Kusunoki, and she nodded back.

"And what may I help you with today, Admiral?"

Sigurdsen looked around and seemed to hesitate.

"I will mention that the house is protected against eavesdropping devices by the very best electronic sensors, and no recording of any kind is being made on my part," Ansen said.

"Ah." Sigurdsen sat back. "I wanted to talk to you about matters of war, Professor. Specifically, how wars might be fought in the future, based on insights from the past."

"A broad topic, Admiral. Should we narrow it down a bit?"

"We could. What I know most about is Jablonka, and, of course, Earth, from my time in the Earth Space Navy. We could hypothesize a war between Earth and Jablonka. Purely as a discussion exercise, of course."

"Of course," Ansen said. "First, give me some broad principles of war, Admiral. Let's see how much the theoretician and the practitioner are on the same page."

"I think most basically, Professor, one needs to understand that war is an engineering discipline, and has been for a very long time."

"At least since the Roman Republic."

"Indeed," Sigurdsen said. "It is the application of force, in the physics sense, to achieve one's political goals. Ballistics, chemistry, hydrodynamics and aerodynamics, metallurgy, propulsion, meteorology, mechanics, biology, quantum mechanics – practically every science and technology is a useful skill in the practice of war."

"In this we are agreed, Admiral. Another basic principle?"

A Charter For The Commonwealth

"Once begun, war will continue until one side is physically, economically, or emotionally unable or unwilling to continue. The other side, regardless of its own losses, is called the victor."

"Again, we are agreed," Ansen said.

"I'll offer one more, Professor. The race does not always go to the fastest, or the fight to the strongest, but that's the way to bet. History is full of famous examples of the underdog pulling out a victory, but those examples are so famous because they are the minority of confrontations. When the underdog has won, it is because they were better prepared or more emotionally invested in the victory, usually both."

"Excellent, Admiral, excellent. Having agreed on basic principles, then, let's move on to specific cases. Were there to be a war between Earth and Jablonka, or, more generally, Earth and its colonies, were Earth to win, how would it do so?"

"By destroying the colonies' will to fight," Sigurdsen said. "Since Earth would want to continue to milk the colonies after winning the war, it would not want to destroy enough population or infrastructure to make it physically or economically impossible to fight. So it would want to dispirit the colonies through a few impressive victories, staged far enough apart to allow the news to spread. To make it readily apparent to all that the Earth will ultimately prevail, and the colonies could short-circuit a lot of suffering and bloodshed if they only gave up the hopeless cause."

"And the colonies? Were they to win, how would they do it?"

"By costing Earth so much money that Earth was not willing to continue the fight."

"An economic win, then," Ansen said.

"Yes, sir."

"What would Earth's biggest potential mistake be, do you think, in waging such a war?"

"Giving the colonies a battle cry," Sigurdsen said.

"Remember the Alamo, eh?"

"Exactly. And the colonies' biggest mistake would be a stand-up battle on equal terms."

"Don't give the Earth the big, demoralizing victories they want. Agreed, agreed." Ansen relit his cigar and stared at the ceiling. Returning his attention to Sigurdsen, he said, "Let us consider the roster of battle, then, Admiral. Let's start with the Earth."

"The Earth has police forces – regime protection forces, to be accurate – on all the colony planets. The Earth Space Navy has approximately three hundred armed frigates available for deployment. There are also a very few larger combat vessels which have never, in fact, been tried in combat."

"No one to fight."

"Correct," Sigurdsen said.

"Of those three hundred armed frigates, Admiral, I suspect more than a few will be on the colonies' side of the ledger at the beginning of actual hostilities."

Sigurdsen raised an eyebrow. "How so?"

"For some period before the actual start of hostilities, whenever such a ship shows up at a colony planet, the colony simply refuses to restock and resupply it. Without reaction mass, they aren't leaving the system, and without food, they have a limited time before they have to surrender. That's now a colony forces frigate."

"What about pirating supplies from other ships?"

"Pirating containerized food and reaction mass? Without a cargo shuttle for the ship-to-ship transfer?" Ansen asked.

"Good point. They could bring along supplies on a freighter."

"And at some point, they no doubt will. But is that policy now?"

"No," Sigurdsen said.

"So that's one thing. The other is that those police forces are primarily recruited locally, and cannot be supplemented from Earth."

Sigurdsen was nodding his head. "Because of the ship resupply problem."

"Exactly. When they show up here with troops, the colonies don't let them come down. They could, I suppose, come down in some sort of assault mode. Do Earth frigates or troopships have armored assault shuttles they could use for that purpose?"

"No. It's never been a requirement before. They're not a Marine force so much as a police force."

"And a regular shuttle is notoriously vulnerable to small-arms fire, such as hand-held rocket launchers, or even a large-caliber hunting rifle," Ansen said. "So what we are left with is the police forces already on the planet. It seems to me one critical thing is the loyalties of the Earth Special Police. It may be worthwhile to consider a name change. Something like Jablonka Protective Service, perhaps."

"What difference would that make, Professor?"

Kusunoki had been quiet during the discussion, but she stirred in her chair and spoke up now.

"More than you might think, Admiral. Humans are social creatures. Tribal. Rename the tribe and you can redirect the loyalties. Earth Special Police is one thing, but Jablonka Protective Service is quite another. If Earth attacks Jablonka, to whom would the Earth Special Police be loyal? Now consider, in the same circumstance, to whom would the Jablonka Protective Service be loyal?"

"All right. I can see that. So Earth's advantages are not as they seem," Sigurdsen said.

"Not completely, anyway," Ansen said. "And what are the colonies' advantages? They have more motivation, because their people are fighting for their homes, while the Earth spacers are fighting on orders alone. That's a big one."

"And the colonies have advantages because most of the fighting would probably be in the colonies, so they have other resources available, like mining equipment."

"Mining equipment, Admiral?"

"Yes," Sigurdsen said. "Take a big ore freighter. Lots of big containers. Put in some iron-nickel-cobalt high-density ore, then a small nuclear demolition, which are used for mining, then a whole bunch of lighter rocks. Do that for several hundred containers. Drop them all like mines in the Earth fleets' path, and as they come up on them, set them all off. The fernico ore isn't going to want to move much, which means there's going to be a whole lot of high-velocity rocks going the other direction."

"Have to be careful of the angles, because the fernico is still going to move. You could shoot your own ships using something like that."

"Yes, but you can figure that into the angles. Another thing the mining people have is really big beam cutters. You can focus them out to a light-second or so. Put some of those on ships. They have a lot longer effective range than the projectile launchers on the Earth frigates. The projectiles themselves continue along at the speed they were launched, but they are easy to avoid at any kind of distance. Even at two miles per second, they take minutes to travel a few hundred miles, and it's hard to hit anything over about a hundred miles. They were basically made for enforcement of commerce regulations against unarmed merchant ships in orbit."

"Beam weapons?" Ansen asked.

"Well, we call them beam cutters, because we use them to cut up bigger asteroids so we can get at veins of metal. That's continuous duty. But you can overpower them by about a factor of ten for a pulse. Those carry for a ways. You have to be careful when using one in pulse mode for that reason. You have to be aware of what's behind what you're firing at."

"You said the Earth ships fire projectiles. What about missiles? Do the Earth ships launch missiles?"

"No," Sigurdsen said. "A missile takes a huge amount of volume compared to a projectile round. A thousand or two thousand to one. There's just not a lot of magazine space on an Earth frigate. Also, missiles are easier to counter. A missile shines like a beacon all the way in, while a projectile is cold once it leaves the launcher. They can be a bugger to detect. It's the difference between seeing a lighted cigarette on your patio on a moonless night, and an unlighted one. And if you do detect it, what are you going to do to a small, solid slug? It's pretty easy in comparison to disrupt a missile's large guidance system and warhead. With a big beam cutter, for example."

"I want to go back to something you said, Admiral. You said most of the fighting would be in the colonies. Wouldn't all the fighting be in the colonies?"

"I don't think so, Professor. The colonies would need to hit Earth infrastructure. Maybe once a month, pop into the Earth system and knock out some installation or other, either in space or on the planet. Something really expensive. Remember the way Earth loses is economically, by being unwilling to take more financial losses. Basically to decide the colonies aren't worth it. The colonies hit something they need, something they'll have to replace at huge expense, that's going to get them thinking it's not worth it."

"OK. That makes sense." Ansen looked at the stub of his cigar, thought about lighting another. He picked up his bourbon instead. "Let's talk about timeframes. If the colonies decided a war like that was coming, how long would it take them to be ready, working from scratch?"

"You mean if they started today? Maybe five years. Perhaps

sooner."

"That's not too bad. It would take some serious money, though."

"I think sufficient funds are available, Professor," Sigurdsen said. "Mining operations are hugely profitable. Most of the colonies with mining operations have a lot higher percentage of fernico asteroids than Earth does. For Earth asteroids, under six percent are fernico asteroids. For Jablonka, it's more like twenty-five percent."

"Where would the beam cutters and nuclear demolitions come from?"

"Mining supplies? The colonies buy them from Earth, with the profits from the sales of fernico ore."

"Really. Interesting," Ansen said. He drained the last of his bourbon. "Well, Admiral, exploring this hypothetical has been a most entertaining diversion. I think we would be open to similar discussions in the future if you were of a mind."

"I've enjoyed it a great deal myself, Professor Ansen, Professor Kusunoki. I think whenever one of us comes up with a topic of similar interest, we should contact the others so we can do it again."

They all stood and Sigurdsen shook hands with Kusunoki first, then Ansen. Ansen did not release his grip.

"You have a deal, Admiral. Very entertaining. Very entertaining indeed."

Ansen and Sigurdsen looked into each other's eyes for a long second, then nodded to each other once, and finished their handshake.

"We'll all be in touch then, from time to time," Sigurdsen said.

Ansen showed him to the door.

Bones Of A Charter

Several weeks later, Ansen and Kusunoki were sitting in the big armchairs in the living room. Both were working on several pieces to be published over time in the Jablonka newsfeeds. They had also sent feelers out via electronic mail to university people they knew on other colonies.

"We need to begin work on a founding document," Kusunoki said.

"Yes, I know. I've been thinking about it," Ansen said.

"Have you even decided what to call this political entity?"

"I've been toying with the Commonwealth of Planets."

"Why commonwealth?" Kusunoki asked.

"It implies a loose grouping. Words like republic, or union, or even confederation are much tighter bondings, and emphasize the central government. I want the central government to be very limited."

"It's still missing something."

Kusunoki sipped her tea, sat back in her chair, and closed her eyes. After a few moments, she reopened them and looked at Ansen.

"How about the Commonwealth of Free Planets?"

"Oh, I like that. A lot," Ansen said. "It emphasizes the planets' independence. Done. And we'll call it a charter. Again, constitution seems too much. Too powerful."

"The Charter of the Commonwealth of Free Planets. That sounds good. What's the structure?"

"I was thinking about a unicameral legislature, more of a council, really. Three representatives from each planet. Period. Having hundreds of politicians in multiple houses and all that complexity would just emphasize the central government."

"That takes no account of population, though. A minority could rule," Kusunoki said.

"What I was going to do is handle that in the vote counting. For something to pass, you need both a majority of council votes in the affirmative, and a majority of per-capita-weighted council votes in the affirmative."

"So each council vote gets multiplied by what, a third of the planetary population for that council member's planet? And then the per-capita votes tallied? That handles the population issue. How do the council members get selected?"

"By each planet, however they want," Ansen said. "They could have elections, or name them outright, or draw straws. That is not the central government's responsibility. It would amount to selecting its own members."

"Do you include an enunciation of powers?"

"Yes, but I think it's more important to include an enunciation of powers not granted. Governments in the past have been very creative in reinterpreting their powers in ever-expansive ways. So a list of what the central government cannot do is also necessary, I think, based on the historical precedents."

"For instance?" Kusunoki asked.

"No authority over food, liquor, tobacco, healthcare, medicine, drugs, weapons, vehicles, fuels, electricity, communications, navigation of commonwealth shipping, imports, exports, or any domestic policy of member planets. No individual crimes at the commonwealth level, and no courts system. Like you said. Free planets."

"Wow. Then what powers does the Commonwealth have?"

"War and common defense. Treaties. Regulation of foreign-flag vessels. Organization, operation, and financing of the navy. Common currency. That's the short list," Ansen said.

"What's the cabinet look like?"

"Prime Minister, Defense Minister, Foreign Minister, Justice Minister, Finance Minister. That's it. Additions to the cabinet are barred by the Charter."

"If there are no Commonwealth crimes, and no Commonwealth courts, why do you have a Justice Minister?" Kusunoki asked.

"Mostly to tell the Council and the Prime Minister, 'You can't do that.' But I said no individual crimes. Planets can be brought up on charges of denying civil rights to Commonwealth citizens."

"With no courts?"

"The Council sits en banc as the court in such a case," Ansen said. "I'm still working on how many votes it takes to initiate sanctions, and what those sanctions are."

"Well, that's a pretty stripped down central government. I like that part of it. What are the civil rights? Are they spelled out?"

"The classics, plus a couple. Freedom of the press, freedom of speech, freedom of religion, freedom of movement, freedom of assembly, freedom from warrantless surveillance, freedom from warrantless search, right to trial by jury and due process, right to own and carry weapons, right to be secure in one's property, papers, and communications. I'm still working on them. Oh, and these rights have to be written into whatever founding document each planet operates under, word for word, with no changes. Their own courts can handle the adjudication of them in most cases. For the exceptional case, a planetary government off the rails, the Commonwealth Council sits en banc as the court."

"What about amendments?" Kusunoki asked.

"Four-fifths vote in the affirmative, per council member, per capita, and of the planets."

"Four-fifths vote? Of the seats or the quorum?"

"Seats."

"You'll never get any amendment passed."

"That's the general idea," Ansen said. "Even a three-quarters vote requirement has resulted in some pretty stupid moves in the past. I want it tighter."

"And financing? What kind of taxes?"

"A head tax on member planets. Period. Nothing else. How the planets collect their levy is up to them."

"Hmm. Well, I like the shape it's taking," Kusunoki said. "Of course, it's going to have to be pounded out in some sort of convention of the planets. You may not like that process."

"I know. I hope to do a good enough job on it to get most of it through as it is. Some of it will depend on who shows up for the convention. We may be able to affect that, sort of help people along in picking delegates with enough knowledge of history to see the problems I am trying to head off."

"Perhaps. There is one thing I think you're missing so far, though."

"What's that?" Ansen asked.

"Make the Commonwealth truly aspirational. Include the right to Commonwealth citizenship to every human being, everywhere."

"Carte blanche?"

"No," Kusunoki said. "There should be some sort of test, I think. A citizenship test. Knowledge of the Commonwealth's structure. Knowledge of the rights and responsibilities of citizens. That sort of thing."

"How about intelligence, education, the ability to contribute to the Commonwealth?"

"Perhaps. But then if you do that, I think you should also finance the new citizen to some extent. Give them some subsidy. If you're looking for people who can make a contribution, you can't simply dump them penniless into the street and expect anything from them."

"I'll think about it. I like the sound of it, but I'll have to think through how it would work. And, of course, the council could also allow additional immigration outside the scope of an absolute right under the charter," Ansen said.

"I think a right to Commonwealth citizenship would make a big difference. The Commonwealth would be the dream of many. 'Not only are we free, but we are open to you as well.' We would draw the best and brightest from across humanity. It would also make us the *de facto* good guys in diplomacy."

"Not a small point, that last. Let me work on it."

Later that evening, they were reading the newsfeeds in the living room.

"Whoa, did you see this?" Ansen asked. "Planetary Governor James Westlake has re-chartered the Earth Special Police as the Jablonka Protective Service. 'We are simply acknowledging the special role our police have in protecting all the citizens of Jablonka, and recognizing their service to the community,' Westlake said."

"Yes, I saw that. And there is an article in the financial news about the Orlov Group placing a huge order for additional mining supplies – including ore freighters, ore containers, heavy beam cutters, and nuclear demolitions – from its Earth suppliers. It is massively expanding its operations in a dozen systems, including Jablonka, Kodu, Calumet, and Bahay. The equipment is to be delivered over the next two years."

Kusunoki looked up from her display to catch Ansen's stunned expression.

"It has begun."

High-Velocity Rocks

It was the weekly crew chief meeting. All the Red Team crew chiefs were there, meeting with the crew boss. With a two-weeks-space, six-weeks-planet schedule, there was also a Blue Team, Green Team, and White Team. When in space, they worked twelve hours on, twelve hours off, so the crew chief meeting took place at crew change time so all the crew chiefs on Red Team could be there.

"You want us to put nukes in the containers?" Bob Dean asked.

"Hey, boss, you realize that nuke goes off you got no container, right?" Theresa Lucas asked.

"And you'll have a ton o' shit flyin' around," Mark Walker said.

"Yeah, and mounting beam cutters on freighters? What's with that shit?" Eben Waters asked.

"Look," Crew Boss Lloyd Behm said. "I'll tell you what the big boss told me, but ya gotta keep it kinda quiet. There's been some shit goin' down in some other systems. Guys come in, shoot up the place, grab a freighter full of fernico, then run off with it. Ain't been in the newsfeeds, because they're tryin' to keep it quiet while they track 'em down."

"No shit," Waters said.

"Yeah, and the Earth cops and the Earth navy are messin' around and gettin' nowhere," Behm said. "So the big boss figures maybe we should set up some surprises for 'em. The idea is, they come in here all hot to trot to steal our shit, and we pop off some of these magic containers at 'em, and then the freighters open up on whatever's left of 'em with the beam cutters in pulse mode."

"Ha, ha, ha. That'll serve 'em right," Lucas said.

"Yeah, I wouldn't want to be on the receivin' end o' one o' those containers. It's gonna shoot that rock outta there like cannonballs," Dean said.

"Yeah, that's what they figure," Behm said. "So I'm thinkin' we could come up with some ideas to make their idea even better. What they got so far is we pack about a quarter of the container with fernico. Shit's heavy as hell, so that gives a good backstop. Then in goes the nuke, one of the little twenty-ton jobs, then we fill the container the rest of the way with rock rubble. That's the basic idea. Now, make it better. Go."

"You want to weaken the end cap of the container, so it gives way first. That'll direct the rock better. You know, cut slots in the seam around the end, like a two-foot cut, then leave six inches, another two-foot cut, leave six inches. All the way around. Something like that," Lucas said.

"All right, I like that," Behm said, making notes. "What else we got?"

"We could put a buncha other stuff in there, too. We use lotsa cable, and once it's been stressed, we can't trust it, so we pitch it. We could put a lotta odds and ends like that in there. Cable in particular would stretch out. Have a lot more chance o' hittin' somethin'. And goin' that fast, it's gonna break whatever it hits," Walker said.

"All right, I like that one, too," Behm said.

"We don't know whether big rocks or small rocks will work better. I think we oughta build one o' each and pop 'em off and see what happens before we build a bunch of 'em," Waters said.

"OK, that makes a lotta sense," Behm said. "I think I can get the OK to do that. We'll set up some remote video cams for analysis afterwards. We'll have to do it somewhere where we ain't trippin' over all that debris forever."

"Aim it north-south so all the debris heads outta the ecliptic. Give it a day or two and it's way outta our way," Dean said.

"OK, that works," Behm said. "What else we got? Anything? Well, think about it. Meantime, let's get those test shots set up. One with big rocks, one with small rocks."

Given a chance to think about it, Dean came up with one more wrinkle: wrap the portion of the container around the nuke with used steel cable. Reinforcing that portion so it held together a fraction of a second longer during the explosion would raise the pressure in the container to a higher peak value, and eject the rock at a higher velocity.

"Are all our people accounted for?" Behm asked.

"Yes, sir. First shift is all in, and we held second shift from going out. We have a good count on everybody," Lucas said.

"All right. Whenever you're ready."

They were in the main facility on a large rocky asteroid named Misty, but which everybody just called Base. With a thousand-mile diameter, Misty was more of a dwarf planet than an asteroid. The two test containers were both located a couple thousand miles from Misty, on the out-system side. The facility was located on the in-system side of Misty currently, so the whole asteroid protected them from the test.

"Five. Four. Three. Two. One."

Lucas pushed the Detonate icon on the console. Several seconds later, on the real-time wide-view display, the two containers both simply exploded and disappeared.

"Damn!" Waters said. "They just vaporized."

"What's our backside radar show?" Behm asked.

"We have two large masses heading out-system south – that must be the fernico end of the two containers – two large clouds of debris heading out-system north at high velocity, and expanding clouds of smaller debris roughly spherical around the explosions," Lucas said.

"So, basically, it worked," Behm said. "Outstanding. All right. Let's get some analysis done on the high-speed, close-in videos and the radar tracks. We need to know which one works better."

"OK, so whatta we got?" Behm asked.

"The test with the large rocks resulted in a shot field of average size o' two to three feet in diameter movin' about ten thousand feet per second," Dean said.

"Nice," Waters said.

"And the small rocks?" Behm asked.

"The test with the small rocks resulted in a shot field of average size o' eight to twelve inches in diameter movin' about fifteen thousand feet per second. Also, the total mass o' the small rocks ejected was about twenty-five percent larger than that o' the large rocks," Dean said.

"Damn," Walker said.

"So how do we get twenty-five percent more mass and half again faster with the small rocks?" Behm asked.

"It's the packing factor, I think," Lucas said. "There's a lot of void when putting the larger rocks into the container. That soaks up some of the initial pressure and lets pressure vent past the projectiles during acceleration. The small rocks are a better tamper."

"That makes sense," Dean said.

"And don't forget twenty-five percent more mass with projectiles that mass about a tenth as much per projectile means more than twelve times as many projectiles down range. Most projectiles will miss in any space battle, but we'll get twelve times as many hits on ships if we have twelve times as many projectiles," Lucas said.

"OK, so are the small rocks big enough?" Behm asked.

"I wouldn't wanna be on a ship that got hit with a rock ten inches in diameter goin' three miles a second, that's for damn sure," Walker said.

"Yeah, I agree. I think that's a killer hit, right there," Waters said.

Lucas and Dean both nodded as well.

"At fifteen thousand feet per second, it's still gonna take over five minutes to go a thousand miles. This is a short-distance weapon," Behm said.

"Yeah, like a mine. You drop 'em in front of the bad guys, and when they come up on 'em, you set 'em off. I think that's how it's got to be," Waters said.

"All right," Behm said. "Let's get to building some o' these. Big boss wants a bunch of 'em – he's talkin' hundreds of 'em – so let's get started. Don't worry about runnin' outta containers. There's a bunch more been ordered. Let's figure we make thirty o' these a month, and figure out how to do that while we're doin' everythin' else. Oh, and document everything so's Blue, Green, and White are up to speed when they come on."

"What about the beam cutters? We gonna start puttin' them on freighters?" Walker asked.

"Not yet," Behm said. "They got some new ones comin'. Bigger'n anything we got right now. So we're gonna wait for the big ones."

Location, Location, Location

"I am stuck on something, my dear, for which I could use your help," Ansen said.

"Of course, if I can," Kusunoki said.

"Clearly things are getting well underway with our friends, and our newsfeed articles have begun a public debate with Mr. Westlake, but we're just puttering around in our musings about a charter. I think we need to step that up, and I'm not sure how to proceed."

"You need to have a constitutional convention."

"Yes, of course," Ansen said. "But these things take time, and they need to be set up well in advance. The clock is running. How do I get sixty or seventy people from thirty-plus planets in one place for up to a year to hammer out a document all will accept?"

"What sort of people?"

"University people mostly, I would think. People not unlike ourselves. History and sociology. Political science. Economics. People who have studied how humanity has organized itself in the past, and know what works and what doesn't. I would like to hand-pick them myself to get the right sort, but I'm not sure I can get away with that. And how do I get them to walk away from whatever they are doing for a year?"

"Hmm." Kusunoki sipped her tea and stared out the window, her eyes unfocused, as she considered the problem. "If we were in Japan, I know what I would do."

"What's that?"

"Have a conference on Hawaii. The Japanese love Hawaii."

"A year-long conference?" Ansen asked.

"Well, it takes six weeks on average for a crossing between planets, and six weeks back. If you are going to have a conference with attendees from multiple planets, there's going to be three months just in traveling both ways. Four for some people. So if you're looking at university people, you're probably talking about something like a sabbatical year."

"That could work. But where would we have it?"

"What planet has the nicest weather, the best resorts, the best food?" Kusunoki asked.

"Doma. No question."

"That's it then. Now the only question is how you pay for it. You have the travel expenses plus all the lodging and food in a resort location for a year. Plus they are going to want a sabbatical stipend. It all adds up. Quickly, in this case."

"That I'm less worried about," Ansen said. "Friends in high places and all that. Money is apparently not a problem. Organization is. How do we get people to want to go? What if they just say, Uh, no, thanks."

"Make it a prize. University people love that sort of thing on their resumes."

"The Westlake Prize. Then you get to go to the Westlake Conference on, what exactly? Something innocuous, clearly."

"Something that's innocuous to the authorities, but will signal your intentions."

"The Westlake Conference on Societies and Structures, sponsored by the Orlov Group," Ansen said.

"And hosted by Gerald Ansen, Professor Emeritus of History at the University of Jablonka. On Doma, at such-and-such resort. All expenses paid, plus stipend. That should do it."

"I still wish I could pick the attendees."

"So do it," Kusunoki said. "When you send this up the chain, send along the list of winners of the Westlake Prize."

"That's pretty brazen."

"Like that's ever stopped you before."

"Admiral Sigurdsen. Come in. Please, come in."

Ansen waved Sigurdsen into the entranceway and closed the door behind him. He showed Sigurdsen into the living room, where Kusunoki was already curled up in her big armchair, and a rocks glass of bourbon and a large cigar awaited Ansen. There was a pitcher of ice water and a glass on the table in front of the armchair Sigurdsen had used during their last discussion.

"You've met my wife, of course," Ansen said.

"Professor Kusunoki," Sigurdsen said as he nodded to her.

Kusunoki nodded back.

"And we have water for you, though other refreshments are available as well," Ansen said.

"Water is fine. Thank you, Professor."

Sigurdsen and Ansen both took their seats, and Ansen jumped in.

"For our last hypothetical discussion, Admiral, we discussed war, in particular how future wars might be fought. For this discussion, I thought we would put the shoe on the other foot. Instead of the military man asking me about war, I thought I would ask the military man about politics."

"Turnabout is fair play, Professor."

"Indeed. So." Ansen took a drag on his cigar and let it out slowly, with a sigh. "If we were to hypothesize a future political structure, one built along largely classical liberal lines – what one might call libertarian, even – that's all well and good. But one quickly comes to the question of origins. How would such a structure get started in the first place, assuming some other structure was in place prior?"

"You asked me for a statement of principles to get started last time, Professor, so let me do the same with this question. What are your basic principles for such a structure?"

"Good, good. That will work. Well, I think the first basic principle is there must be a founding document of some sort. A charter or constitution. Rule of law in such a structure is important, and some basic law to which all others are subservient seems required."

"I'm with you so far. Another basic principle?" Sigurdsen asked.

"For such a structure to be truly libertarian, most decisions should be outside of the control of the central government and left to the planets and the citizens. And such controls should be designed to be more robust than such controls have proved throughout history."

"Yes, there are several tragic examples. France. The United States of America. All right, we're together so far. I believe I gave you three basic principles last time, Professor. Have you a third on this question?"

"Yes," Ansen said. "Such a founding document must be drawn up with the participation of all the individual sovereignties – in this case, planets – of which it is to be ultimately composed. For psychological reasons, if none other, it cannot be implemented across those multiple sovereignties without their participation."

"Again, I am in agreement. So, Professor, having found agreement on basic principles, I believe we are down to specific cases. How does this founding document get written? From what venue does it emerge?"

"A constitutional convention has been the traditional mechanism, and I think it could work in our hypothetical case. Delegates from all the individual sovereignties, drawn together in one place to hammer out the structure and its implementation on paper."

"One problem then is that a predecessor structure to this hypothetical emergent structure is unlikely to appoint such delegates, or to appoint such delegates as would have a classical liberal structure as an end goal," Sigurdsen said.

"Indeed, Admiral. The delegates would likely have to be well-known eminent individuals of certain dedication to the goal, selected primarily from academia. The question then is, given how long it could take to get the job done, How does one get them to attend?"

"I would think it to be the task of no more than a year."

"And I agree," Ansen said. "Much less than a year, and one simply runs out of time, given that the travel time to collect everyone in a single location is itself four months of round-trip travel. At the same time, a year away from one's other work, away from one's home, is likely the maximum. The question remains, How does one get them to attend?"

"Hold the meeting someplace really nice and pay all their expenses would be two obvious measures, I would think."

"Including all the expenses for their spouse and family to accompany them. But don't forget they are currently employed by their universities, which largely do not pay salaries during sabbaticals."

"Ah. So a salary as well, then," Sigurdsen said.

"For a sabbatical, the traditional term is a stipend, but, yes, that is the solution. A stipend rather larger than their normal salaries would be an additional inducement. A further inducement would be to make it a prize."

"A prize?"

"Yes," Ansen said. "University people love that sort of thing. Some sort of prize, with an impressive name behind it. The Westlake Prize, say."

"One cannot, however, call it a constitutional convention,

Professor. That would certainly raise the suspicions if not the reaction of the predecessor regime."

"Clearly some subterfuge is necessary, Admiral. But something that would signal to the recipients themselves what is going on. The actual winners of the Westlake Prize could meet for the Westlake Conference on Societies and Structures, for example."

Sigurdsen was nodding his head.

"Sponsored, perhaps, by the Orlov Group," Ansen said.

"And hosted by Gerald Ansen, Professor Emeritus of History at the University of Jablonka," Kusunoki put in.

"Very interesting, Professor. At the end of this conference, presumably, one emerges with the founding document in hand and has checked all the boxes, including having had participation from all the individual sovereignties."

Ansen nodded. "That is the goal."

"I do see one problem, however, Professor," Sigurdsen said. "How does one keep such a classical liberal project from being infected with statist authoritarians of one form or another? Fascism. Communism. State socialism. State capitalism. They all have their adherents in the target academia group. The classical liberals would be a minority, I would think."

"The selection process would have to be very carefully done, Admiral. There is no doubt about that at all. I wasn't at all sure it was possible, so I took the liberty, purely for purposes of our discussions, of attempting to draw up a list of such individuals from the existing environment, just to see if it could be done. It turned out rather better than I had hoped."

Ansen picked up a single sheet of paper from his side table and handed it to Sigurdsen.

"Here is the list I came up with for our purely hypothetical discussions, Admiral."

Sigurdsen looked the paper over carefully.

"Two people each from thirty-three planets?" Sigurdsen asked.

"Those thirty-three are all the first-round colony planets, and all have larger economies. There is a rather large break between the last of them and the next colony on a complete list, in terms of economy, population, and the like. In particular, those others as yet have no university structures from which to draw the appropriate individuals."

"And two from each?"

"One academic is too easily run roughshod over by his fellows, I think, Admiral. Two, however, can play 'good cop, bad cop' in dealing with ideological opposition."

"I see." Sigurdsen folded the paper and put it in his pocket. "For our future discussions, then."

"By all means."

"One last thing, Professor. You seem to have two events there, the awarding of the prize and the attendance at the conference. How would you see that playing out, in our hypothetical situation?"

"Oh, I would think the prize award could occur at any time. The conference should be no less than two years later," Ansen said.

"Two years? That seems long."

"There is preparatory work that would make a conference much easier and its outcome more assured. A circle of correspondence. And it is three weeks per leg to transfer such correspondence among individuals on different planets, even using the fast courier ships. Three years might be even better."

"I see. So access to fast mails, then. And the conference should be someplace really nice, some resort? Doma is the obvious choice," Sigurdsen said.

"That was my thought as well, Admiral."

Sigurdsen stood up, followed by Ansen and Kusunoki.

"Well, Professor, I must say, I really do enjoy our discussions. Thank you for calling this one."

"No problem at all, Admiral. We enjoy them as well. Until next time then?"

A Dangerous Game

They were in Westlake's office in the Planetary Governor's Mansion in the government center north of Jezgra. They were seated in the same side arrangement where Ansen and Kusunoki sat with Westlake the month before. Georgy Orlov had just laid out Ansen and Sigurdsen's hypothetical discussion of a few days before.

"Well, there's his plan for a constitutional convention," Westlake said.

"Agreed. What do we think about it? That's the question, Jim," Orlov said.

"I think we have to do something like it, Georgy. The question of legitimacy always comes up. If all the planets aren't involved, if it's just Jablonka's plan, then there's no chance it holds."

"Thirty-three planets. Not all of them."

"Most of the rest are only fifty years old or so," Westlake said. "Some maybe seventy-five. The thirty-three he chose were all in the first wave of colonization, between a hundred twenty-five and a hundred fifty years ago now. That's a big difference. I hate to leave them all out – there's over a hundred of them now – but they just aren't ready."

"Compromises, compromises."

"As always."

"Fair enough. What about using our names, though?" Orlov asked.

"I know why he's doing it. If it has our names on it, the other planetary governors won't interfere. Won't inquire too deeply. And it signals to his delegates that they're protected, at least somewhat."

"Are they, though? Can we protect them?"

"I think so," Westlake said. "There're no guarantees, though, for any of us. We're playing a dangerous game, Georgy. Ansen knows that. He's not a child, and he's not stupid."

"Well, you've met him. I haven't."

"No, he's not stupid, and his wife is his secret weapon. She's very quiet, but she's got him covered where he's intellectually weakest, on the people side of things. They're a powerful pair."

A Charter For The Commonwealth

"So they're the two Jablonka delegates?" Orlov asked.

"Yes, and I'm good with that. They're who I would have picked. Did pick, in fact. And I've spot checked some of the rest of these people. Solid, one and all. Not a statist in the bunch."

"Good. It would be silly to do all this work and take all these risks to replace one totalitarian government with another. At least with only one, there are no wars. With two, they would be fighting it out all the time. At least if it was only the peasants getting killed."

Westlake nodded.

"What about the costs on this, Georgy? Sixty-six academics, their spouses and families, round-trip to Doma, resort accommodations for the best part of a year, and a generous stipend into the mix."

"Not a problem, Jim. I have a thousand times that many people back and forth to the asteroid belt every other week in a dozen different systems. Those expenses are a nit in my cash flow. We do a certain amount of community work anyway. This will come out of that fund."

"All right. I just wanted to be sure."

Westlake looked down at the list of academics again. Georgy sat quietly, smoking a cigar. Their friendship went way back, and Westlake had always been the deeper thinker of the two. Now they were finally coming to the culmination of their plans.

"Yeah, let's do it," Westlake finally said.

"OK. I'm on it."

It was a bit over a week after their last conversation with Admiral Sigurdsen that Ansen and Kusunoki were notified of their selection as awardees of the Westlake Prize.

"Wow. These guys don't fool around," Ansen said.

"Why is it I keep thinking we're a part of someone else's larger plan?" Kusunoki asked.

"Well, for the time being at least, their plan is our plan."

Ansen scanned down the list of awardees.

"It's the whole list. Everyone I sent them. I can't believe they just took my list verbatim."

"I'm sure they at least spot-checked them to make sure we were all on the same page."

"Probably so, probably so," Ansen said. "Well, I guess it's time I

got started on my 'Dear Colleague' letter."
"Now that should be an interesting read."

Dear Colleague:

Congratulations on your selection for the Westlake Prize.

As you know from the materials you were sent by the selection committee, the Westlake Prize includes an invitation to the Westlake Conference, to be held in three years' time, at The Dachas, Doma's premiere vacation resort. Round-trip transport, resort fees, and meals for you and your family will all be paid by our sponsor, the Orlov Group, including private schooling for your children, for this sabbatical year. In addition, a generous stipend will be paid for your attendance.

The Westlake Conference will consider in detail a single academic question. First, however, some background is necessary.

As you know, there have been numerous instances of decolonization in Earth's history. These decolonizations have had mixed results. When structures were in place for the post-colonial period, the transitions have usually been smooth and orderly. When decolonization resulted in a power vacuum, transitions have often been violent, and the resulting situations unstable.

It is the goal of the Westlake Conference to determine an appropriate post-colonial structure to ensure that, were a decolonization event to occur, the transition to a post-colonial environment would be smooth and orderly, avoiding the chaos of a power vacuum.

We will work together for these next three years toward this end, preparing for the Westlake Conference, where all outstanding issues will be resolved. We hope to issue a conference paper detailing our recommended post-colonial structure at that time.

I look forward to working with you all on this important project.

And, once again, congratulations on your selection for the Westlake Prize.

Most sincerely yours,
Gerald Ansen
Professor Emeritus of History
University of Jablonka
Jezgra, Jablonka

A Charter For The Commonwealth

Three weeks later, on Calumet, Matheus Oliveira was reading his latest mail. He got the letter from the Orlov Group and the letter from Gerald Ansen in the same batch. They were marked as having come in on the latest courier ship from Jablonka.

"What the hell?" Oliveira muttered as he read first one, then the other.

His wife, Sania Mehta, walked into his home office.

"I just got a mail saying I won something called the Westlake Prize," she said.

"Me, too. Never heard of it."

"Isn't Westlake the planetary governor of Jablonka?"

"Yeah. Oh, great. There go all our friends," Oliveira said.

"Not necessarily. Did you read the letter from Gerald Ansen?"

"Yeah. I couldn't make heads or tails of it. Who's Gerald Ansen?"

"Gerald Ansen," Mehta said. "The author of 'Human Rights: A History of Freedom' and 'A History of Statism: Legacy of Failure.'"

"*That* Gerald Ansen? What's he doing clowning around with the likes of Westlake?"

"Read his letter again. Read between the lines."

Oliveira turned back to his display and read Ansen's letter again carefully.

"Oh, my God."

"That's what I said. Now look at the list of our fellow awardees. Mineko Kusunoki is Ansen's wife and a respected libertarian sociologist."

Oliveira scanned down the list of names, now keyed to the context. He turned back to Mehta with wonder in his eyes.

"That's a short list of all the most radical libertarian academics on the thirty-three most well-established colony planets."

"It sure is," Mehta said. "Some husband-and-wife teams there, like us and the Ansens. Most aren't. But what is true of all of them is that they are ideologically aligned with Enlightenment principles. That is *not* an accident."

"What does he mean by 'post-colonial structure?' The only colonies of any kind now are Earth's colony planets. He wants to design an 'appropriate post-colonial structure' in the event of a 'decolonization event?' That's setting the stage for colony independence."

"Yes, it is. What he's doing is planning a revolution. Right out in front of God and everybody."

"They'll string him up. And I mean that literally," Oliveira said.

"I don't think so. That's why it's called the Westlake Prize, why it's sponsored by the Orlov Group. Big establishment names. The biggest. Ansen has powerful sponsors, and he's letting everybody know that."

"So should we go?"

"Absolutely. I wouldn't miss this for the world," Mehta said.

"A year on Doma sounds nice, I admit. But what do you do at a year-long conference?"

"You still don't get it, do you? That's not a conference. It's a constitutional convention."

Oliveira merely stared at her, his jaw slack. Mehta was smiling hugely, and her eyes danced.

All across Earth's largest colonies, academics who had worked toward human freedom in obscurity for years read and reread their mail, and wondered they had lived to see such times.

Warships

It was the weekly crew chief meeting. All of the Red Team crew chiefs were there, meeting with the crew boss, Lloyd Behm.

"OK, so some of the new beam cutters are here, and the big boss sent me some plans for what he wants us to do with 'em."

Behm rolled the plans out on the table so everybody could see.

"What we got here is one o' the new freighters came in last month. It has four cylinders o' ten decks each, which is a lotta deck space for a freighter, but the thought is to sell passage as well, so there's lotsa passenger cabins and all the extra crap that goes with that. It's been plumbed up for triple water stocks in the front containers, so it can go anywhere to anywhere and back without needin' to rebunker reaction mass at the other end. Same for food.

"What we want to do is mount those big beam cutters here on the first ring of freight racks. Eight o' them big bastards here around the front. We'll use some of the control runs that are already there for container release, and run them to a couple extra consoles we can use for beam focus and aiming and shit. We're still gonna have the other rings of container racks, and we're gonna work up some stuff there, too. They're makin' some special containers on Jablonka that will be able to push out nuclear demos. And of course we have our own rock-throwing mines.

"Finally, the new freighters have racks between the radiator fins behind the cylinders. We want four more o' the big beam cutters here on these extra freight racks, pointed aft. What that does is provide a field of fire aft for beam weapons located behind the cylinders."

"Sweet baby Jesus," Eben Waters said.

"Damn," Mark Walker said.

"Uh, boss?" Theresa Lucas asked. "That's not a freighter anymore. That looks like a warship, and a really nasty one at that."

Behm put his hands on the table and leaned across to be face to face with Lucas.

"Looks like a freighter to me, Lucas. And that's what we're callin' it. OK?"

Behm held her eye, and she nodded.

"Sorry, boss. My mistake."

"Look like a warship to anybody else?" Behm asked as he scanned faces left and right.

"Nope," Bob Dean said. "Straight up freighter to me."

Waters and Walker both nodded.

"Me, too, boss."

"Yeah. Me, too."

"Good. Don't forget it."

"How many of these are we gonna work up?" Dean asked.

"A dozen," Behm said.

"Holy shit," Waters said softly.

"We got a couple years, so figure gettin' one done every two months or so. If it takes us three, four months to get the first one right, that's OK. What we don't wanna do is screw it up somehow, right? So let's get the first one right so we know what we're doin', then we can ramp up."

Mark Walker watched as his crew mounted one of the big beam cutters on the first freighter to be converted, the OGS *Stardust*. The big units were two containers wide and high, and full depth – twenty four feet high by twenty four feet wide, and eighty feet long – with the big circular beam emitter exposed on one end. About the size of a big two-story house in the suburbs. It still looked small compared to the fifteen-hundred-foot-long freighter.

He looked along the length of the freighter. It was bigger than the ones he was used to, but all the same elements were there. The shuttle racks were on the bow, really just a set of protruding frameworks with latches to hook the shuttles on. *Stardust* had two big cargo shuttle racks and two small passenger shuttle racks, and all the shuttles were currently aboard.

Behind that, down the length of the ship perhaps three-quarters of the way, were the cargo racks. There was no cargo hold on a space freighter. The cargo was all in containers latched onto the ship. The cargo racks on the frame of the ship held the first layer of containers, the next layer of containers latched to the previous layer, and so on, until you had five or six layers of containers girdling the ship. Right now there were no containers on *Stardust* other than the ones they were wrestling into place, and all the innards of the ship's engines and plumbing were exposed. Unlike an aircraft or an ocean-going ship, there was no reason to skin over a starship for aerodynamic or hydrodynamic reasons.

At the rear of the ship were the cylinders for the crew and passengers. These and their connecting corridors were the only part of the ship sealed against vacuum. *Stardust* had four cylinders. They were currently unfolded, sticking out from the ship at right angles. When stationary, the ship could be set spinning, which provided apparent gravity in the cylinders. For spacing, the cylinders, which were mounted in huge yokes, were folded back along the length of the ship. The acceleration of the ship provided apparent gravity.

Between the cylinders, the four massive black radiators stuck out from the ship. Huge rectangles of black, two hundred feet on a side, stuck straight out from the ship at ninety-degree angles like fins. Whenever humans used energy, there was waste heat, and *Stardust* used a lot of energy. The radiators radiated the waste heat into space.

Walker brought his attention back to the here and now. They had settled on four twelve-hour shifts out of every two week rotation working on the 'freighters,' one first shift and one second shift per week. All the hundreds of people working on them in orbit about Misty knew what they were working on, but the word had gone out. Freighters they were, and that's what everyone called them.

A beam cutter designed to carve up asteroids was big, but size wasn't the problem in space. Mass was. If that big bastard got moving, it would crush one of his spacers with no problem at all, so the key was to take it slow. They had some of their heavy scaffolding rigs lashed to the freighter with cables, and dozens of cables restrained the big unit as they slowly moved it into place with motorized come-alongs.

Walker and all his people were on lines clipped to the scaffolding. Breaking loose and going adrift was a special terror of the job. You would think it would be easy to go and retrieve someone, but it wasn't. They had given up trying. Simplest thing to do if you went adrift is pop your face mask. At least it was quick.

"McBride! Take it easy, dammit. We don't want that big bastard to swing," Walker said over the crew radio channel.

"All right, boss," Jack McBride's voice came back.

There was always one guy on a crew who was in a goddamn hurry all the time, and for Walker it was Jack McBride.

The good part was those issues usually resolved themselves. He would be a man short until the next rotation, but everybody would start being more careful again.

Theresa Lucas' crew was connecting control runs into a couple of extra consoles on the bridge. There were always a lot of extra consoles, each with their own display and configurable interface. Ships lasted a long time, and might go through several different phases of their careers. Engineers and shipping companies kept coming up with new capabilities. You couldn't predict what future uses would be needed, so there were always extra consoles on the bridge, extra control runs in the chaseways. Every console had its own computer capability as well, for the same reason.

They were connecting control runs from the ship's radar processors' extra outputs into the gunnery consoles, for targeting, and connecting control runs from the chaseways coming in from the front container racks, for weapons control. The nice thing about this work is it was inside the ship, so her crew wasn't EVA this shift. It was still in zero-gravity, though. You couldn't exactly spin the ship while they were mounting the beam cutters.

"We've got connectivity to beams 1, 2, and 3, boss," Kevin Walsh said as he checked one of the gunnery panels. "We can talk to 'em."

"OK, good. What about radars? We seeing them?" Lucas asked.

"Yeah. We're not getting any feed because the radar's not hot, what with people EVA and all, but the processors are talking to us."

"OK. What about you, Little? You up?"

Paul Little was sitting at the second gunnery panel.

"Radar's talking, and I can see beams 1 and 2. I'm showing no connection to beam 3," Little said.

"I'm on it," Kevin Steverson said.

Steverson and Jim McCoy had the back of both consoles open, and Steverson bent down to check the control run connection for beam 3 coming into the bottom of the console from the bridge chaseway.

"What about that?" Steverson asked.

"OK, I got beam 3 now," Little said.

"What about the other beam cutters, boss? We gonna hook 'em up now?" McCoy asked.

"Might as well," Lucas said. "As they mount each one, we'll check them out, but no reason not to hook them up now. How're the control runs from beams 9 through 12 coming?"

"We're good on those. They were easier, 'cause they're at this end of the ship."

"All right. So let's get them connected up. There's another crew starting to mount the aft cutters. We might as well be ready."

Francis Turner opened the door and stuck his head into Tully Roberts' office in the Orlov Group's downtown Jezgra headquarters.

"Hey, Tully. Whatcha up to?"

Roberts jumped, then blanked his display.

"Christ, Frank. Don't you ever knock?"

"That's OK, Tully. I won't tell the boss you were screwin' off. You wanna do lunch today? It's beautiful out."

"Nah. I got some stuff I gotta get done."

"Well, then, you better stop playin' and start workin'."

Turner laughed and left. Roberts thought about it, then turned his desk around so he faced the door. This way, people coming into his office wouldn't be able to see his display.

But it wasn't surprising Turner thought the beam cutter targeting software for the freighter conversions was some kind of game. The gunnery console code was coming along nicely.

"Welcome aboard, sir," Lloyd Behm said to Jarl Sigurdsen when he came out of the stairway down from the shuttle bay on the front of the *Stardust*. The ship was spinning, but there wasn't much gravity this close to its axis.

"Behm, isn't it?" Sigurdsen asked.

"Yes, sir. Red Team Crew Boss."

"And you're going along for the testing?"

"Yes, sir. I have a contingent aboard. In case there's anything needs clearing up," Behm said.

"Excellent."

"This way, sir."

Behm led Sigurdsen aft, outboard to the circular main corridor, and down the stairs into Cylinder One to the bridge.

"Welcome aboard, Admiral," Captain Marc Heller said. As Heller was the captain of the freighter, and not a military captain, and Sigurdsen's title was that of a retired admiral of the ESN, there was no saluting. It wasn't a military operation, though Sigurdsen was in fact Heller's two-up superior in the corporate structure. Heller's direct superior, Rick Ewald, was the Director of Shipping Operations under Sigurdsen.

"Thank you, Captain," Sigurdsen said.

"If you'll step this way, sir, we can brief you on where we're at."

"Very good."

Heller led Sigurdsen from the bridge to a meeting room off the corridor behind it. Waiting there was Bryan Jones, Heller's first officer.

"Admiral Sigurdsen, Bryan Jones, my first officer."

"Good to meet you, sir."

Sigurdsen nodded to him, and Heller waved Sigurdsen to a seat.

"Our status right now is we are ready to move on out from Misty and test the main weapons, the beam cutters," Heller said. "We have done some testing from here at minimal power settings, just to light things up enough to tell whether we hit them or not. Tully Roberts has been up here from Jezgra making tweaks in his gunnery code, and right now he's got us to where we can pretty much hit what we aim at out to a couple light-seconds."

"Well, that's good news," Sigurdsen said.

"Indeed. What we don't know yet is if, when we dial the beams up to full power, they'll do any damage at anything like that distance. That's what we're about to find out. Our plan is to move out several light-seconds from Misty and see if we can't, um, disassemble some asteroids."

"That's what I'm here for, Captain. You could do all this and report it to me, sitting in my office groundside. But this is something I need to see."

"Understood, sir. Mr. Jones, could you please run through the detailed plans for the Admiral?"

The *Stardust* folded cylinder and got underway at her normal cruise of 0.5 gravity. That was at eighty percent power. Pushing the engines to the redline would yield just over 0.6 g, but the additional speed and extra gravity shipboard wasn't normally worth the wear-and-tear on the engines and the much higher drain on reaction mass, which went up faster than linearly as you approached the engines' limits.

In three hours, she was a light-second out from Misty, and they began hunting targets. Sigurdsen was on the bridge as an observer, Heller and his first-shift bridge crew were at their positions, and Shell Scott, who was a retired Earth navy weapons officer and got no end of grief about his first name because of it, was at the main gunnery panel, with the gunnery console programmer Tully Roberts on the auxiliary gunnery panel.

"What have we got, Mr. Scott? Any good candidates within range?" Heller asked.

"We have a rocky asteroid, couple hundred meters diameter, at half a light-second dead ahead, sir," Scott said.

"Light it up first. Make sure we can hit it."

"Yes, sir."

Scott targeted the asteroid, set the beam strength at one-tenth percent, and fired.

"Confirmed, sir. We can hit it."

"Full power on one beam, then, Mr. Scott."

Scott fired again.

"Confirmed hit, sir. We heated it up a bit, but we didn't hurt it."

"Adjusting the focus for range," Roberts said. He busied himself at his panel. "We have focus now, sir."

"Again, Mr. Scott," Heller said.

Scott fired again, and the asteroid blew apart. Of course, at one-half light-second no one could see it, but radar confirmed multiple small targets where there had been one large one before.

"Direct hit. She's broken up, sir. Velocity of fragments indicates 'exploded' might be a better term."

"Outstanding. Good shooting, Mr. Scott. Now let's find us something out about one light-second."

"We have a rocky asteroid at 1.05 light-seconds, fifteen mark thirty on the ship. Four hundred meter diameter, sir."

"Helm, come to fifteen mark thirty on the ship. Target and engage when in your sights, Mr. Scott."

This time Scott was careful to adjust focus to range. He targeted the asteroid with one full-power beam and fired.

"Target has broken up, sir. Slow-moving fragments, so this one was not an explosion like the other."

"Excellent, Mr. Scott. Now find me a big one."

"We have a large rocky asteroid at 0.95 light-second, ninety minus forty-five on the ship, sir. One kilometer diameter, give or take."

"Helm, come to ninety minus forty-five on the ship. Target and engage with all eight beams when in your sights, Mr. Scott."

Scott selected all eight beams, adjusted the group for focus to range, and fired.

"She broke up, sir. She's not flying apart, but she broke up."

"Excellent shooting, Mr. Scott. Now let's see if we can scratch the paint at one-and-a-half and two light-seconds."

"Thanks for letting me ride shotgun during your exercises, Captain. I hope I wasn't too much in the way," Sigurdsen said.

"Not at all, Admiral. We were happy to have you," Heller said.

"I have a little present for you, Captain. You can't hang it yet. For right now it has to be our little secret. I'll tell you when you can screw it to the bridge bulkhead in place of what's there."

Sigurdsen handed Heller a flat box, eighteen inches by six inches and an inch thick. Heller cut the tape and opened the top flaps to reveal a bronze plaque:

COMMONWEALTH SPACE SHIP

INDEPENDENCE
BATTLESHIP BB-001

Heller looked at it for several minutes. When he looked up at Sigurdsen again, there were tears in his eyes.

"It's true, then?" Heller asked.

"It will be, if we can pull it off. I'll let you know when you can hang it, Captain. You and your crew have earned it. You just can't let them know yet. Couple years, I think. In the meantime, you need to fill out your crew complement from Orlov Group employees, and drill them to be ready.

"Because, while we don't know when you will be needed, Captain, you and the CSS *Independence* will be needed before it's over, that's sure."

"We'll be ready, Admiral Sigurdsen. When we get the call, we'll be ready."

The Public Debate

Ansen stepped up his criticism of the Earth's colonial policies in the Jablonka newsfeeds, and many of his fellow Westlake Prize winners did the same. Ansen was careful not to criticize the planetary governors, though, putting the spotlight on the costs and benefits of Jablonka's relationship with Earth. He concentrated on the policies coming out of Earth, and not the local officials whose job it was to carry them out.

Westlake himself took to the newsfeeds and argued the benefits to the colonies of Earth's oversight, as did many of his fellow planetary governors as the debate spread across the colonies. As the debate heated up, some of the Westlake Prize winners got less than subtle hints their own planetary governor was less tolerant than Mr. Westlake and his friends. Visits by government agents to suggest they knock it off if they wanted to avoid prison, and even some being taken into custody and questioned, sent the message, and they backed out of the debate.

But as the debate raged on, and was carried on all the colony newsfeeds, the public began to take notice.

Connie Elliott, Vanessa Crum, and Karen Myers were having coffee and croissant at a table on the sidewalk of a little cafe across the street from Kabisera City Park on Bahay. The weather in Bahay's capital was beautiful on this late spring morning, and they had just finished a long morning walk on the trails in the park, which ran well up into the hills north of the city.

"Have you been following these debates in the newsfeeds?" Elliott asked.

"On Earth and the colonies and all that?" Crum asked.

"Yes. I've never seen anything so up front before about what Earth costs us in taxes and fees every year."

"It's ridiculous," Myers said. "Those Earth bastards bleed us for every nickel and dime. The colonies would be rich if they just left us alone."

A Charter For The Commonwealth

"I'm not so sure," Crum said. "They do keep the peace among all the colonies. That's the counterargument, right?"

"Yes," Elliott said. "And Westlake and other planetary governors, including ours, make that argument, but it's not very convincing to me. Their arguments seem kind of thin in comparison to some of the economic analysis the other side is doing."

"Thin?" Myers asked. "I'll say. His Excellency Richard Mcenroe, the Planetary Governor of Bahay, couldn't find his ass with both hands if you kicked him there to give him a head start. Westlake is doing his best, but Gerald Ansen just shredded his argument in his latest piece. And our own Jane Paxton wrote a scathing piece on civil rights violations in the colonies. I heard her talk once. She's got her head on straight."

"I hope she's careful, or she's going to have trouble keeping her head on, period," Crum said.

"I don't know about that. This is starting to look like the sort of thing, the more you clamp down on it, the more out of control it gets. Like squeezing a wet bar of soap. Sooner or later, it squirts out of your grip," Elliott said.

"Yes, but where does it land? That's the question," Crum said.

His Excellency Richard Mcenroe was also enjoying the beautiful morning. He was out on the patio of the Planetary Governor's Mansion on Bahay, looking out over another portion of the Kabisera City Park.

"But, sir, shouldn't we do something about Jane Paxton? Her latest piece in the newsfeeds was way over the line," Michael Jacobus asked.

"To what end, Michael? Do you want to prove her point? She has advocated no violence, no treason, no action. It is, pure and simple, an analysis of civil rights violations in the colonies. For the most part, in other colonies. Your own police force came out relatively unscathed. Should I then have you arrest her for complimenting your restraint?

"No, I think Westlake has it right here. In his letter, he said this was a way to let people blow off some steam, and if we suppressed it, it would just blow up in our faces. I think he's right. As long as there's no violence, no call to arms, we let it go."

"And if it turns?"

"Then we follow Westlake's lead. I can't help thinking he's got something up his sleeve. The fellow's very bright, and he's at the center of things. I'm content to let him call the shots."

The debate in the colony newsfeeds did not go unnoticed on Earth.

"Have you seen the colony newsfeeds, sir?" Andy Hasper asked.

"Yes, I was going to ask you about it," Arlan Andrews said. "What's going on out there?"

"A few dozen academics spread across the larger colonies have begun something of a media campaign against Earth's taxes and duties on the colonies. This Gerald Ansen on Jablonka looks to be the ringleader."

"And what's Westlake doing about it?"

"He and several of the other planetary governors are vigorously making the counterargument."

"But no arrests?" Andrews asked.

"No, sir. It's all being fought out in the newsfeeds."

"Young Westlake is weak, like his father. That Ansen fellow should be in jail. I knew it was going to be trouble when Fournier gave his son-in-law the Jablonka charter like some sort of damned wedding present, but he was calling the shots then."

"Should we try canceling the Jablonka charter, sir?"

"No. That's not how the game is played. That charter was granted by the families, and so it stands. Just because I'm leading the families now doesn't mean I can go revoking charters and the like. Everybody's got things they don't want to lose. It would open up everything, and probably mean I end up being pushed out and Fournier's faction takes over again. No, I can't do anything. At least not until Westlake loses control out there.

"When that happens, though, I damn well can do something, and I will. So keep an eye on those newsfeeds for me."

Costing Them Money

Ansen, Kusunoki, and Sigurdsen were meeting once again, for another of their hypothetical discussions. They were all seated in the big armchairs in the living room, Ansen and Sigurdsen across from each other, and Kusunoki curled up in her chair next to Ansen.

"You called this one, Admiral, so what is our topic today?" Ansen asked.

"It's actually a continuation of our first topic, Professor. A further hypothetical of our first discussion on fighting wars in the future."

"Ah. Interesting. Do we have further explorations to make in this area?"

"I think so," Sigurdsen said. "Let's start out our discussion today assuming everything we discussed in that first discussion."

"It was a while back, but, as I recall, we discussed how such a war would end and spent quite a bit of time on warships and the like."

"Yes, Professor. So let's assume for today all those things are true. The warships exist, and they have the capabilities we discussed previously."

Ansen and Kusunoki glanced at each other.

"This means," Sigurdsen continued, "in our hypothetical war between Jablonka and Earth, a force of Jablonka warships is likely to be able to attack Earth and escape again. Of course, no plan survives contact with the enemy, but assume for today's discussion that is true."

"Very well," Ansen said.

"And we previously agreed, were Jablonka to win such a war, it would be because Earth lost the will to fight on economic grounds."

"That the war was costing them so much, they would prefer it to end than to continue. Yes. That is easier to achieve with a situation such as the Earth government is now, for example, as plutocrats would rather not fight wars, which is not true of all autocratic states."

"Correct," Sigurdsen said. "Given that, what would the Jablonka forces be best employed doing? In short, how could Jablonka cost them the most money, while not making any of the big strategic mistakes."

"Such as killing a huge number of civilians and uniting the population behind an increased war effort."

"Or destroying something of huge sentimental value and little contribution to the war effort," Kusunoki put in.

"Exactly. Correct on both counts," Sigurdsen said.

"That's an interesting question, Admiral," Ansen said. "I think you need to separate the costs into two parts. The cost to replace anything destroyed, and the cost in the meantime to make do with another solution while the thing destroyed is replaced. The first one is straightforward. The important thing about the second one is to make it something for which the workarounds are much more expensive and yet absolutely necessary."

"All right. I can see that."

"I'll give some examples. I am most familiar with Europe and North America, so I can give you examples there, but there are likely similar targets in the rest of the world.

"First, I believe you could cut off a large part of New York City from rail traffic with a few well placed hits on tunnels and bridges. This does several things. Commuters can no longer get to their jobs, which disrupts the business of the city. Food and energy now need to be delivered by alternate means, such as the highways, which are already overcrowded. A massive effort would need to be mounted on an ongoing basis just to keep everyone fed, and that would go on for the years it would take to replace those structures.

"Second, you could break Copenhagen off from the rest of Denmark, and all Scandinavia from the continent, by bringing down two bridges over the Denmark Strait, north and south of Copenhagen. That would throw all road traffic back onto ferries, and the number of ferries available for that high level of traffic is lower than it was before the bridges, when traffic was much less.

"You could also separate England from Europe with a hit on either end of the Channel Tunnel. If it were in the water at either end, the tunnel would fill with water and be hugely expensive to repair. Same thing for the Japan-Korea rail tunnel, the Bering Strait rail tunnel, and the Denmark-Sweden rail tunnels.

"Let's see. You could also go after water and electricity. If you broke Hoover Dam, the resulting rush of water would probably also take out a couple of other dams downstream. It would disrupt fresh water and electricity supplies in a large area, all of which have to be made up from other sources. Same thing with the Grand Coulee Dam. Kentucky Dam. There's a couple big ones on the Tennessee River, I think. That sort of thing. You'd have to look to see what's downstream, how many people would be killed in the flooding.

"You could disrupt the water supply for southern California with a few well-placed hits on reservoirs there, too. And, of course, there's Three Gorges Dam in China, but I don't think you could break that with anything short of full-up nuclear weapons, and the flooding would kill tens of millions."

"That's a very interesting list, Professor. What else?" Sigurdsen asked.

"Well, there are locks on the Great Lakes and St. Lawrence Seaway. If those were broken, all the commerce on those lakes would come to a halt for years. The locks of the Panama Canal. You might also be able to block the Suez Canal by nudging a bunch of dirt over to block the narrow channel. I'm not sure if you could block the Dardanelles or the Gibraltar Straits or not, but those would be hugely disruptive."

"Keep going. Anything else, Professor?"

"Well," Ansen said, "There are very few road and rail connections through mountain ranges. The Alps, for example. The Pyrenees. The Rockies. Hits on tunnel portals of some of the big tunnels would disrupt a lot of traffic and be hard to clear.

"Oh, and oil pipelines. The ones that are very far north, such as in Alaska and Siberia, have to keep flowing to keep them from clogging up. Once the oil gets cold enough, it is impossible to pump and you have a thousand-mile-long yard decoration. It's impossible to repair, and hugely expensive to replace.

"Other oil pipelines, like the ones from Russia into Europe, and the ones from central North America to the coasts, would be disruptive but easily fixed. There's no problem of those congealing like the northerly ones.

"Water pipelines as well, I suppose, for fresh water to cities, but those are easy to repair. The better way there is to go after the dam that creates the reservoir. We already talked about those."

"What about space assets?" Sigurdsen asked.

"I don't know enough about Earth's space assets. Give me some examples."

"Asteroid mining from Ceres. There's a camp on Ceres, much like we have one on Misty."

"You would kill all the miners, and space infrastructure of that sort is normally built on the planet in pieces and assembled on site, so it's easy to replace. Bad target," Ansen said.

"The base on the Moon?"

"Again, I think you kill everyone in it, when you pop it open to vacuum, but it's relatively easy to reseal and repump full of air, so too many dead and not enough disruption. Bad target."

"The Quito Elevator?" Sigurdsen asked.

Ansen looked at the ceiling, taking a drag on his cigar.

"That one's different. Vastly expensive to replace, but it allows taking a lot of tonnage to orbit cheaply. Arguably of use in a war. It takes a long time to build the tether, because it has to be spun and layered and bonded in place, and because it's so large. Limited number of people killed.

"Um, that last assumes you break the tether toward the bottom, so the tether and the station continue on into space, rather than you break it toward the top and the whole mass of the tether comes crashing down onto the planet. Thirty thousand miles of anything weighs a lot."

"Infrastructure in orbit?"

"Depends on what it is," Ansen said. "A space station full of people? No. A big facility for spacedocking and building ships, including military ships? Sure. The latter is a valid military target, and has relatively few people on it compared to a space habitat."

"All right. I see the pattern. Most interesting, Professor."

"I think there's one thing you're missing in this discussion," Kusunoki said.

"What would that be, my dear?"

"We want to be friends with these people afterwards, right?"

"Yes, at least friendly enough to resume trade," Sigurdsen said.

"But the things you are talking about breaking are likely to make the powers that be very angry, and cost them a lot of money and a long time to fix."

"Costing them money is the general idea," Ansen said.

A Charter For The Commonwealth

"Yes, but you can do that by breaking things that are easy to fix once the peace treaty is signed. For example, instead of breaking Hoover Dam, you could take out the power lines and water pipes that come from it, achieve the same disruption, but they could be easily fixed once the treaty is signed. That's a further incentive to sign."

"Huh," Ansen said. He took a drag from his cigar and looked up at the ceiling for a moment, then turned back to her. "I think you're right, my dear, but why did you wait so long to bring this up? We generated an entire list of things that would take a long time to repair, to no end."

"No, the list of things you could break, and which would take a long time and a lot of money to repair, is very useful. Send it to them once you have proved you can bomb them with impunity."

"Oh, ho! Break the things that are disruptive but cheap to fix, and then tell them that if they don't sign, we'll start breaking real infrastructure."

"Yes. I think there's a way to disrupt just about everything you mentioned, but without breaking the big piece. You could halt the Channel Tunnel, for example, by bombing the electric substation that feeds the trains. You could disrupt bridge traffic by bombing holes in the pavement of the approaches. That sort of thing. But then give them your second-stage target list. Tell them you will make that disruption a longer-term and much more expensive problem."

"That's excellent tactics, Professor. I like it." Sigurdsen thought a moment, then nodded and turned from her to Ansen. "Well, I think with that, I have exhausted my topic, Professor. And I thank you for an entertaining discussion."

"Yes, our discussions are always very enjoyable, Admiral."

"And what about a follow-up to our last discussion, Professor? The one you called," Sigurdsen said.

"About founding documents and academic prizes and the like? We're a few months from being prepared for that discussion, Admiral, but it is surely one we will need to have."

"Excellent, Professor. I look forward to it."

After Sigurdsen left, Ansen and Kusunoki were sitting in the living room.

"Did you hear what he said about the ships?" Kusunoki asked.

"Yes, but that was all part of our hypothetical discussion," Ansen said.

"I don't think so. Admiral Sigurdsen is always precise. There was no hypothetical, no maybe in what he said specifically about the ships. He said, 'The warships exist, and they have the capabilities we discussed previously.' That's pretty definite."

"Well, if that's correct, I feel a lot better about our chances. The big concern is how many people will die before we can prove to Earth's plutocrats it's a lost cause."

"We'll see," Kusunoki said. "You and I need to keep thinking about how to convince them. I had one thought in that direction. What if, in addition to the treaty, we offer a free trade deal?"

"What? You mean try to make peace and make friends at the same time?"

"Sort of. What the plutocrats really want is trade with the colonies. They don't care about actual sovereignty over us as long as they can profit. Of course, they want to do it on mercantilist terms, and we won't accept that, but offering a trade deal, promising not to become a closed trading consortium that locks out Earth commerce, in either direction, might be enough of a sweetener to clinch a deal."

"But we would do that anyway," Ansen said.

"Of course, but they don't know that. Put it in the deal."

"It's a concession that doesn't cost us anything."

"That's the very best kind," Kusunoki said.

"Happy anniversary. Twelve years," Orlov said.

"Yes, and still another year until Ansen's conference even starts," Westlake said.

"Your conference, you mean. The Westlake Conference."

"Whatever. It's Ansen's ball and he's running with it. The problem is I can't see the game clock, so I have no idea when the whistle's going to blow."

"Well, we haven't seen any concerns expressed by Earth yet. At least I haven't," Orlov said, and raised an eyebrow at Westlake.

"No, me neither. I just have this feeling like I'm being watched, and I don't know where it's coming from. Besides, they're all taken up by their own internal politics, among the families. The colonies just aren't that important to them."

A Charter For The Commonwealth

"Understood. Of course, if things kick off early, we're already in pretty good position."

"How many of the ships are complete now?" Westlake asked.

"Ten. Two more are being assembled. And that's just in Jablonka. There are another thirty-four in the other eleven systems in which I have a charter. Four in some and two in others. And my competitors are doing the same thing in other systems. We'll have a total of almost seventy ships within another six months."

"That's remarkable."

"It's still only about two per planet, and it's not that hard to do," Orlov said. "Oh, it's expensive, but that's manageable. What's hard to do is cover for the fact they never show up back on Earth. These are supposed to be freighters for the Earth run."

"How are you managing?"

"Various excuses. We ordered a bunch of spare reaction mass pumps and injectors on the grounds there was an unacceptable level of failures in their space trials. And of course those had to be installed and adjusted on every ship. All very complex stuff. All complete bullshit, too, but it bought us time."

"There's another two years to go, though," Westlake said.

"Oh, we bought some other freighters of the same type that we haven't converted. We're running them as hard as we can, and rotating transponder codes every time they go to Earth, so it looks like all the ships are cycling through."

"There's no problems with names painted on the ships and such?"

"We named them, but never painted the names on them so we could play a shell game with them."

"One thing I don't understand. Can't you still use the converted freighters as freighters? I mean, if you cover up or disguise the weapons systems for now, can't you still carry all the freight containers?"

"There's an idea. I like it. It would also get the crews experienced with spacing to Earth and back. I'll look into it."

"What about manpower?"

"We're good there, too," Orlov said. "We hire new people, then use them for backfill as we crew the ships from more experienced hands. It's only money."

Orlov shrugged.

"What do you think their first move will be?" Westlake asked.

"The one that makes the most sense is to send the navy here. Jablonka is the richest, most productive of the colonies. It's the biggest chip on the table. Take it and the rest fall."

"They may not, though."

"In which case," Orlov said, "if it's a planet that's not a hard nut for them to crack, the planet surrenders. Sooner or later they'll trip a trap somewhere. And then we'll take out their ability to threaten our planets."

"You're sure about that?"

"No doubt. Jarl Sigurdsen went up to Misty for the weapons tests on the first of the ships. He said it was unbelievable. That's not to say Earth can't respond in kind, but it will take time, and in the meantime, we can force a treaty by costing them money."

"How are we doing on target selection?" Westlake asked.

"Ansen was a big help with that. With his and Kusunoki's input, we've been working on target selection. We can cost them money, all right. Lots of money."

"Enough to force a treaty?"

"Oh, yeah. By the way, in that regard, do you want to exempt your family's holdings?" Orlov asked.

"No, I don't think that would be fair. Let's pick the targets with an eye to what's best for us, what's most likely to force a treaty, and without adding any other constraints."

"Fair enough. And relax, will you? You're starting to make *me* nervous."

Flying Nukes

"You want what?" Ken Prescott asked.

"Flying nukes," Sigurdsen said.

"I don't even know what that is."

"Nukes we can drop, have them brake into the atmosphere, and then we can steer them to target as they fall to the planet."

"I thought most things you could break with a ballistic drop," Prescott said. "You know, you drop a container of fernico on it – nine thousand cubic feet of fernico is about twenty-two hundred tons, with a terminal velocity over twenty-five hundred miles per hour – that's like a three-hundred-ton nuke. That's gonna break damn near anything."

"Hoover Dam."

"Forget I said anything."

"We've been looking into it," Sigurdsen said, "and there's actually been a fair amount of work done on what it takes to break a dam. The critical issue is to explode a demolition behind the dam, and up against what you might call the wet side. As water is incompressible, pretty much the entire shock of the explosion is delivered against the dam. In contrast, when striking a dam on the front side, the dry side, the water behind it serves as a reinforcement. So delivering a suitable explosion against the back side of the dam, and at sufficient depth, is the controlling issue.

"Which is why my request for flying nukes. We want to drop a small twenty-ton nuke against the back side of several dams, and break them."

"Twenty-ton nukes? Not bigger ones?"

"No. We have plenty of the small mining demolitions. Anything like a warhead – kiloton or megaton or anything like that – we would have to design and build. But we bought a lot of the mining demolitions."

"What if the explosion is insufficient? Twenty-ton nuke isn't much."

"Then we'll hit it again, and again, until we pop it. The nice thing

61

about using water as a tamper is it flows back into the hole after every shot."

"All right," Prescott said. "We'll get right on it. I take it what you want is more of something where you tell it where to go and it goes there, not something where you actually have joystick control."

"Yes, we don't need or want the flight control loop going through a remote pilot, but we need to be able to specify the target and modify it as it goes if necessary."

"OK. So a self-steering directed aerial munition. Assuming we come up with something, how are we going to test it?"

"We'll try it out on Jablonka. Dummy warhead, and we'll steer it down someplace empty, like the middle of the Voda Ocean. We can always say we're trying to develop a new reentry system for shuttles or escape pods or something."

Ken Prescott, who was the head of the Orlov Group's research division, was meeting with some of his staff on the flying nukes problem.

"We looked into this, and it turns out the technology is centuries old. It just hasn't been used much in the last couple hundred years," Dave Leigh said.

"Really," Prescott said.

"Oh, yes. It was common in the late 20th and early 21st centuries. Aerial gravity bombs segued into directed gravity bombs. Eventually everything moved on to cruise missiles. By the time hyperspace was discovered and space colonization began, the directed gravity bomb technology was out of use and never came back," Kirsi Niskala said.

"So are we wrong to use it? Should we be doing something else?" Prescott asked.

"No, I think it's a good fit for us. It's cheap, quick to develop, and effective if you have control of the space. That's why it fell out of favor. You need control of the air space for it to work, whereas with cruise missiles you don't," Leigh said.

"All right. Good. So how does it work?"

Leigh and Niskala both looked to Dustin Martin, who had done the detail work on the proposal.

"Assuming you're in low orbit within some cone of space over your target, you drop the munition – which from orbit means you eject it backwards so it no longer has orbital velocity – and it starts to fall. It has all its steering flaps open, so it's in a high-drag configuration. When it hits the thin upper atmosphere, it deploys a small parachute for a while, then a larger one. Once it's safely down into the atmosphere, it sheds the chute and uses the steering flaps to direct itself to the selected target," Martin said.

"It's still going to heat up on reentry," Prescott said.

"Yes, but not enough to affect the munition," Niskala said.

"How precise do we think we can be in placement?" Prescott asked her.

"We're not completely sure, but we think we can drop it on target plus or minus a foot or two," Niskala said.

"Really. And how long will it take to have a prototype?"

"Oh, we weren't supposed to go ahead on that yet?" Leigh asked with a smile. "The shop is building up half a dozen test units now. This isn't a final design, mind you, but a test device to gain data from."

"When will those be ready?"

"Another couple weeks. Then we need six months or so to turn around a final production design. After that, you can just turn the crank on production. They're pretty simple," Leigh said.

Prescott and his whole crew were on *Stardust* for the test shots. A shuttle had dropped half a dozen three-foot-diameter buoys out in the Voda Ocean well away from land or shipping lanes, and maintained a radar watch for boats wandering into the area. They would be dropping dummy munitions – no nuclear demolition aboard, just an equivalent weight.

Two more spare consoles on the *Stardust*'s bridge were devoted to the planetary bombardment weapons, as opposed to the anti-ship weapons. Dustin Martin was at the secondary panel, while the primary panel was being manned by James Pramann, one of *Stardust*'s crew and another Earth Space Navy vet.

"All right, everybody. We can't forget we're testing on a populated planet. Let's make sure we at least hit the ocean," Captain Heller told the bridge crew.

There were chuckles all around, then the navigator, Matt Asnip, said, "We're approaching the target cone, sir."

"Whenever you're ready, Mr. Pramann."

"Bring ship's bows to zero minus one hundred thirty-five on orbit vector," Pramann said.

Since the ship was spinning to maintain internal gravity, Asnip applied thrust at ninety degrees to the desired rotation, and the ship rotated it's bows down to a forty-five degree angle to a radius from the planet, pointing back along its orbit and down.

"Orientation at zero minus one-hundred thirty-five on orbit vector," Asnip said. "Entering target cone. Center of target cone in five minutes."

Pramann and Martin were huddled over Pramann's console checking everything one last time as the minutes ticked by.

"Center of target cone," Asnip said.

Pramann pushed the Launch icon. At the front of the ship, more than a thousand feet away, a two-foot diameter cover blew off one corner of a container in the racks between two of the big beam cutters. Compressed air accelerated the dummy munition down a tube the length of the container and out into space. It fell rapidly behind *Stardust*.

There was a subtle bump to the ship you could just feel on the bridge.

"Munition away," Pramann said.

In a relative sense, the dummy munition dropped back and down from *Stardust*, but it was still headed in *Stardust*'s orbital direction, but at a much slower velocity. It angled down toward Jablonka.

As it fell, it assumed a high-drag configuration, unfolding its directional vanes straight out to the side, with their surfaces perpendicular to its velocity. When it hit the upper reaches of the atmosphere, it started to heat up, still accelerating as gravity pulled at it harder than its drag in such thin air could slow it. It deployed a small drogue chute on a long line behind it. As the atmosphere thickened, its high-drag configuration and the drogue chute together halted its acceleration and started to slow it down. The dummy munition released the drogue chute and deployed a slightly larger chute. Its deceleration increased.

The dummy munition was tracking its location relative to the coordinates of its intended target. It began to manipulate its vanes to alter its direction slightly, aiming for the target. It then released the second chute and came barreling down out of the sky, adjusting its impact with finicky precision.

"Holy shit, *Stardust*. That was awesome. We didn't even see it coming. Just BAM and the buoy is gone. Damn," the voice of shuttle pilot Nathan Davis came over the radio.

"*Stardust* confirms. Positive impact on target. Roger," *Stardust*'s radio operator, James Oconnell radioed back.

"Boy, I'll say, *Stardust*. We have little bits and pieces of buoy around where it used to be, but none of them is more 'n a couple inches across. It's like it just exploded. And the water spout went a hunnert feet in the air," Davis came back.

"Good shooting, Mr. Pramann. Now you have ninety minutes to set up to see if you can do it again. Two at a time, this time around," Captain Heller said.

"Yes, sir. We're on it."

The two-at-a-time test the next orbit, and the three-at-a-time test the orbit after that, were as successful as the first shot, to the delight of shuttle pilot Davis, who got even more expressive as the tests went on. Prescott and his crew took a shuttle back down to Jezgra even as divers were retrieving the dummy munitions from the shallow water of the test site for analysis.

Learning From The Past

It had been several months since their last meeting. It was, as always, at the home of Ansen and Kusunoki.

"So, Professor, are you ready to continue the discussion with regard to founding documents?" Sigurdsen asked.

"Yes, Admiral," Ansen said. "We have been corresponding among the Westlake Prize winners, and the essentials of a founding document have been decided."

"Excellent. Then let me ask you for a statement of basic principles, as we have done before."

"The primary role of the central government is providing military defense for its member planets, with the secondary roles of conducting foreign policy, providing a common currency, and ensuring civil rights. That's basically it."

"A short list, then. And your second principle?" Sigurdsen asked.

"That the document explicitly spell out the only powers of the central government, and further explicitly spell out a long list of the powers that the central government does not have."

"Belt and suspenders. Makes sense. Do you have a third?"

"Yes," Ansen said. "That amendment of the document should be the next thing to impossible. Historically, they seldom go well."

"A good set of principles, I think, Professor. But you called this discussion, so you must have questions for me."

"Indeed, Admiral. They all have to do with the management of the military. What should such a basic document include? What does your study of military history indicate to you would be most appropriate in a founding document?"

"There are a few things that are known to have worked in the past, and a few that have failed miserably. Successes first, or failures?" Sigurdsen asked.

"Failures, I think."

"Very well. The first has to do with the makeup of the service, in how its members are selected. Three things there that have failed miserably in the past are conscription, mercenaries, and foreign fighters. All should be banned in your basic document."

"Well, conscription we already had banned, in a human right to be exempt from involuntary servitude, in which we explicitly included conscription. If the nation is to be defended, its citizens must rise to do it voluntarily. A failure there means the fight is not seen as necessary, or the military is under-compensated, or both," Ansen said.

"Exactly correct."

"With mercenaries and foreign fighters, you are thinking about the Roman Empire, I think?"

"Among others," Sigurdsen said. "Why would you want an armed military force of strangers within your country? Ultimately, your government only operates with their dispensation. Or not. And it is unclear whether they actually will defend your country when push comes to shove. They certainly have no patriotic reasons to do so."

"Fair enough. Another failure?"

"Placing control of specific military expenditures under the control of the legislature. Not just how much is spent – that's the proper role of the legislature – but how much is spent on specific programs."

"Because the legislature doesn't have the knowledge or experience to make those decisions?" Ansen asked.

"Worse. They have institutional biases on such decisions. They literally cannot make them correctly."

"Examples?"

"Spending more than needed on fancy new systems, and less than needed on the maintenance of critical existing systems. Spending money on systems rather than manpower. Under-financing payroll, medical expenses, and retirements. Spending money on the basis of where it is spent – in which politician's territory – rather than on what it is spent for. Making basing decisions on the basis of which politician's territory it favors. The list goes on and on," Sigurdsen said.

"So military spending decisions –"

"Should be made by the military and the executive. Not the legislature, other than the overall level of military spending."

"Interesting. That makes for a powerful executive," Ansen said.

"Who is subject to a no-confidence vote by the legislature."

"Understood. Other failures? Or are we on to successes?"

"Successes, I think. Officers of flag rank should be approved by the legislature," Sigurdsen said.

"Which is another control on the executive."

"Correct. It also gives the military an institutional continuity across administrations."

"So flag-rank positions don't become patronage jobs," Ansen said.

"That's right. Another success is having the military swear oath to the founding document rather than to the government or to the administration."

"Yes. There were some interesting failures there, with oaths being sworn to the leadership."

"Fascist Germany and Italy stand out, as well as Imperial Rome, but there are many examples. If the leadership goes off the rails, departs from the founding document, the military should be oath-sworn to disobey them," Sigurdsen said.

"Any others?"

"One more. Military operations and military intelligence shouldn't be in the same chain of command."

"That one's fairly obvious, I should think," Ansen said. "Otherwise the intelligence unit simply argues operations' position."

"And covers operations on its failures. And yet, this is a very common organizational mistake. There are inefficiencies in having them be separate, to be sure, but to have really colossal failures, they need to be under unified command."

"And civilian leadership benefits from a diversity of opinion."

"Talking about civilian leadership," Sigurdsen said, "there should also be a ban on currently serving military personnel holding civilian positions in the government."

"That we already had, I think."

"Excellent. Well, that pretty much covers it for me, Professor. Did you have other questions for discussion?"

"Not at the present time, Admiral. But, as always, a most enjoyable discussion. Most enjoyable, indeed."

Wolf In Sheep's Clothing

About half of Red Team had been sucked into the ship's crew for *Stardust*. The crew chiefs were doing their best with half of their crews being green spacers.

"Now what do they want? We're having a hard time keeping up as it is, and the ore containers are piling up without enough tonnage to get them to Earth," Theresa Lucas said.

"Well, they want us to fix that," crew boss Lloyd Behm said. "They need to have ships showing up in Earth orbit, unloading fernico, we need to get some o' this stuff that's stackin' up outta here, and *Stardust*'s crew needs some experience spacin' around. So they want us to disguise the ships."

"Disguise *Stardust*? As what?" Eben Waters asked.

"As *Stardust*. The freighter. Disguise her weapons. So we can let her run her normal freight runs."

"Those beam cutters are pretty big, boss," Mark Walker said.

"Yeah, but other than the beam emitters, they're just a big steel box. Can we cover over the beam emitter end with some thin steel plate, and paint some markings on 'em like they're oversize water containers or something? You know, so-and-so many thousand gallons? 'Cause they might be big, but compared to the ship, they're not."

"Yeah, maybe," Robert Dean said. "All twelve together are forty-eight containers' worth of volume, and on a ship that'll take a couple thousand containers, that's not a lot. Couple percent. We should be able to make it work."

"We could put explosive bolts on them, to allow the covers to be blown off if they need the emitters," Lucas said.

"That won't work on the front ones. If the ship is under acceleration, those covers will fall back along the length of the ship, ripping up stuff as they go. The back ones would work, though. Those are more important, if you're making a run for it," Dean said.

"Yeah, but if the ship's not acceleratin', blowin' the front ones off is still easier than goin' out there with a wrench or a torch or somethin'. Especially if ya spin the ship first. They'll drift out, then it's OK to go," Walker said.

"Fair enough," Dean said.

"OK, that sounds good," Behm said. "And document everything for the other teams. *Stardust*'s our baby, along with *Starlight* and *Starhome*, but the other teams have their own ships to modify. We need to get these babies shipping, and their crews need the spacing time."

When it was all said and done, all the teams had major management changes. Once the disguises were done, Red Team Crew Boss Lloyd Behm moved aboard *Stardust* under Captain Marc Heller as the senior non-com, Robert Dean moved aboard *Starlight* under Captain Pamela Wright as the senior non-com, and Theresa Lucas moved aboard *Starhome* under Captain Bokerah Brumley as the senior non-com. Mark Walker would be Red Team Crew Boss of the mining operations on Misty going forward, and Eben Waters would be his assistant, while all the assistant crew chiefs moved up.

Starhome's secret name was CSS *Victory*, while *Starlight*'s was CSS *Vengeance*.

The secure video conference had twenty-six attendees: Jarl Sigurdsen, the Orlov Group's VP of Mining Operations, his subordinate, Rick Ewald, the Director of Shipping Operations, and the captains and first officers of all twelve of the converted freighters.

"Good morning, gentlemen, ladies. Thank you for hooking in to this conference," Sigurdsen said. "We are going to begin using your ships for freight operations to and from Earth. We need the tonnage, and your crews need the practice.

"This will necessarily require some caution on your part to maintain the secrecy of your ships' modifications. We have disguised some of their capability as extra reaction mass storage and extra supplies. You will also have a much larger than normal crew complement, which we are attributing to training missions for the new crew members required for so many ships.

"We do want you to maintain the secrecy of your modifications. However, if you are fired on, you may fight your ships as required to escape. Our preference is you blow the covers and use the aft beam weapons, because that will leave behind little evidence of what actually happened for Earth to make heads or tails of. Their ship was simply lost. It happens. But we need you to make it back here so you can tell us Earth has turned belligerent.

"We also need to emplace a more strict organizational structure aboard ship. We will be using naval ratings and organization charts we have devised from both the Earth Space Navy and from prior Earth sea-faring navies. We have sent you all materials on these ratings and organizational structures for your use in implementing them aboard your ships.

"Finally, we need to train these crews so you can be effective. We also sent you materials on training scenarios you can use while under way, as well as some you have to do here, like gunnery practice. You have to do those last carefully, out of sight of the Earth's commerce enforcement ships in the system, so coordinate that with us."

Stardust Captain Marc Heller and his XO, Bryan Jones, met with Lloyd Behm, the senior crew boss on *Stardust*.

"Your rank, Mr. Behm, is Senior Chief Petty Officer, or simply Senior Chief. We are giving you seniority stripes for your years of service in the Orlov Group, which make you senior of all non-commissioned crew aboard. The senior non-com. We need you to sort out what you have for crew and make recommendations of ratings for all non-commissioned crew aboard."

Behm was looking over the table of ratings.

"I understand, sir," Behm said. "Seaman Recruit, Seaman 2nd, Seaman 1st, Petty Officer 3rd, Petty Officer 2nd, Petty Officer 1st, Chief Petty Officer, and Senior Chief Petty Officer. Makes sense to me, sir."

"Good. I want you, as the senior non-com, to have a weekly meeting with the First Officer here, to discuss anything that needs discussing. Problem children, whether officers or enlisted, status of the ship, any issues that come up. We want to keep good communications between the two sides of the house."

Jones and Behm nodded to each other. They had both been with the Orlov Group and known each other for years, mostly from ferry rides from Jezgra to Misty and back early in Jones' career.

"Not a problem, sir," Behm said.

"There's something else I want you to do, Senior Chief," Heller said. "I've been reading up a lot on naval organization, particularly ship organization, and there's a tradition I really like. It's really important to have all the chiefs and senior chiefs on board ship be in cahoots with each other to keep things running smoothly. I don't want the ship's organization fracturing up into departments that are competitive with each other instead of cooperative. Some seafaring navies had a Chief's Mess, where all the chiefs and senior chiefs ate and bunked together, rather than with their departments. I want you to look into that and implement it aboard *Stardust*. I've sent you a couple articles on that."

"I saw those, sir. The Goat Locker."

"Yes, that's what they called it. Unofficially."

"No problem, sir."

"Great. Now that we have all that out of the way, we need to talk about training exercises. On our way to Earth, we need to start shaking out the crew. General quarters drills, maneuvering drills, that sort of thing. Commander Jones has some ideas on that. Go ahead, Bryan."

Marc Heller had left the *Independence* name plate in his house in Jezgra. No sense providing proof positive of anything untoward if they were searched. It would take a pretty thorough search to turn up anything on *Stardust*. With the weapons consoles powered down, they were just the spare consoles she shipped with, and the beam cutters were pretty cleverly concealed, all in all.

They were all loaded, with a thousand containers of fernico, and had completed ship and cargo checks.

"All right, Mr. Asnip, is our course set?"

"Yes, sir. Departure on your order."

"You may proceed. Very gently, please. Call them out."

"Sounding maneuvering alarm."

The klaxon blared, then three bells sounded.

"Halting ship spin."

They gradually went from maybe one-half gravity to weightless.

"Ship spin at zero. Folding cylinders."

There were some side thrusts on the bridge as the crew cylinders, including the one the bridge was in, folded against the ship's sides, then some distant clanking as they were latched.

"Confirming positive latch on all cylinders. Powering up main drive to ten percent."

Gravity gradually increased to just above zero. There was a change in the ship's background noise, barely noticeable, but one every spacer knew.

"Underway. Coming to zero mark ninety on Misty."

Stars panned across and down the ship's display as she reoriented toward the hyper limit.

"On course zero mark ninety on Misty. Bringing engines gradually to eighty percent."

The barely perceptible engine note in the background noise became slightly louder as the engines came up, and gravity increased over several minutes to one-half g.

Greg Yetter, the loadmaster, was fussing over first one set of external cameras and then another as *Stardust*'s acceleration slowly grew. He also monitored various strain gauges and seismic sensors throughout the ship.

"Engines stable at eighty percent," Asnip said.

Yetter looked up to see Heller looking at him with a raised eyebrow.

"Load secure, sir. No shifts, no breakaways. We're good."

"Excellent, Mr. Yetter. Nicely done, Mr. Asnip. Secure from maneuvering."

Two tones sounded throughout the ship.

"Secured from maneuvering, sir."

Senior Chief Lloyd Behm was meeting in the Chief's Mess with the other chiefs on the *Stardust*. *Stardust*'s original crew spaces in Cylinder One had been deemed "topside" and refitted for officers. Her mechanical spaces in Cylinder Two and her passenger cabins in Cylinders Three and Four had been deemed "below decks," and her passenger cabins refitted as bunk rooms. Whereas normal crew complement was forty, with a hundred passengers, *Stardust* now had forty officers and two hundred enlisted aboard, including eleven chiefs and three senior chiefs.

"OK, so this is gonna be a quick trip," Behm said. "Here to Earth, unload and reload, and back to Jablonka. And there's gonna be no liberty on Earth. Too much chance o' somebody gettin' drunk and spillin' the beans."

"Crew's not gonna like that, Lloyd," Senior Chief Abigail Swogger said.

"Yeah, I know, Abby, but nothin' I can do about it. Lotta guys turn into big mouths when they get a couple drinks in 'em. Especially if there's ESN guys around. We just can't take the risk."

"Well, we'll deal with it," Swogger said.

And she would, too, Behm knew. The XO, Bryan Jones, had questioned having a female senior chief, especially with only three senior chief positions for a two-hundred-person crew. Behm had told him, "Anybody stupid enough to give Abby Swogger a hard time will get a quick education. She don't take no shit offa nobody and that's a fact." Jones had signed off on it, and she had more than lived up to her billing.

"What about having liberty on ship? You know, let a third of the crew or so get into the booze for two days, then the next third, then the next. But keep them all on ship," Chief Robert Wood asked.

"We'll have to think about that one, Bob," Behm said. "There may be a way to pull it off. Everybody give some thought to that. How do we do it without somebody gettin' drunk and mouthin' off to an officer or somethin'?"

"We could maybe isolate the off-duty guys somehow. You know, like a liberty mess or something," Chief Shannon Gaffney said.

"Letting them blow off some steam would help a lot," Swogger said, "as long as it doesn't get out of hand."

"Well, we're not bringin' any hookers on board, so that will limit some of the shenanigans," Senior Chief Larry Southard said.

"And female crew is off-limits," Swogger said. "Out the airlock off-limits."

"You know somebody's gonna test that, Abby," Southard said.

"Then I'll space him myself," Swogger said.

And she would, too, Behm thought. *Without hesitation and without regret. Which would also put an end to the problem.*

A loud harsh klaxon sounded throughout the ship, followed by the five bells of the general quarters alarm, at 3:00 AM their second night under way.

A Charter For The Commonwealth

"C'mon! Move it, move it, move it," Chief Don Thibodeau said. He was at the base of the stairs down into Cylinder Two from the central corridor. "Let's go!"

"Twenty-five minutes. That's pathetic," Behm said.

"What's your goal?" Thibodeau asked.

"I don't know, Don, but it sure as hell ain't twenty-five minutes. I'm thinkin' more like five minutes."

"The problem is nobody prepped for general quarters," Wood said. "They should have their general quarters clothes and equipment laid out ready when they go to bed."

"Bob's right," Swogger said. "We need to have everybody lay out their clothes at the ready when they go to bed. No exceptions."

"All right. So everybody needs to tell your monkeys to prep for general quarters before they hit the rack," Behm said.

"You know some guys are gonna resist that," Gaffney said.

"Then you tell 'em Momma Swogger will come explain it to 'em, and help 'em dress themselves," Behm said.

"Yeah. That'll do it," Gaffney said.

"I like it," Swogger said.

"What?" Petty Officer 1st Michael Kouvatsos asked. "You think you're special, Teuber? You got some kinda special dispensation?"

"Nah, Petty Officer. I just think it's silly, is all," Seaman 1st Steve Teuber said.

"Silly, is it? You want I should ask Senior Chief Swogger to come down here and you can tell her that? Have Momma explain it to you why she thinks it's important? Have Momma help you lay out your clothes at night?"

Teuber blanched.

"No, Petty Officer. That won't be necessary."

"Well, then, you better get with the program, Teuber. 'Cause the next time I catch you slackin', Swogger's comin' down here. And you know what they say. If Momma ain't happy, ain't nobody happy."

Stardust was almost two weeks out from Misty before she was far enough away from the system for the big ship to transition to hyperspace. There had been four more general quarters drills during those two weeks.

When they sounded general quarters for the hyperspace transition, it took eight minutes for all hands to be in place.

"Now that's more like it," Swogger said.

"We're gettin' there," Behm said. "Now we can start drilling damage control."

The Big Question

"I'm sorry for jumping turn on you, Admiral, but we need to have one more hypothetical discussion before Mineko and I leave for the Westlake Conference," Ansen said.

"Certainly, Professor. I always look forward to our discussions, and I'll miss them while you're gone," Sigurdsen said.

"This discussion is a continuation of our last one. If such a situation were to come to pass – the founding document and all the rest – the obvious question is, What then? What is the next step? The document is presumably finished, and is also secret. It exists, but no one knows it exists. What then?"

"What is the triggering event for an announcement, you mean?"

"That, and how does it all get started. How does the initial Council get selected, for example?" Ansen asked.

"It seems to me you have two choices there, Professor. One is to wait for some triggering event. I'm not sure what that might be, but we could bandy it about. Perhaps it might be announced in response to some unpopular decision by Earth with regard to the colonies. Those seem to come along regularly. Or one could simply declare the government in operation immediately."

"That leaves the question of how the council is initially selected."

"What is your quorum requirement for the council?" Sigurdsen asked.

"Well, we won't know until the conference hammers out the final form of the document, but we were thinking of at least two councilors from eighty percent of the member planets. In practice that would be a minimum of fifty-four councilors of the ninety-nine, two from each of twenty-seven planets."

"It seems to me the Westlake Conference itself constitutes a quorum under those rules, so the founding document could name the conference attendees to be the initial council. Say for a four-year term, after which the planets would be able to name their councilors."

Ansen opened his mouth to respond, then closed it. He stared out the picture window for several minutes before responding.

"That actually could work, Admiral, but it raises several questions. First, a response from Earth might follow almost immediately. A military response. Would we be able to defend ourselves on that timeframe? Say one year?"

"Yes, no question."

"Truly?"

"Truly," Sigurdsen said.

"The second question raised is, Would a four-year term be sufficient to ensure, whatever confrontation with Earth did ensue, it would be over within that timeframe?"

"Yes. Probably less than two years. I picked four years to have sufficient cushion."

"That quickly?" Ansen asked.

"We'll have had almost four years to prepare by that point, Professor, while Earth will be scrambling to respond. We have a window of opportunity to prevail. Then it's a race to stay ahead of them, but we will have the more competitive structure and a more loyal and motivated military."

"Understood. The third question it raises is, What about the third councilor from each planet? Do we just operate in the interim with two from each planet?"

"You could. Or you could name a third yourselves. You will have two people from each planet already. They can nominate someone."

Kusunoki stirred in her chair, muttering something under her breath. Ansen and Sigurdsen turned to her, and she was looking out the big picture window, wide-eyed with sudden insight.

"What was that, my dear?" Ansen asked.

Kusunoki turned her head to look at them, and her eyes were sparkling. "The governors. Make the planetary governors the third councilor from each planet."

"That is an interesting – and counterintuitive – proposal, Professor. Why would you make Earth's current planetary governors members of the council of a new, free polity?" Sigurdsen asked.

"Think about it, Admiral. One, they are the legitimate authority now, which adds immediate legitimacy to the council.

"Two, it will confuse and divide the Earth government. These are the sons and daughters of some of Earth's most powerful families. Do they want to hang their own children for treason? We will get some of the Earth family patriarchs to at least think about backing us, particularly if we throw in a free-trade treaty.

"Three, it will get at least some of the planetary governors, who are used to being in charge of things in the colonies, to throw in with us, because then they will still be in charge, at least partially. And they'll be independent of oversight from their families. We'll probably get more of them than you think. Instead of fighting against us, they'll be fighting for us.

"Four, the planetary governors who do throw in with us already know all the levers of power within the colonies, have the allegiance of the police forces, have their existing bureaucracy, have the relationship with the business community. They also have relationships with the other planetary governors, and may be able to convince others to throw in with us.

"Five, the initial council is all academics. The planetary governors are all administrators. We need administrative experience, badly, and they are the best source of it we have."

"That, my dear, is brilliant," Ansen said.

"I like it as well," Sigurdsen said. "I like it a lot, actually. Especially the part about dividing the loyalties of Earth's ruling families. Anything to sow discord within the enemy's high councils is a big positive with me."

"But what if they vote to dissolve the commonwealth, or turn everything over to Earth again, or some such?" Ansen asked.

"They're still a minority in the council. You simply outvote them," Kusunoki said.

Ansen and Sigurdsen both nodded.

"We come to the last question, then. Who is the first chairman of the council? Who is the executive?" Ansen asked.

Sigurdsen looked at Kusunoki with a raised eyebrow, and she smiled and nodded to him.

"Westlake," Sigurdsen said. "Has to be."

"Well, it has to be one of the planetary governors, Admiral," Kusunoki said. "As noted, they are the only ones with administrative experience. And Westlake is the obvious choice. Jablonka – centrally located, the largest economy among all the colonies, and a hub of colonial shipping – is the logical choice for the capital, as well. And we have the advantage of being able to float it past Mr. Westlake –

very quietly, of course – before we set out for the conference."

After Admiral Sigurdsen left, Ansen returned to the living room and sat with Kusunoki.

"Well, that was interesting," Ansen said. "How long have you been thinking of co-opting the planetary governors to the council?"

"I would love to claim I thought it all along, but in fact it just occurred to me. A flash of insight."

"It's brilliant. I said it and I meant it. It makes more and more sense the longer I think about it. You not only co-opt the governors and divide loyalties among our opponents both here and on Earth, but you co-opt their legitimacy and the structures of authority that report to them, all at once. Together with a trade deal built into the treaty, it makes the likelihood of success in negotiating a settlement much more likely."

"I think so. The only real question now is what does Mr. Westlake think."

"So what do you think, Georgy?" Westlake asked.

"It's a brilliant move. They co-opt the existing authorities, divide Earth's councils, and get all the administrative experience a bunch of academics is sorely lacking. Sigurdsen said it was Kusunoki's idea, apparently on the spot," Orlov said.

"I told you, she's Ansen's secret weapon. But being chairman of the council also raises the stakes considerably for me, personally."

"Yes, it does. But co-opting the planetary governors also greatly increases the odds of success. Together with the military side of things. The converted freighters aren't just Q-ships any more, they're full up warships. Oh, they don't have the redundancy and such I would like, but they've become really serious offensive weapons."

"I wonder how many governors will opt in to the commonwealth, and how many will work against us," Westlake said.

"Some of that you can affect, Jim. I suspect a lot of them will take a wait-and-see attitude. These are people who are accustomed to coming out on the winning side in the families' never-ending political gamesmanship. I don't think most will jump one way or the other until they see which way the wind is blowing. You might be able to encourage that in your contacts. Have you taken a count of which way you think people will go?"

"Yes. I make it eight hard against us, maybe as many as ten for us. The rest could go either way."

"I think they'll try to straddle the fence," Orlov said.

"Perhaps."

Westlake looked down at his hands, clasped between his knees, for several minutes. Orlov knew that pose, and simply waited. At length, Westlake looked up at Orlov, looked directly into his eyes.

"You think I should do this, don't you, Georgy?"

"Right now, I don't think you should do anything. Let the conference proceed. A document is probably almost a year off. Ask for an early copy. But yes, I think once they go public you should publicly sign on. And have letters to your contacts in the colonies, and to your father, ready to go."

Westlake nodded.

"Will you be my defense minister, Georgy?"

"Well, I won't be on the council. From Jablonka, that'll be you, Ansen, and Kusunoki. But, as long as at least the interim ministers don't need to be on the council, then yes, Jim, I'll be your defense minister."

"With Sigurdsen as chief of operations, I suppose?"

"No. That'll be Rick Ewald. He's director of my shipping operations now, and chief of naval operations is mostly an administrative position. I want Admiral Sigurdsen out in the field, with the fleet."

"The fleet. The Commonwealth Space Force. Who'd have thought?"

Westlake took a drink of his coffee, set the cup down and stared at it for a while. He looked back up at Orlov.

"I suppose at some point we'll have to buy all those ships from you, Georgy."

"I'd rather you spent your tax money on keel-out warships, Jim. Those ships are still useful to me as freighters once you replace them. Having armed freighters, at least for a little while, seems prudent to me."

"We'll need our own shipyards."

"Clearly."

"There's a lot of work ahead, Georgy."

"That's why they need administrators. You're a good choice for chairman, Jim."

"All right. I suppose I can meet with Ansen and Kusunoki now. They're the winners of the Westlake Prize, after all. Tag up before they head off to the conference."

"Professors, come in, come in. Please, be seated."

As he had three years before, Westlake waved his guests to his side seating arrangement, where the refreshments requested last time had already been laid out. He shook hands with both before they all took their seats.

Westlake waved to the humidor on the table, already placed for Ansen's use.

"Go ahead, Professor Ansen. Please."

"Thank you, Excellency."

Ansen took one of the Earth-import cigars, long missing from his humidor, cut the end, and lit it. He drew in the first puff and then exhaled luxuriously, while Westlake and Kusunoki poured their coffee and tea, respectively.

"Thank you so much for stopping by to meet with me. I will mention that this meeting, like our last, is not being recorded and is off the record," Westlake said.

Ansen nodded. He had already put Westlake's invitation on the coffee table.

"Understood, Excellency."

"So here we are. Remarkable. With many thanks to the two of you, we have a good framework for a charter, we have a navy, and we are on the verge of becoming our own polity. I wanted to express my thanks personally for your roles in making my dreams possible."

"We're not quite there yet, Excellency."

"No, Professor Ansen. But we are very close. Closer than I dreamed we could be."

"But you set all this in motion, Excellency."

"Yes, Professor Kusunoki. But a life in administration teaches you not to be too hopeful. Many things one starts in motion either do not play out as one might hope, or fizzle out altogether. I'm happy this has not been one of them."

Kusunoki nodded.

A Charter For The Commonwealth

"That being said, with you having done so much already, I nevertheless have some further requests to make of you."

"Please, go ahead," Ansen said.

"First, Georgy has told me of your plans to name the planetary governors to the council and to nominate me as council chairman. Despite the increased risk to me personally, I think – as you do, Professor Kusunoki – this greatly increases our chances of success. I have already begun thinking through my approach to my fellow governors and to Earth.

"But it would greatly assist me if you would send me a copy of your charter as it then stands perhaps two months before you pass it. With six weeks round-trip travel time on fast mail courier ships, that gives me a chance to look through it and get back to you before final passage."

Ansen nodded. "Sensible."

"I hoped you would think so. Also, I would like you to advise me on final passage, and then hold your announcement for two weeks. That means I will be able to get a message to my father on Earth before he gets news of the charter."

"Agreed."

"Thank you. I think it will help our chances considerably to get our argument before my father. Suzette's father as well, for that matter." Westlake sipped his coffee, then set the cup back on the table. "Finally, I would ask that at least interim ministers in the government not be required to be members of the council. I need Georgy Orlov at defense."

"That makes sense as well, Excellency. Since we don't know which planetary governors will side with us, and the academics that comprise two-thirds of the initial council have little or no administrative experience, requiring that ministers be from the council in the first, oh, ten years or so, is a recipe for disaster." Ansen considered. "Should ministers be from the council on the longer term, though? That's an interesting question."

"That's for the conference to decide, I think. My only caution would be that it might give individual planets too much power. Were the minister to do something their own planet doesn't like, they could replace him on the council, and now you're out one minister. It might make ministers too compliant to their planet's policy preferences."

"An interesting point. Well, we will consider the longer term requirement, and put in the short-term exemption as well."

"Thank you, Professor. And with that, my own questions are complete. Unless you have any questions for me?"

Both Ansen and Kusunoki shook their heads.

"Very well, then. Good travels, my friends, and the best of luck in your endeavors at the conference. You hold all our futures in your hands."

When Ansen and Kusunoki arrived at the Jablonka shuttleport for transfer up to their ship to Doma, porters carried their substantial trunks into the shuttleport terminal building. Packing for a year was no small matter. Thankfully, the days of carrying one's books and papers in physical hard copy were long gone, or there would have been twice as much.

The head porter greeted them inside. Several hundred other passengers bound for Doma were already there.

"Professor Ansen? Professor Kusunoki?"

"Yes."

"Ah. Very good." He checked them off a list. "Your other trunk arrived earlier."

"What other trunk?"

The head porter waved to another trunk, every bit as large as theirs, sitting over by the pile of luggage to be boarded. Ansen walked over to it curiously. It was already tagged for Doma, and had his name prominently labeled on it. He unlatched the lid with a thumb swipe, glanced inside, and closed it again. He walked back to the head porter.

"Ah, yes. Of course. I had completely forgotten about it."

He and Kusunoki walked over to waiting area chairs to wait for the arrival of the shuttle.

When they were out of earshot of the porters, Kusunoki asked, "What's in the other trunk?"

"It is full to the brim – to the very brim, my dear – with those wonderful cigars, bourbon, and tea. And this."

Ansen handed her a small card, inscribed in a precise, decorative hand she recognized.

With all best wishes. W.

In Transit

They were in the Goat Locker, and Senior Chief Lloyd Behm had the floor. *Stardust* had made its transition to hyperspace on departing Jablonka yesterday.

"OK, so now that we can get to general quarters the same day they're sounded, we need to practice what we do when we get there. Some people have obvious assignments, like the computers, engines, weapons, and environmental sections. Everybody else goes on damage control parties. So what kind of damage are we likely to take in a battle?"

"Punctures from ESN projectile launchers," Chief Wood said.

"Right. Now on this trip, we're not gonna be doing any attacking. We're just gonna defend ourselves if we need to run away. So where are we likely to take punctures? What's our aft aspect look like?"

"Deck One of the cylinders," Senior Chief Southard said.

"Engines," Chief Tom Wallace said.

"Radiators," Senior Chief Swogger said.

"Aft beam cutters. You know, beams 9 through 12," Chief Gaffney said.

"Right. All the above. Now, if we're runnin' away, and the engines are runnin' hard, we don't need to worry about engines because any projectile headed for the engines is gonna be vaporized before it hits us. If we lose a beam cutter, we lose one. Can't do anything about that on the run, but we could mount a spare once we escape, if we carried spares. I should look into that for next trip.

"Cylinders and radiators is the issue. So we need damage control parties suited up, with patches and shit, on the lower decks of every cylinder. And we gotta have all the airtight doors shut so we can limit air loss, particularly on lower decks. We don't know how many decks those damn things will go through."

"Sounds right. What about the radiators?" Swogger asked.

"We need to be monitoring all four radiators for pressure. Any pressure drop on a radiator, we can assume it's been holed and we need to valve it off and lean harder on the others. We can fix it and refill it once we escape. So that's all on the engines people."

"We'll run hot if we lose a radiator," Chief Wallace said.

"Yup. Don't know how hot, but we probably ought to try it in one o' these drills and see what we get. Could get warm in here. We'll deal with it. We wanna figure it out now, not then.

"But that's what we're about. So let's think up some ways to practice this stuff. Then I'll run it all past the XO and get approvals. And then we're gonna drill patching, and valving off radiators, and anything else we can think of. Our job is to preserve the ship and the crew while continuing to carry the fight to the enemy. We better figure out how to do that, ladies and gentlemen. We got two months in hyper before we get to Earth. I wanna know – not guess; *know* – we can do that before we get there."

Seamen 1st Garland Noel and Toby Cobb and Seamen 2nd Jason O'Toole and Paul Clithero were in the stairwell on Deck One of Cylinder Two. Petty Officer 2nd Pamela Stump was in charge.

"All right. So what we're gonna do is patch the deck, like we got a hole from a projectile launcher. I put a screamer on the ceilin' somewhere on Deck One. It's gonna make a loud whistlin' sound, and shine a spot o' light down on the deck. That's your hole. You gotta find it and patch it. Got it?"

"Sure, Petty Officer," Noel said.

"Yeah. No problem, Petty Officer," Cobb said.

"OK. Noel and O'Toole, you're first up." Stump pushed a button on a remote, and a loud whistling noise started off in the distance. "Go."

O'Toole picked up the patch, a flexible eighth-inch steel-mesh-and-rubber plate twenty-four inches in diameter with two folding handles on one side, and Noel grabbed the tool box. They walked off down the aisle after the sound. Stump watched dumbfounded, but said nothing.

They found the screamer in one of the bunkrooms. Noel put down the toolbox and rummaged for the spray can of rubber gasketing. He found it and sprayed it around the light spot on the floor. O'Toole set the patch plate on it.

They looked up to see Stump standing in the doorway. She turned off the screamer with her remote, and they all went back to the stairwell.

"OK, Cobb and Clithero. Your turn."

Stump turned on another screamer, and Cobb and Clithero set off to find the screamer and patch the 'hole' much as Noel and O'Toole had. They all met up back in the stairwell.

"OK. First, you guys did it just like a trainin' movie. Problem is, those movies are an hour long. Both teams took almost fifteen minutes to find and seal the damn hole. This whole deck would be depressurized in that time, as well as any decks further up that got punched as well.

"I wanna count the time it takes to seal a hole in *seconds*, not minutes. You need to arrange your toolboxes so the items needed most often are on top, not rummage around for 'em. You need to head off down the aisle at a dead run to find that hole. And you can slam the plate over it and spray the gasketing around it after the plate is down. Vacuum will pull the gasketing into the gap. Got all that?"

"Yes, Petty Officer," Cobb and Noel said together.

"All right, then. Organize your stuff and then let's try it again."

They made four more practice runs before Stump was satisfied.

"OK. That's it for now. Tomorrow we do it suited up."

They didn't audibly groan. Not quite.

"Hey, you guys wanna get home or not? We could get GQed in the middle of the night. You guys gotta be able to do this in your sleep. And we're gonna practice it until you can."

Stump practiced the other two teams for Deck One that afternoon. There would be four teams on each of the lower decks of each cylinder.

"So how we doin' on the patchin' teams?" Behm asked.

"Libis, Stump, Kuhn, and Edwards have their teams performing pretty well. Most of the others, not so much," Chief Christine Chase said.

"That's Steven Libis, Pamela Stump, Alan Kuhn, and Valerie Edwards?" Behm asked, looking at his crew roster.

"Yeah. They have their times down under three minutes. Pami Stump says if we keep the decks sealed but leave all the compartment doors on each deck open in GQ, four teams per deck ought to be able to get their time down around a minute. Checking compartments takes up a lot of the time. With the doors open, they can hear where it is."

"Well, this is a freighter. The compartments on a deck aren't airtight from each other anyway."

"That's what Pami said," Chase said.

"All right, Chris. Let's do that. And I think what we ought to do is bump these four to petty officer 1st, and have them each supervise all the patching crews in one of the cylinders. I left some openings in the petty officer ranks so we could promote people who earned it."

"I think that makes a lot of sense, Lloyd. They clearly know how to get teams to perform. Let's see if they can teach others how to get teams to perform."

Chief Wallace was in Radiator Control in Cylinder Two for a test of shutting down one radiator to see how bad their heating problem would be.

"We have all the readings on our current status?" Wallace asked.

"Yes, Chief. We have our recordings running all the time, and we're showing they're updating," Petty Officer 1st Lindsay Harwood said.

"All right. Let's go ahead and shut one of 'em down."

"You heard the man. Shut down the coolant pump on Radiator One."

"Shutting down the coolant pump on Radiator One," Seaman 1st Jennifer Lowenthal said. "Radiator One flow rate dropping. Radiator One flow rate zero."

"Close inlet valve on Radiator One."

"Closing inlet valve on Radiator One. Radiator One pressure dropping."

"Close outlet valve on Radiator One."

"Closing outlet valve on Radiator One. Radiator One isolated."

"Yount. Watch your temps. Call 'em out," Harwood said.

"Monitoring temps. Stable at 180 degrees inlet temperatures on Radiators Two, Three, and Four. No significant rise yet," Seaman 1st James Yount said.

They all watched for several minutes.

"Inlet temperatures now at 190 degrees.

"Inlet temperatures now at 200 degrees.

"Inlet temperatures now at 210 degrees.

"Inlet temperatures now at 220 degrees.

"Inlet temperatures now at 230 degrees.

"Inlet temperatures now at 240 degrees.

"Temperatures stable at 240 degrees."

"And that's at eighty percent on the engines, Chief," Harwood said to Wallace. "If we're running at a hundred percent, they're going to go higher."

"And our safety limit is, what? 280 degrees?"

"Yes, Chief. Though I hope not to go that high. The option is to shut off the air conditioning compressors in the crew spaces and go to emergency lighting systems to cut back on waste heat in electricity generation."

"Well, if we gotta do it, we gotta do it. Cutting back on the engines when somebody's shootin' at us ain't my idea of a good time."

"I'm with you there, Chief. I guess the bottom line is, as long as we only lose one radiator, we're good."

Stardust continued to have patching drills and general quarters drills throughout the first month of the hyperspace transit.

They were into the second half of the transit, after they had flipped ship for the long deceleration to Earth, when the klaxon sounded and five bells rang general quarters at 3:00 in the morning. About five minutes into general quarters, two screamers went off without warning on Decks One through Five in each of the four cylinders, the first time a screamer had sounded during general quarters. The patching crews reacted automatically, without thinking, and all forty of the 'holes' were patched and the entire ship sealed within two minutes.

That night, Chief Christine Chase invited Petty Officers 1st Steven Libis, Pamela Stump, Alan Kuhn, and Valerie Edwards to dinner in the Chief's Mess. When they entered, Senior Chief Lloyd Behm led the assembled chiefs and senior chiefs in a standing ovation.

Stardust was ready for battle.

Gerald Ansen and Mineko Kusunoki had a first-class suite on the passenger liner *Jewel Of Space*. A central sitting room connected to a small office, bedroom, and bathroom on each side. It was luxurious accommodations shipboard, and they appreciated each having an office in which to work in addition to the central suite for their conversations. They had the porters fold up the double bed in one bedroom and strap their three trunks to the floor stanchions, as a measure against having them fly around in zero-gravity.

The *Jewel Of Space*, plying routinely between Jablonka, the largest and richest of the colonies, and Doma, the premier resort planet, was one of the most luxurious liners in service, and they had its premier accommodations. They were thus not crowded in the way typically associated with space travel.

"Well, this is very nice for being aboard ship," Kusunoki said. "I remember my trip out from Earth as being much more crowded than this."

"Indeed," Ansen said. "As with my student travels to and from Earth decades ago. Still, six weeks is a long time. It's particularly a long time to do without cigars."

"Did you not see there was a first-class smoking lounge on this floor?"

"Excuse me. What did you say?"

"There's a first-class smoking lounge across the hall. I'm not sure how that works with recycled air, but there it is."

Ansen jumped up from his chair in the sitting room and went out the door. He returned three minutes later.

"Marvelous. Momentous. Miraculous." Ansen reseated himself next to Kusunoki. "I have decided I will not, in fact, go out of my mind on this trip. Thank you, my dear."

"You're welcome," Kusunoki said, smiling hugely. "So, if you are not going to go out of your mind during the trip, what are you going to do for the next six weeks?"

"Build a decision tree for the charter, with historical references for each of the branches."

"Every decision, from the beginning?"

"Yes," Ansen said. "Every decision I can think of. Unicameral or bicameral. Per planet or per capita. How many legislators. President or prime minister. Which cabinet ministers. Each civil right, in or out. Each government power or authority, in or out. Commonwealth crimes, in or out. Commonwealth courts, in or out. Requirement for amendments. Everything. Top to bottom."

"That's quite a job."

A Charter For The Commonwealth

"Yes, but I have six weeks and there is quite literally nothing else I can do. No parties. No newsfeeds. No correspondence. No meetings. No classes. No walks on the quad. Nothing except smoke cigars and get drunk, or work."

"While smoking cigars and drinking," Kusunoki said.

"Well, yes. Of course."

As a passenger liner, *Jewel of Space* could and did maintain 0.8 g acceleration, and so there was near normal gravity except during maneuvering. Both Ansen and Kusunoki knew from their previous voyages neither was bothered by zero-g, so there were no pills to take against weightlessness sickness on hyperspace transitions or when flipping the ship mid-transit.

As the occupants of the Owner's Suite for the passage, they were invited to sit at the Captain's Table in the First-Class Dining Room, which they did regularly once Ansen discovered the bourbon served at the Captain's Table was a better brand than that available otherwise.

Ansen spent many of his waking hours in the First-Class smoking lounge, smoking cigars and drinking bourbon, and working on his decision tree. The computer graph grew and grew, as he and Kusunoki in their evening conversations revisited every decision they had considered and added more. His goal was a complete map by the time they reached Doma, with all the historical precedents annotated, to assist the conference in its deliberations.

There is nothing to match the food served at the Captain's Table in the First-Class Dining Room of a luxury liner. Between the food, the drink, the cigars, and the work on the decision tree, the six weeks passed swiftly.

The shuttle down to Doma from the *Jewel Of Space* delivered them to the Doma shuttleport in Nadezhda. As they debarked, they were greeted by a young man in a light khaki uniform with "The Dachas" embroidered on the breast.

"Professor Ansen? Professor Kusunoki?"

"Yes," Ansen said.

"I'll drive you to The Dachas, sir. This way, please."

Ansen and Kusunoki followed him through the terminal and out the front door. It was a beautiful day, of the sort for which Doma is famous. Temperature in the mid-70s, a clear blue sky, and a cool breeze blowing, just enough to wave the lush tropical foliage back and forth.

Porters followed with their three trunks. As they walked down the sidewalk, Ansen signaled to the porters on one trunk.

"You there. Set that right here, please."

Ansen pointed to a spot to the edge of the broad walk. The porters were confused, but set the trunk down where indicated. Ansen walked over to the trunk and sat down.

"Have a seat, my dear."

To the consternation of the driver and the porters, Ansen and Kusunoki sat on the trunk, holding hands, while Ansen smoked one of the lovely Earth-import cigars he had pulled from Westlake's gift trunk back on the ship.

To the driver, Ansen said, "I have been in motion constantly for the last six weeks. For just a few minutes, I simply want to sit still."

He looked around with interest, then to Kusunoki said, "Lovely place, isn't it, my dear?"

"Absolutely beautiful," she said.

Earth

Stardust made her hyperspace transition into normal space about ten percent farther from Earth then the published system periphery, just as they had in Jablonka. No sense in taking chances with a thousand containers – 2.2 million tons – of fernico aboard.

The gunnery and bombardment consoles were manned, but not powered up at the moment.

"Mr. Stodden, what have you got?" Captain Heller asked.

"Nothing nearby, sir. Not way out here," radar operator Karl Stodden said.

"Send our arrival announcement, Mr. Oconnell, and request arrival instructions."

"Yes, sir."

"Flip ship and lay in a course for the planet, Mr. Asnip."

As *Stardust* had been decelerating for the last month, and the hyperspace generator was tied in with the engines, she emerged from hyperspace with her bows pointing away from Earth. Flipping ship with that much mass of cargo was a slow business, and it was several minutes before *Stardust* was pointed in-system.

"Ship flipped and course laid in, sir."

"Get us under way, Mr. Asnip. Gently, please."

"Yes, sir."

Lieutenant Commander John Rebori had the current watch on Earth's northern approaches in the frigate ENS *Moses Lambert*, of which he was the first officer. It was nearing the end of their four-weeks-on/two-weeks-off rotation. Some of that two weeks off would be spent in transit to Earth and back, which always ticked him off. It used to be four-weeks-on/four-weeks-off, which was a different thing altogether. But they were short of ships, and this looked like it was going to become the new normal.

So he was not in a particularly good mood when the *Stardust*'s arrival announcement came in. He also suffered from the ESN's institutional arrogance, the by-product of being the only navy in

93

space, and never having been seriously challenged.

"*Moses Lambert* here. What's with you, *Stardust*? Miscalculate your hyperspace transition?" Rebori asked with barely concealed contempt.

"*Stardust* here. Just taking it easy with a couple million tons of fernico aboard, *Moses Lambert*," the answer came back.

Huh. Clearly they didn't know how to space that big bastard. Then again, it was a colony freighter, a bunch of spacer wannabes, so what could you expect.

"Well, call us again when you hit the system periphery, *Stardust*. You know, sometime next week."

"Boy, this guy really has his attitude on sideways, sir," Oconnell said to Captain Heller.

"That's not unusual, I'm afraid, Mr. Oconnell. Picket duty is not a popular assignment, and, at the same time, the ESN has more than its share of jumped-up junior officers. His captain is probably a commander, and may well be worse. We'll see."

A day and a half later, when *Stardust* reached the published system periphery, Oconnell retransmitted their arrival announcement.

"I have a Commander Patrick Viebey, sir. He demands to speak to the captain."

"Put him on, Mr. Oconnell," Captain Heller said.

"You're live, sir."

"Captain Heller here, Commander Viebey. Go ahead."

"What the hell's your problem, Heller? You know you're supposed to send an arrival announcement when you transition."

"We did send the arrival announcement immediately upon transition, Commander. Thirty-seven hours ago. Lieutenant Commander Rebori instructed us to send it again once we reached the published system periphery."

"Why are you transitioning so far out then, Heller? There's a reason for a published system periphery."

"We have green crew, Commander, and over two million tons of fernico aboard. It seemed prudent to allow plenty of safety margin."

"Yeah, I suppose if you don't know how to space a ship, you have to tip-toe around to keep from breaking it. Your form says a thousand containers of fernico, Heller?"

"That's correct, Commander."

"How many crew and passengers do you have aboard?"

"Two hundred forty crew, no passengers."

"Two hundred forty crew, Heller? What's up with that?"

"It's more like forty crew and two hundred green trainees, Commander. It was some corporate type's great idea to pack in green trainees to the deckheads and see if they learned anything."

"Oh, so *Stardust*'s not a spaceship, it's a kindergarten. Is that it, Heller?"

"Something like that, Commander."

"All right. You're cleared for passage, Heller. But keep your nose clean from here in."

"Yes, Commander. Thank you."

Heller signaled Oconnell, who cut the connection. The first officer walked up to Heller's seat.

"Wow. That guy sure is obnoxious, sir. Made me want to fire up the weapons consoles."

"Now, now, Bryan," Heller said. "We're just a peaceful, unarmed freighter, remember. It's not our time. Not yet."

"Well, when we unmask this ship and come back here, I hope we run into Commander Viebey again."

"So what have we come up with for ideas about liberty? We're only a week out now, and we gotta tell the crew something," Lloyd Behm said.

"My issue is we may have to fight our way out of the system if something goes wrong. I don't want to have half the crew down drunk and be short of damage control parties if that happens. We need to be able to fight this ship until we're out of here," Abby Swogger said.

"How about we tell everyone no liberty on-planet, but as soon as we transition to hyperspace on the way back, we'll have on-board liberty in Cylinder Three for three days, and then a day to transition, and then on-board liberty in Cylinder Four for three days? But no leaving your cylinder during that period. That'll allow us to keep the officers out. We'll just sequester half the crew spaces at a time," Shannon Gaffney said.

"OK, that could work," Behm said.

"But no fraternizing," Swogger said. "That can get out of control fast. And I'm serious about spacing anybody who takes advantage. Don't anybody doubt that for a second."

"I'll take it to the exec and see what he says. We may get shut down there, and then the details don't matter."

"So what do you think, sir?" the exec asked.

"I think it's probably a bad idea, but it may be less bad than all the alternatives," Captain Heller said. "We can't let people loose on the planet. Hell, Bryan, half the bridge was ready to swim vacuum to get their hands around Viebey's neck just from a five-minute radio conversation. We put a hundred or more ratings down on the planet and they get drinking, there's no keeping our secret.

"At the same time, I worry about things getting out of hand. Bryan, you and I have both been around the block enough times to know how badly this can go. And what about people who don't want a big party? Who just want to sit in their quarters and have a beer?"

"I've been thinking about that, sir. It seems to me we need an internal police force – you know, an MPs sort of thing – to break up anything that gets out of hand. That's what we would have on planet with the Shore Police. As for the other, sir, I think we could limit this to lower decks in each cylinder in turn, and let people swap around bunks to get themselves on the side of the line they want to be on. All the quarters are pretty much the same anyway. Then MPs patrol the landing at the boundary."

"Well, I think we need to do something to blow off some steam once we get free of Earth. People are pretty stressed at the moment, worrying we could be found out. So I'll leave it up to you and Senior Chief Behm to figure it out. Err on the side of caution, because this already sounds pretty stupid, but I don't think we can go on five months spacing without some relief, and planet leave isn't in it."

"We'll figure it out, sir."

Lloyd Behm and Abby Swogger were meeting privately in Behm's office just outside the Chief's Mess. As senior non-com, he was the go-to guy for problems below decks, and that often meant private meetings. Like this one.

"OK, so the exec got it past the captain. But that means it's on us to make it work, Abby. Coupla ideas there I think are pretty good. We find out how many people want to party, then let people re-bunk to separate them out. Bottom decks get the party, upper decks get a couple beers in quarters, hopefully everybody's happy."

"Scuttlebutt I'm getting is nobody wants planet leave. They're all afraid somebody else will get drunk and spill the beans, and they'll all end up in prison."

"Good. So at least we won't get a buncha grief about that. But five months is a long time to keep people bottled up aboard ship without 'em letting off any steam. One thing we do need, though, is the equivalent of Shore Police. We need everybody to know there's a limit, and we're gonna enforce it. Then hopefully we don't have to. I want you to take that. Put a force together. Figure out who you want, talk to 'em, sign 'em up. Some people who have prior, maybe."

"I'll run some filters past the ship's personnel files and see what I find. You want some big guys, right? Maybe some police service or MP or something?"

"Or a job as bouncer in a bar. Whatever. Some big guys everybody knows you don't wanna mess with. That oughta hold the lid on right there."

"All right, Lloyd. I'm on it."

Stardust had performed her flip halfway in from her hyperspace transition, and was now decelerating as it approached Earth.

"We have orbit instructions from Orbit Control, sir, and the Orlov Group Cargo Center has a shuttle schedule for us."

"Transfer the orbit instructions to Navigation, Mr. Oconnell. What's our shuttle schedule look like?"

"Pretty good, sir. There are twenty five cargo shuttles actually standing by. They said don't even bother to spin up, they'll meet us on orbit insertion."

"Outstanding. All right. Let's get into orbit and start offloading. Send the Cargo Center our container map, Mr. Oconnell. We want to make sure they only take the containers we're here to offload."

"Yes, sir."

A thousand containers takes a long time to unload, especially if they're loaded with fernico. The big cargo shuttles could only take four of the 2200-ton containers per trip, and it was three hours round trip, so it took a day and a half to unload and reload *Stardust*. The container map indicated which containers to unload, and which containers remained latched to the freighter.

Once the shuttles had dug down to *Stardust*'s core on one band of containers, they began bringing outbound containers up. They latched those to the empty portion of *Stardust*'s container racks, then picked up more fernico containers for the trip down. The outbound containers were lighter, and there were two thousand containers brought up before loading was complete.

At least that was the usual procedure. But for this trip there were a hundred containers that came in on *Stardust*, right up against the core of the ship, and stayed for the return trip.

"Shuttle OG-197 here. That looks like it to me, *Stardust*. Can you confirm?" shuttle pilot Megan Welch asked.

"Confirmed, OG-197. That's all we got for you. One thousand fernico inbound," Oconnell transmitted.

"And two thousand miscellaneous outbound for you. Hey, what's with all the through containers, *Stardust*? You guys got another stop?" Welch asked.

"Negative, OG-197. We're pre-stocked for both directions, and we brought along a lot of spares. *Stardust* is pretty new, and we wanted to make sure we could get home."

"Roger that, *Stardust*. Well, you're good to go. Happy spacing."

"Thanks, OG-197. You, too. *Stardust* out."

"All right, Mr. Oconnell. Do we have a departure window?"

"Yes, sir. We're actually good to go right now."

"Transfer departure instructions to Navigation. Mr. Asnip, you may proceed when ready."

"Yes, sir. Laying in course now.

"Course laid in.

"Bringing engines up to ten percent."

Gravity finally returned, though only .05 g. *Stardust*'s crew had been dealing with weightless conditions aboard the ship for the last day and a half as the shuttles unloaded her. They were getting pretty tired of cold meals and sleeping strapped down to their bunks by this point, but it was pretty standard fare for freighter crews.

"Coming to course zero mark ninety on the planet.

"Steady on course zero mark ninety on the planet.

"Bringing engines up to eighty percent."

Gravity slowly increased to .5 g throughout the ship as *Stardust* accelerated.

"Engines steady at eighty percent."

"Excellent, Mr. Asnip."

Stardust looked a lot bigger for the trip back. With twenty-one hundred containers latched around her circumference and down her length, she was a lot bigger volume going back to Jablonka than she was with eleven hundred containers coming in to Earth, but she was actually a lot lighter. The Earth exports heading out to Jablonka weren't even close to half the weight per container of the fernico loads.

After a week in transit to the system periphery, heading out the way they had come in, *Stardust* was approaching the system pickets. The ENS *Moses Lambert* had been rotated out, and the ENS *Joshua Kanapkey* was on station.

"Transmit our departure announcement, Mr. Oconnell."

"Transmitting, sir."

"ESN Commander Tamara Wilhite requesting the captain, sir."

Here we go again, Heller thought.

"Put her on, Mr. Oconnell," Heller said.

"You're live, sir."

"Captain Heller here, Commander Wilhite. Go ahead."

The voice that came back was cool, calm, and professional.

"Wilhite here. Good morning, Captain. I show *Stardust* inbound one thousand fernico, outbound two thousand miscellaneous, customs declared and fees paid. Two hundred forty aboard, no deletions, no additions. Bound for Jablonka."

"That's all correct, Commander."

"Very well, Captain. You are cleared for departure. Good spacing. Wilhite out."

The connection broke.

"Well, XO, it appears the ESN has some professional officers after all," Heller said to Bryan Jones.

"There was always a rumor to that effect, sir. I could never confirm it, though. Not until now."

There was no need to play it safe with two thousand containers of miscellaneous cargo aboard. *Stardust* no longer had over two million tons of cargo aboard. It was more like half a million tons, despite double the number of containers.

"Crossing the system periphery now, sir," Asnip said.

"Sound hyperspace warning."

"Sounding hyperspace warning, sir."

"You may proceed when ready, Mr. Asnip."

Asnip cut the engines to zero, flipped the ship, brought the hyperspace generator up, and transitioned the *Stardust* into hyperspace. Once in hyperspace, he flipped the ship again, transitioned the engines to hyperspace configuration, and engaged the engines, bringing them up to ten percent. He came around to course eighty-seven mark fifteen on the galactic center, and gradually increased the engines back up to eighty percent.

"Hyperspace transition complete, sir. Steady on course eighty-seven mark fifteen on the galactic center, engines steady at eighty percent."

"Excellent, Mr. Asnip. Secure from hyperspace warning."

"Secured from hyperspace warning, sir."

The tension on *Stardust* had ratcheted ever higher the longer they were in the Earth system. When the all-clear from hyperspace warning sounded, a cheer went up below decks.

They had made it out of the Earth system without being discovered.

A week later, Lloyd Behm and Abby Swogger were again meeting privately in Behm's office just outside the Chief's Mess.

"All right, Abby. How did it go?"

"Not too bad, Lloyd. We had five fist fights broken up, a dozen confined to quarters, and three cases of acute ethanol poisoning in sick bay."

"That sounds like a pretty quiet shore leave for a couple hundred ratings."

"Yeah, and nobody went out the air lock."

"I think you having a crew of MPs standing ready at the airlock probably helped that, don't you think, Abby?"

"Perhaps. Anyway, all in all, it worked out pretty well. And everybody got to blow off all that tension that built up in the Earth system."

"OK. Well, write me up a report on it. Especially what you did prepping for it. We'll file it with Operations when we get back. Some other ships can learn from what you did."

"Sure, Lloyd."

"And good work."

"Thanks."

Doma

The Dachas were located southwest of Nadezhda, on the shore of the Bolshoye More, the 'great sea,' Doma's largest ocean. The ground car took about thirty minutes to get there from the shuttleport.

There was no check-in at The Dachas. The entire stay for the eight months the conference would be meeting was being picked up by the Orlov Group. The ground car brought Ansen and Kusunoki through the front entrance into the grounds, at which point they transferred to a small driverless electric cart for the trip through the grounds to their unit. The porters loaded their trunks on another little shuttle, and followed.

The housing units themselves were small houses built directly on the beach. A combination of landscape walls and vegetation hid the units each from the next. Facing the ocean, the living room had a glass wall that opened onto a lanai with a pergola. There was a gas fire pit on the lanai, as well as a gas fireplace on the wall in the living room.

"Well, this is very pleasant," Ansen said as they were let into the unit and shown past the bedroom into the living room. The glass wall was completely open, and the gentle ocean breeze carried the salt air into the room.

"Beautiful," Kusunoki said.

The porters brought their trunks in and placed two of them in the bedroom at Ansen's direction. The third went into the living room against the back wall, near a small bar in the back corner.

The head porter explained the accommodations.

"For anything you want, you simply say what it is. To get the computer's attention, say 'dacha' followed by what you would like. If you then say 'shuttle,' a shuttle will show up at the front door to take you wherever in the resort you would like to go. You can give the shuttle directions by the name of the guest, rather than the unit number. You can also request the conference center. This end of the resort and its conference center has been reserved exclusively for your meeting.

A Charter For The Commonwealth

"When you wish to eat, simply say 'dacha' followed by what you would like. You can request specific food and drink items, or make a general request, such as 'a light lunch, with white wine.' Similarly with turning on or off the fire pit and fireplaces, opening or closing the glass door, adjusting the temperature. Anything you would like, we will try to provide."

"I imagine you get stumped once in a while, though," Ansen said.

"We do, but then we cover that for the next time. Our offerings have become pretty complete over time. If you have no other questions, then?"

"I have one," Ansen said. "Can I smoke in here?"

"Yes, Professor Ansen. The Orlov Group has paid a smoking premium on units reserved for guests who indicated a smoking preference on the questionnaire everyone was sent to determine their needs. As you recall, it inquired as to spouses, children, pets, allergies, and other things. If the guest indicated they preferred a smoking unit, as you did, they have been accommodated. You will note ashtrays and cigar lighters have been provided."

Ansen looked around the room, and spotted the ashtrays on the coffee table and side tables in the living room as well as on the lanai, each including a butane lighter.

"And the conference center?"

"There as well, Professor Ansen."

"Remarkable. Well, I think we're all set then."

Ansen tried to tip the head porter, but he waved it off.

"Everything has been taken care of, sir. You have no need of money for anything on the grounds, including gratuities, for the duration of your stay. Any office services needs you have, either here or at the conference center, as well. Enjoy your stay, sir, ma'am."

And with that, the porters withdrew and left them alone.

Ansen and Kusunoki sat on the lanai, in two very comfortable cushioned bamboo armchairs, facing out to the beach and the ocean beyond. He had one of the Earth-import cigars and a bourbon from Westlake's trunk, having found rocks glasses and an icemaker behind the bar in the living room. The crossbars of the pergola were set to allow the morning and evening sun onto the lanai, but to block the sun mid-day, as now.

"Should we get some lunch, my dear?"

"Certainly. It would be nice to eat something that wasn't super fancy ship food."

"You order then."

"Dacha," Kusunoki said. "Lunch. Cold ham and Swiss cheese sandwich on toasted light rye, mayonnaise and Dijon mustard on the side. Two servings. Also, small garden salad. Two servings. One salad with raspberry vinaigrette dressing on the side, and one with balsamic vinaigrette dressing on the side. Also, one sweet iced tea."

A voice came back from somewhere near the center of the pergola. "Understood. Twenty minutes."

They sat and looked out to sea, holding hands, just watching the surf and enjoying the down time.

Eighteen minutes after their order, the voice interrupted their reverie.

"Lunch is here. Server awaits admittance."

"Admit server," Kusunoki said. There was no response.

"You forgot the 'dacha,'" Ansen said.

"Dacha. Admit server," Kusunoki said.

"Admitting server."

A room service waiter came in from the front door with a motorized rolling cart. He said "Good day," and without any other speech or fanfare laid out their lunch on a pair of folding tables he retrieved from a corner of the lanai and set up in front of them. He made a guess on the iced tea and salad dressings – getting them right – and departed without a word.

"This. This I could get used to," Ansen said as he put balsamic vinaigrette on his salad.

"Indeed. I had heard The Dachas was the premier resort on Doma, but I guess my imagination wasn't up to the task."

After lunch, Ansen relighted his cigar, and sat back with a sigh.

"Dacha," Kusunoki said. "How many of the sixty-six conferees have arrived?"

"Forty-two of the conferees have arrived. Two more are currently on their way from the shuttleport."

"Dacha, when will the other conferees arrive?"

"Twenty additional conferees are scheduled to arrive over the next three days."

"Dacha, that only adds up to sixty-four. Explain."

"The delegation from Calumet was not included as either here or scheduled. Their ship is overdue. No update is available."

"Dacha, who is in the delegation from Calumet?"

"Matheus Oliveira and Sania Mehta."

"Well, now that's troubling," Ansen said. "I hope they're OK."

"Probably delayed due to some mechanical breakdown. Losing a ship is relatively rare. Dacha, let us know immediately if and when their ship arrives in system."

"Understood."

"I hope it's something that minor. I had planned on nominating Mehta as chair of the conference."

"Not yourself? You're the host, you know," Kusunoki said.

"Yes, but I think the conference should elect its own chairman. Also, I intend to be an outspoken advocate for certain features and structures in the document. More outspoken than a chairman probably should be. I should give those speeches from the floor, not from the chair."

"What about Mehta?"

"Well, I've read her writings," Ansen said, "and she's likely with me on almost every issue. But she can keep a lower profile than I would like to myself. I've also seen some videos of her in debate and interview, and she's very quick. Perfect for chairman. But I have to ask her about it. See if she's willing."

"How long can you hold back from selecting a chairman, to see if they show up?"

"Probably a couple of weeks. Not much more."

"Who's likely to be your biggest nemesis of the coming eight months?" Kusunoki asked.

"Patryk Mazur. He's a tough old bastard, and he's a brilliant speaker. I expect some of the debate to be oratory for the ages."

"Why'd you invite him, then?"

"Because he's a deep thinker, and he's honest," Ansen said. "If he sees a problem in your proposal, you probably have a hidden problem. A problem you didn't see. But, by the same token, if you win the rational argument on an issue, he will concede the point and then be committed to supporting it. And he's a great big gun to have on your side."

"So you won't be able to just ram things through."

"Not likely."

"Good."

Ansen looked over at her, saw the twinkle in her eye, and, like so many times before, fell in love all over again. He lifted her hand to his mouth and kissed it.

He fell asleep in his chair to the sound of the surf, as the sun moved into mid afternoon. Once he was snoring softly, she got up quietly and went into the bedroom to unpack and hang their clothes.

The computer spoke to Kusunoki in the bedroom, pitched low so as not to wake Ansen, sleeping on the lanai.

"Professor Ansen has a communications request from Patryk Mazur."

"Dacha, hold the request a moment."

Kusunoki walked out onto the lanai. Ansen had been asleep for about two hours, which was as much nap as he should have mid-day if he was to sleep that night. Kusunoki touched his shoulder.

"Mmf. Wha'? Yes, dear. What is it?"

"You have a communications request from Patryk Mazur."

"Put it through, put it though."

"Dacha, put the communication through."

"Mazur here. Gerry, are you there?" a baritone voice asked.

"Yes, Patryk, I'm here," Ansen said.

"I thought we might get together. Have you two had dinner yet?"

"No, I was just napping on the lanai."

"How about I come over then? We can eat at your place."

"That would be fine, Patryk."

"See you in half an hour."

When the call cut off, Kusunoki had a question.

"How do you know Professor Mazur?"

"We were at Oxford at the same time. He was a year or two ahead of me in graduate school. We debated, and I watched him challenge speakers in the Oxford Union. He was a tremendous debater then, and his skills have not lessened with age."

"Is there a Mrs. Mazur? Will we be four for dinner?"

"No," Ansen said. "Malwina passed away – what? Five years ago, maybe. I think that's what the bio I reviewed said. She was a bit older than he."

"Did you know her?"

"No, she was after Oxford. I think he met her on Kodu."

"You have a guest. Patryk Mazur awaits admittance."

"Dacha, admit Patryk Mazur," Kusunoki said.

A tall, thin man in his mid-70s came out onto the lanai from the house.

"Hi, Gerry."

Ansen got up from his chair to shake hands.

"Hi, Patryk. Long time."

"Almost fifty years."

"And my wife, Mineko Kusunoki."

Mazur and Kusunoki shook hands.

"Pleased to meet you," Mazur said.

"And you, sir."

"Patryk, would you like a bourbon?" Ansen asked.

Mazur looked at the open bottle on the table.

"Is that a Jablonka knock-off?"

"No. It's Earth-import. I've been making friends in high places."

"I noticed that. Sure, I'll take a bourbon.

Ansen pushed the small tray, with an extra glass, a bowl of ice, and the open bottle, to Mazur.

"Help yourself."

Mazur poured for himself and added a couple ice cubes as they all took their seats.

"I was saddened to note your wife's having passed when I was reviewing biographies for the Westlake Prize."

"Thank you. I still miss her terribly." Mazur sipped the bourbon, sighed with satisfaction. "So you picked the conferees. I thought it looked like your list."

"I didn't say I picked the conferees."

"Oh, yes, you did, Gerry. You just said you were reviewing biographies for the Prize, not reviewing biographies of the winners. No matter. It's a good list, without regard to who drew it up."

Ansen conceded the point with a small wave of his hand. Mazur still didn't miss much.

"Perhaps we should order dinner before we get down to business. It will take some time, I imagine," Ansen said.

They each ordered dinner – Kusunoki ordered seafood, Ansen a steak, Mazur ordered a large salad with grilled chicken, and the computer specified one hour – before Mazur took up business again.

"So what are we really about here, Gerry? I have my guesses, of course, but I want to hear it from you."

"Anyone with a little study and their wits about them knows sooner or later the colonies will split off from Earth and become one or more independent entities. I was asked to design a government – a classical liberal, open-society government – to be the successor government in the colonies."

"And you have money behind you."

Ansen opened his arms out to encompass the lanai. "Obviously."

"Revolution always was the hobby of the upper classes. And, of course, you have this conference so you can at least pretend this isn't the product of one old coot from Jablonka."

"It really needs not to be, Patryk. The various issues need to be dragged out in the open and debated. There's no way other way, I don't think, to do it."

"Agreed. And to that point, one of the reasons I came over this evening was to ask you to refrain from using your position as chair to stifle debate and ram your vision through."

"I don't intend to be the chair."

"Really."

"Really. Patryk, this is too important. Everything needs to be hammered out with all the due diligence we can muster. And I don't want to be hamstrung by being the chair. I want to argue my points from the floor."

"Which is why you included me."

"Which is why I included you. I figured we would have a lot of fun debating the issues. And you're an honest debater. We'll actually get somewhere."

"Oh, this will be fun. Gerry, it will be like one of those godawful historical simulations, where the two dinosaurs take the field and fight it out, with all the stomping and bellowing."

Kusunoki tittered and covered her mouth.

"I thought you'd enjoy it. One last go at each other, eh, Patryk?"

A Charter For The Commonwealth

"I'm looking forward to it. I don't agree with all your ideas, you know."

"Any hints?" Ansen asked.

"No, no. I think I'll just waylay you on the floor. So who were you thinking of as chairman?"

"Sania Mehta."

"Good choice," Mazur said. "She's quick, and she won't take any crap from either of us. I've seen her in videos. Debates, conferences, that sort of thing. Composed. Professional. She's perfect."

"That's what I figured, too. One problem. Her ship didn't show on schedule. It may be lost, but that's a pretty low probability. Probably just delayed with mechanical problems. But transit delays can get into a couple weeks or more pretty fast."

"How late are they now?"

"Four days," Ansen said.

"And the rest of the attendees will all be here when?"

"Three days."

"So to accommodate a two week delay, we only need a week of doing something else, right?" Mazur asked.

"Right."

"I think we should have you present your proposal in full, with handouts and markups. The whole whoop-te-do. You got enough for a week?"

"Oh, sure," Ansen said. "I built a decision tree on the way here. Everything from basic principles to minor details. I could distribute the file to everyone, and present it as a framework for our discussions."

"Perfect. Once you've given your welcome speech, Gerry, open the floor to motions. I'll move we have you walk us through your decision tree. Professor Kusunoki here can second.

"And once you're done, assuming Professor Mehta is here, I'm going to move to have you replaced as chair, so you can properly defend your proposals without being fettered by protocol.

"And then you and I are gonna have some fun."

Distinguished Colleagues

Once sixty-four of the sixty-six attendees of the Westlake Conference had arrived at The Dachas on Doma, Gerald Ansen sent an announcement to everyone that the opening session of the conference would convene in the large hall of the conference center the next morning, Tuesday, at 11:00. Only Matheus Oliveira and Sania Mehta were missing. The ship from Calumet, the *Nebula Queen*, was now eight days late.

"Distinguished Colleagues:

"Thank you all for attending the Westlake Conference. I am your host, Gerald Ansen.

"As we have discussed in our letters, we are all aware any colonial arrangement, such as between Earth and the other human-settled planets, is by its very nature temporary. This is borne out by the historical evidence that all other colonial arrangements in human history have in fact expired.

"The events that precipitated the end of those relationships have ranged from peaceful agreements to bloody wars of independence. The situations that subsequently emerged in the colonies have ranged from spectacular successes to dismal failures.

"The largest determining factor of success on the part of the newly independent colony is the structures in place before independence. When such structures were insufficient to the task, dictatorships and totalitarian states were often the result.

"During the course of the next eight months, it is our goal to design a post-colonial structure for the thirty-three planets of Earth's first-round colonization of space, the thirty-three planets you represent. We will write the founding document, the charter, of a new polity to step into the void left behind when the current colonial arrangement expires.

"In so doing, we hope to spare our planets and populations, our families and friends, the chaos of a disorganized interregnum, and the tragedy of totalitarianism that would otherwise be the likely result.

A Charter For The Commonwealth

"Our first step along this path will be to get to know one another better, at formal events like this luncheon, and at less formal gatherings and meals among ourselves over the next several weeks. I would encourage you to get together with other delegates, those whose work has interested you as well as those with whom you disagree, to discuss the possibilities.

"At the same time, we will also be presenting our ideas, and I invite any who would like to make such a presentation to let me know so we can schedule you. The presentations will be to get all our ideas out on the table so we can consider them, debate them, and assemble our document.

"Before we bring in lunch, are there any questions?"

"Here!" called out Patryk Mazur.

"Mr. Mazur."

"Mister Chairman, you distributed a decision tree you worked up on the way here. At least I got a copy. Did everyone else get a copy?" Mazur asked as he looked around.

Several delegates indicated they had, and Ansen said, "Yes, I sent the file to everyone."

"Mister Chairman, I move you present that decision tree first, and you walk us through that, because it seems to me that other proposals could be worked into that decision tree."

"Seconded," called out Mineko Kusunoki.

"The motion has been made and seconded that we start the presentations with the decision tree I distributed three days ago. Ayes? Nays? The Ayes have it. We'll start on that after lunch.

"OK, everybody. Let's eat."

Gerald Ansen took the rest of that week and into Monday to walk the conferees through his detailed decision tree. They then started into presentations by several other attendees who had prepared formal proposals.

The *Nebula Queen* was now fourteen days late.

By the end of the second Friday session, the *Nebula Queen* had still not arrived. At this point she was nineteen days late, and concern was growing the ship may have been lost.

"We may have to pick another chairman, Gerry."

"Yes, Patryk, I know. That's an inconvenience for us, but, more than that, it's a terrible loss. *Nebula Queen* was carrying a thousand passengers and another five hundred crew."

"Well, let's think about it over the weekend. We don't have to do anything now until Monday."

It was 3:00 in the morning on Saturday when the computer voice woke Ansen and Kusunoki.

"Wake up.... Wake up.... Wake up...."

"Dacha, we're awake. What is it?" Ansen asked.

"Pardon me, but you asked to be informed immediately if there was news of the *Nebula Queen*."

"Yes, dacha, go ahead."

"The *Nebula Queen* has made her hyperspace transition into the Doma system. All aboard are reported fine."

"Thank God."

"Dacha, what is their expected timetable for arrival on Doma?" Kusunoki asked.

"The *Nebula Queen* has suffered a failure of one of her reaction mass injectors. This limits her acceleration to two-thirds normal, or 0.5 g. Her scheduled arrival is now set for Friday."

"How does this affect your timetable?" Kusunoki asked.

"We'll work around it," Ansen said. "Now that we know they're safe, everybody is going to want to wait for the last two delegates to arrive before we begin serious debate. We'll do more preliminary work, have longer lunches, have more getting-acquainted time. It'll be fine.

"I'm just happy everybody's OK. I was really starting to worry about them."

Often, when Ansen was awakened in the middle of the night, he had trouble falling back asleep. But after being told *Nebula Queen* was safe, he fell back asleep instantly, and slept like a baby.

The *Nebula Queen* finally limped into Doma orbit Friday morning at the end of the third week of the conference. She was twenty-six days late.

When Matheus Oliveira and Sania Mehta finally arrived at The Dachas, they found a message waiting for them from Gerald Ansen, inviting them to dinner with him, his wife Mineko Kusunoki, and fellow delegate Patryk Mazur. They accepted the invitation, had lunch, and spent the afternoon decompressing on the lanai after ten weeks aboard the Nebula Queen, the last seven of which were on conservation protocols to make sure the food and water lasted.

"You have guests. Matheus Oliveira and Sania Mehta await admittance."

"Dacha, admit our guests."

Oliveira was fiftyish, and Mediterranean swarthy, while Mehta was south-Asian Indian and in her mid-40s. They were quite a contrast to Ansen and Mazur, both pale northern Europeans in their 70s, and Kusunoki, Japanese and in her early 40s.

Kusunoki, Ansen, and Mazur stood to greet them as Oliveira and Mehta came out on the lanai. The low coffee table and padded lounge chairs had been augmented this evening by a dinner table and five straight chairs.

After they had greeted each other and shook hands all around, they sat at the table, Ansen with his ever-present cigar and bourbon, Mazur and Oliveira with bourbon, and Kusunoki and Mehta with summery drinks from a pitcher Kusunoki had ordered earlier. They ordered supper before getting down to business, and Oliveira lit a cigarette.

"Matheus, Sania, I can't begin to express our relief you are all right. We were quite concerned," Ansen said.

"It was something of an adventure, although one I would rather not repeat," Oliveira said. "We were halfway here, in hyperspace, at the point where they had flipped the ship to begin decelerating to Doma. When they reengaged the engines, there was a loud bang you could feel throughout the ship, and then alarms went off. We stayed at zero gravity for an hour while they figured out what was going on and got everything secured. Apparently a reaction mass injector let go, and sort of exited the ship. We were streaming reaction mass until they got the valves all changed around and such."

"So there we were, at our fastest speed in hyperspace, minus one-third of our deceleration, and no way to slow down in time to not go flying past Doma," Mehta said.

"Oh, my," Kusunoki said.

"And it's not a field repair. Oh, ships carry the spares, to make sure they can get a replacement installed at their destination, but you don't go outside in hyperspace and tend to it. Only at a planetary repair facility," Oliveira said.

"So what they did was aim to one side of Doma, and use some of our deceleration to keep pushing us in a spiral around the Doma system while using the other part of our deceleration to burn off speed. So we spent the last several weeks going around and around the system out there," Mehta said.

"And we've spent the last seven weeks on emergency food and water protocols to make sure we wouldn't all be dead by the time we could slow down enough to make transition," Oliveira concluded.

"That is an amazing story. I guess it's heartening to know, even though such failures can occur, the crew knows what to do to get everyone safely to their destination," Mazur said.

"Most of the crew had not had such a failure before, but the captain and the chief engineer were both old hands and I guess that sort of thing was once more common. They had sort of a ho-hum attitude that helped keep everybody calm about it," Oliveira said.

"All that being said, we're three weeks late. What have we missed?" Mehta asked.

"Actually, not much," Ansen said. "We hoped you were simply delayed and not lost, and so I purposely dragged my feet. We spent the first two weeks presenting our various proposals to each other, and getting to know one another before beginning serious debate. When we heard last Saturday you had made your hyperspace transition, we continued those activities into this week. No one wanted to get into serious business without everyone here, especially not once we all knew you had made it."

"That was very considerate," Oliveira said.

"We also had an ulterior motive," Mazur said.

"Oh?" Mehta asked.

"Yes. Gerry and I are old acquaintances. We were both in the Oxford Union fifty years ago, and we have sparred before."

"The Oxford Union?" Oliveira asked.

"Probably the premier debating society on Earth," Mehta said.

"And it has been for over four hundred years," Ansen said. "As Patryk says, he and I were both in the Union. We have debated each other before, and we have our differences now. Some of the debate ahead on the charter is likely to be epic. But I find myself hobbled. As host, I am the default for chairman of the conference, but I cannot debate freely as chair."

"We were wondering, Sania, if you would chair the conference," Mazur said.

"Thank God," Oliveira said, and both Ansen and Mazur looked at him quizzically while Mehta sat stunned.

"I was afraid you were going to ask me, and I don't have the patience for it. Within two days, I would be using the gavel on people's heads," Oliveira explained.

"Chair the conference? But, but I haven't even been here the last three weeks," Mehta said.

"That's actually an advantage," Ansen said. "You haven't formed any opinions on anything, you haven't settled into any of the little cliques that always form. You're sort of coming into the whole thing from outside the process, which makes it easier to keep your distance and be even-handed."

"And we need someone both even-handed and strict, because Gerry and I are going to go at it. As will others. I've seen videos of you in conferences and debates before. You have the patience, you have – or can produce on demand, which is just as good – an air of authority, and you don't put up with any nonsense," Mazur said.

"We need you," Ansen said simply.

Mehta looked around, stopped at Kusunoki, who was nodding.

"You're a good choice, Sania. You'll do fine. We'll help," Kusunoki said. "Even Gerry and Patryk. When they aren't trying to kill each other."

"Well, if you're all agreed, I'll give it a go."

"Excellent," Ansen said. "But one thing. Once you are chairman, give no deference to either of us. You need to be hard as nails to keep everyone in line, us included."

"Agreed," Mazur said. "An even playing field for everyone, and strict adherence to the rules of debate. That's what we need to be successful."

"One last thing," Ansen said. "I've sent you all the proposals from the last three weeks for your review. I've also sent you my summary of what happened the last three weeks –"

"As have I, for a second point of view," Mazur said with a wink.

"You should feel free to review these or ignore them at your discretion. On Monday morning, I will convene the conference –"

"At which point, I will challenge him to recuse himself as chair on a point of order," Mazur said.

"I will then open the floor to nominations for chairman."

"But you can't be sure I'll be elected chair," Mehta said.

"I'm sure," Kusunoki said. "Leave that to me."

Ansen banged the gavel several times.

"Please be seated, everyone."

The conversations died down and everyone took their seats.

"Welcome to the fourth week of the Westlake Conference."

"This morning I would like to welcome our last two attendees. Matheus Oliveira and Sania Mehta have made it to Doma after their ship from Calumet suffered mechanical difficulties on the transit here. We are so happy they are safe and have joined us."

Ansen applauded and all the room joined in as Oliveira and Mehta stood and waved to the room.

When the applause died down and Oliveira and Mehta resumed their seats, Ansen opened the floor for business.

"Today we begin the business of considering the proposals brought before the conference over the last three weeks."

"Point of order," Mazur called out.

"Mr. Mazur," Ansen said.

"Mr. Chairman, as you are the author and presenter of the largest and most complete proposal of the last three weeks, I assert you cannot be evenhanded as chair and ask you to recuse yourself as chairman of the conference."

There was a stir of conversation and remarks from the attendees at that pronouncement, and Ansen banged the gavel three times. He seemed to consider before speaking.

"Mr. Mazur is correct." More stir, more gavel. "Therefore I will recuse myself upon the agreement of this conference to a new chairman. Do I hear nominations?"

"Here!"

"Ms. Kusunoki," Ansen said.

"As one person who did not hear any of the presentations of the last three weeks, and has not already formed any opinions or alliances on any subject up for debate, I move Sania Mehta as chairman."

"Seconded." That was Hu Mingli, from Meili, Ansen noted.

"We have a nomination and a second. Are there other nominations?" Ansen asked and waited.

The attendees stirred, but, as no one other than Mehta and Oliveira met the criteria of Kusunoki's carefully worded motion, there were no other nominations.

Ansen banged the gavel.

"Nominations are closed. We are voting on the replacement of the current chairman with Sania Mehta as chair of this conference. Ayes? Nays? The Ayes have it. Congratulations, Madam Chairman."

Sania Mehta got up and walked up to the chairman's dais, where Ansen stood and met her at the edge of the dais. He gave her the gavel as he shook her hand, then walked out onto the floor and sat down with Kusunoki. The attendees applauded.

Sania Mehta, Chairman of the Westlake Conference, took her seat at the chairman's desk and gaveled the meeting to order.

Earth

"You wanted me to keep an eye on the colony newsfeeds, sir," Andy Hasper said.

"Yes. Has something changed?" Arlan Andrews asked.

"Yes, sir, but I'm not sure exactly what. The debate grew and drew in more participants, some of whom were pretty far over the line, in my opinion. On some of the colonies, Westlake and a number of other planetary governors made the counter-argument, some more effectively than others. On other colonies, the planetary governors actively suppressed the biggest troublemakers, usually bringing them in for questioning and letting them know the next time they wouldn't be going home any time soon. That was the pattern, sir, but –"

"Go ahead, Andy. What changed?"

"Well, some of the biggest participants, the early participants, have gone silent, sir. Ansen, Paxton, Rivera. A bunch of others. They haven't published anything in a couple months. It was subtle enough it took me that long to twinge to it."

"Any clues of what's going on?" Andrews asked.

"They're all listed by their universities as being on sabbatical, sir."

"All of them? At the same time?"

"Yes, sir."

"Anything else?"

"They are all listed as winners of something called the Westlake Prize, sir."

"Oh, I don't like the sound of that."

"No, sir. I also got wind of something called the Westlake Conference. Sponsored by the Orlov Group."

"What's that? Where's it held?" Andrews asked.

"No idea what it's about, sir, but it's on Doma."

"Shit. Fournier's private little paradise. We don't have anybody there, do we?"

"No, sir. It's mostly a vacation and retirement spot. Hard to get any kind of agent in there permanently. Not enough business activity for most of the decent covers to work."

A Charter For The Commonwealth

"Well, ain't that just dandy. Fournier, Westlake, and Orlov. How did I guess? And they rounded up all the key people bitching about Earth policy into one place, eh?" Andrews asked.

"Apparently so, sir."

"Fuck. I don't know what they're up to, but I don't like it. See what else you can find out, but quietly. Whatever you do, don't let them know we're on to anything. Also, we should probably review what resources we have in Jablonka in case we need to take some kind of direct action. We may need to move assets into place."

"Yes, sir. I'm on it."

The Census Debate

"We now come to the next item, the determination by the Commonwealth government of the population of each member planet for purposes of determining the weighting of votes in the Council and collecting a head tax on member planets," Sania Mehta said.

"Madam Chairman, I move the language proposed be included in the Charter as drafted," said Gerald Ansen, standing at one of the two lecterns in the well of the floor.

"Seconded," Ikaika Kalani called out. He was one of the delegates from Hutan.

"Debate," Patryk Mazur said.

"We have a call for debate on this issue. Is there an objection, Mr. Ansen?"

"No objection, Madam Chairman."

"Your opening statement, Mr. Mazur."

"Thank you, Madam Chairman."

Patryk Mazur collected his notes and advanced to the other lectern.

"Madam Chairman, distinguished colleagues.

"This subject has come up before, often before, in human history. The Romans are reputed to have gathered census data by requiring everyone to report to the village of their birth, causing disruptions which became famous in another context."

There was some chuckling among the delegates to that.

"More recently, a republic founded on the highest of principles made the same mistake Mr. Ansen now puts forward for our proposed Commonwealth. If I may point out to you the enabling language within the Constitution of the United States of America, dated 1789."

Mazur manipulated the controls on the lectern and the large overhead display showed a portion of a handwritten document, with one sentence highlighted.

"They, too, had provided for a representation based upon the population of their member states, a concept to which I do not object. And they provided means within their founding document for their federal government to determine the populations of their member states. 'The actual Enumeration shall be made within three Years after the first Meeting of the Congress of the United States, and within every subsequent Term of ten Years, in such Manner as they shall by Law direct.'

"So there we have it. An 'enumeration,' to be made every ten years. Now, enumeration is a very precise word. It is 'to make a counting of.' We have here a very limited authorization for a specific purpose, the sort of thing Mr. Ansen and I might both applaud.

"Shall we now proceed two hundred and thirty years forward and see what grew out of this innocuous language?"

Mazur manipulated the lectern controls, and a new document appeared on the large display, and slowly scrolled through multiple pages as he talked.

"We have here the 'American Community Survey' of 2018, promulgated by the Census Bureau of the United States of America, an agency that by that time employed over four thousand permanent bureaucrats and over six hundred thousand census takers. This questionnaire runs to eleven pages, in three columns, the last four pages of which are repeated for each person in the household. If four people live in this household, this survey runs to twenty-three pages.

"And what sort of data is being collected by the federal government of the United States of America under that simple enabling language within their Constitution?

"The name of each person living there. Fair enough, I suppose, for while that exceeds the nature of a simple count, the word 'enumeration' can also mean a complete listing.

"The race of each person. A curious inquiry for a republic whose declaration of existence loudly and proudly declared all people to be created equal. If you are not going to treat people differently on the basis of race, then for what purpose do you need to know it?

"The relationship of each person in the household to the other, with choices like 'Husband or wife' or 'Unmarried partner' or 'Housemate or roommate.' Now what business is it of the government, with whom I am engaging in sexual relations, and the commitments my partner and I have or have not made to each other? If my housemate and I engage in the occasional sexual congress, is that person then my 'Unmarried partner?' Even if we do so only once? If one act of sexual congress is not enough for such a change in status, then what is the threshold count? Must I keep an accounting? And why is any of this any of the government's business?

"The education of each person in the household, by level of education attained and even the subject matter of their studies. By what person or company each person in the household was employed. How much money each person made. Whether the house was owned or rented, and the amount of the rent or mortgage payment.

"How the house was heated. How the computers in the house were connected to the network. How much the electricity bill was last month. How much the gas bill was last month. How each person got to work, and how many minutes it took them to get there.

"Note that answering this ridiculous intrusion of the government into people's lives, pending by the most tenuous thread from that enabling language, language similar to what Mr. Ansen here proposes, was mandated by law. One could be fined one hundred United States Dollars for not complying, an amount equal at the time to two bottles of good bourbon, a measure of value Mr. Ansen and I both understand."

There was general laughter from the delegates.

"Further, one could be fined five hundred dollars – we are now up to ten bottles of good bourbon – for providing false information. How anyone could be expected to fill out such a lengthy and detailed questionnaire and not make any mistakes in its performance is beyond my comprehension. What if I misstated the number of minutes I took to get to work? Is it twelve, or is it thirteen? It seems to me the only sane response to this survey is to decline to respond and pay the two bottles of bourbon, keeping the other eight bottles for myself. Perhaps I'll even share them with Mr. Ansen."

Mazur sorted his papers until the laughter died down.

"My fellow delegates, I cannot support the inclusion of a provision in the Charter of the Commonwealth that would, by the historical evidence, enable the Commonwealth government to so pry into the private affairs of its citizens."

Mazur shut off the overhead display but remained at the lectern. He turned and nodded to Mehta.

"Mr. Ansen. The floor is open for debate."

"Thank you, Madam Chairman. Mr. Mazur, I note you do not object to the weighting of Council votes by population. By what means then is the population of the member planets to be determined?"

"Let the member planets conduct their own counting."

"And if they cheat?"

"In which direction would they cheat, Mr. Ansen? If they understate their population to reduce their tax burden, they reduce the impact of their vote in the Council. If they overstate their population to gain advantage in the Council, they must pay a higher head tax."

"It's like asking students to grade their own exams."

"But having students grade the exams can work, especially if the students don't grade their own papers."

Mazur stopped for a moment, then thumped his fingertips on the lectern.

"Ah! Now there's an idea. What about having some other member planet make the count or certify the results of a member planet's count?"

"So Kodu could certify Jablonka's population count?" Ansen asked.

"Yes, or Jablonka could simply hire Kodu to do the count. The count doesn't have to be terribly accurate, after all. The difference between one hundred million and one hundred and one million makes little difference, either for the head tax or on the Council."

"Madam Chairman, I think Mr. Mazur and I have come to sufficient agreement on this point to be able to work out some new language that will avoid the historical danger he has so eloquently described. I withdraw my motion, and propose Mr. Mazur and I be charged with redrafting the proposal on this point."

"Mr. Mazur?" Mehta asked.

"No objection, Madam Chairman."

"Very well. The motion is withdrawn. Mr. Ansen and Mr. Mazur will draft new language on this point, and this point is set aside for future consideration of the new language. We move on to the next item of business."

The Citizenship Debate

"We now come to the next item, the right of every human being over the age of fourteen solar years to petition for and be admitted to citizenship in the Commonwealth upon passing a citizenship exam," Sania Mehta said.

"Madam Chairman, I move the language proposed be included in the Charter as drafted," said Gerald Ansen, standing at one of the two lecterns in the well of the floor.

"Seconded," Mineko Kusunoki called out. This clause had been her idea and was her pet project.

"Debate," Patryk Mazur said.

"Counter," Kusunoki said.

"We have a call for debate and counter on this issue. Is there an objection, Mr. Ansen?"

"No objection, Madam Chairman."

"Debate and counter will begin on the matter. Mr. Mazur, Ms. Kusunoki."

"Thank you, Madam Chairman," they both said.

Ansen stepped down from one lectern, yielding it to Kusunoki, while Mazur advanced to the other lectern. Mazur looked a little discomfited to find himself opposite Kusunoki.

"Mr. Mazur, your opening statement."

"Madam Chairman, distinguished colleagues.

"My issue with this provision is one of both appearance and substance. My understanding is that this Citizenship Exam is to presume, in addition to the standard fare of a knowledge of the Charter and the structure of government, the equivalent of a college education.

"Are we then to be an elitist nation, one which admits people only on the basis of intelligence and privilege? Do we not desire also citizens who may contribute in other roles than those enabled by such an education? Will we turn away all those who do not or cannot, by innate ability or circumstance of fortune, meet the requirement of a college education?

A Charter For The Commonwealth

"My fellow delegates, I object to this provision on those grounds, and ask that it be dropped from consideration."

Mazur turned and nodded to Mehta.

"Ms. Kusunoki. Your opening statement."

"Thank you, Madam Chairman. Mr. Mazur, I'm afraid you misunderstand this provision and its application, its intent and its scope.

"It is not only under this provision that citizenship in the Commonwealth may be granted under this Charter. The powers granted to the Council in Article 2 of the proposal include that of determining rules, regulations, and quotas for immigration and the granting of citizenship by other means.

"This provision is a limit on the Council's power to regulate immigration. It states that in no case, regardless of the Council's regulations, shall citizenship be denied to any person who meets this admittedly high bar.

"It is a constraint on the Council's power to limit citizenship."

Kusunoki nodded to Mehta.

"Mr. Mazur, the floor is open for debate."

"Thank you, Madam Chairman. Ms. Kusunoki, I must ask under what imaginable set of circumstances the Council would deprive granting citizenship to a person who met the requirements of the proposed language?"

"Mr. Mazur, I will use your own previous example of the United States of America in the year 2018. A hard quota on immigration was first set by their Congress. Special preferences were then granted to various people who suffered one circumstance or another – political refugees, economic refugees, refugees from natural disasters, family members of people already admitted under the previous three categories – until that hard quota was almost completely filled. The remaining positions of the quota were filled by a lottery of the open applications.

"At that point, and to its own detriment, the United States of America denied entry and citizenship to the rest of the open applications, people who not only met but greatly exceeded the requirements of the language proposed here. University professors with PhDs, entrepreneurs who had built whole industries, doctors, engineers, scientists. When their visas expired, they were sent home –

deported! – despite their desire for citizenship.

"Further, the process of immigration and citizenship had become a set of hurdles and mazes only a lawyer could navigate. People without means were seldom capable of following all the ins and outs of these procedures on their own. Regardless of how qualified otherwise, the poor, it seemed, need not apply.

"That is an historical precedent, Mr. Mazur. It has happened before, and therefore it can again, under the proposed language of the Charter absent this provision.

"With this provision, however, it is a simple matter. Present oneself at the nearest Commonwealth embassy, consulate, or planetary headquarters, anywhere in human space, petition for citizenship and take the citizenship exam. If you pass it, you are at once and always a citizen of the Commonwealth, and no act or regulation of the Council can ever deny that right, whether tycoon or pauper, wearing tuxedo or rags."

Mazur looked at Kusunoki for a long minute. He looked back down to the proposed language, then thumbed back to Article 2 of the proposal and the powers of the Council to regulate immigration.

"Mr. Mazur?"

"A moment, please, Madam Chairman."

Mehta was content to wait. Mazur finally looked back up from his papers.

"Thank you, Ms. Kusunoki. Madam Chairman, I withdraw my objection to the proposed language. Further, I encourage my fellow delegates to vote in favor of the proposal, as I shall myself."

Mazur and Kusunoki both returned to their seats, and Ansen returned to his lectern.

"We have a motion and second on the proposed language regarding the right of every human being over the age of fourteen solar years to petition for and be admitted to citizenship in the Commonwealth upon passing a citizenship exam," Sania Mehta said. "Are there other objections?

"Hearing none, we will proceed to a vote. Ayes? Nays? The Ayes have it, and the proposed language is adopted."

Mehta looked at the clock on the wall.

"It is now time for a break. We will reconvene at 3:00."

Mehta banged the gavel once, and rose from her seat as the

delegates got up and stretched, some of them heading to the refreshments in the back of the room, and others to the restrooms in the hallway.

Kusunoki walked across the room to Mazur, and surprised him with a hug and a kiss on the cheek.

"Thank you," Kusunoki said.

"For what?" Mazur asked.

"For being who you are."

Halfway

Gerald Ansen, Mineko Kusunoki, Patryk Mazur, Aluna Kamau, Ikaika Kalani, and Manfred Koch were having dinner at Ansen's and Kusunoki's dacha. Aluna Kamau was a very dark black woman from Courtney, Ikaika Kalani was a very large Polynesian man from Hutan, and Manfred Koch was a pale, blue-eyed northern European from Waldheim.

Ansen and Kusunoki, and the single (and lonely) Mazur, had been having dinners and weekend meals with small groups of other delegates throughout the months of the conference. Every delegate had by this time been their guest several times, but they kept changing around the invitations so the mix of people was always different.

The dinner table on the lanai had now become a permanent fixture. Dinner had been ordered and they sat around the table and chatted while they waited.

"So here we are. The end of our seventeenth week. Halfway through the conference," Ansen said.

"It's amazing," Kamau said. "At once it seems like the time is flying by, and at the same time everything before the conference seems like a different life."

"Indeed," Koch said. "It has been an incredible experience thus far. To see all the ideas we had all been working on separately come together in such a way. And in what is, really, a very short time."

"It is the advance work that made that possible," Kalani said. His voice was a deep rumble, as much felt as heard. "Three years of correspondence paved the way."

"I think by now we are more than halfway complete with the Charter, though, don't you?" Kamau asked. "My estimate is we're two-thirds complete, or even a bit more."

"Agreed. Perhaps two more months of work, and we will be finished, I think," Koch said. "The question then is, what do we do with it?"

"We should all be thinking of our options there, I think," Mazur said. "We'll have plenty of time to debate those in the last two months."

"And I should have more information to share by that point, which would help in debating those options," Ansen said.

"Some of those options, the ones where this all becomes something more than an intellectual exercise, are pretty scary," Kalani said.

There was general agreement and nodding of heads. Everyone knew what Kalani meant, and no one thought the big Polynesian talking about being afraid was at all incongruous.

Other dinner parties among the delegates also had been going on all along throughout the conference. At the halfway point, another included Donal McNee, red-haired and green-eyed, from Bliss, Guadalupe Rivera, dark and beautiful, from Parchman, Jacques Cotillard, impeccably dressed, from Valore, Nils Isacsson, tall and big-boned, from Boomgaard, Willard Dempsey, built like a fireplug, from Mountainhome, and Jane Paxton, the blond-haired, blue-eyed firebrand from Bahay.

They were seated around a similar table on another lanai. Dinner had been ordered, and drinks served.

"Two months more, I figure, and then the document's done. Then what do we do?" McNee asked.

"Two months of vacation? Works for me. Hard not to like it here," Dempsey said.

"No, what do we do with the document?" McNee asked.

"Well, that's the question, isn't it," Isacsson said. "And Ansen's being cagey about it. He never talks about what's next. Just a lot of babbling about 'post-colonial structures' and the like."

"What we ought to do is put the document in force. Declare the Commonwealth," Rivera said.

"And then who's the Council, and who's the executive?" Cotillard asked. "And what do we do when Earth comes calling?"

"That's the big question," Paxton said. "What will Earth do, and where does that leave us? And yet, there's something going on behind the scenes here. As Nils said, Ansen's being cagey. And there's money behind this. Westlake. The Orlov Group. I don't even want to think about the bill for a hundred and twenty round-trip interstellar passages, what with spouses and kids and all. And taking one whole section of The Dachas for eight months? That's big money."

"Not for Orlov," Cotillard said. "Pocket change. The actual numbers on what the Earth is making off the colonies are huge beyond belief. We could be no more than someone's hobby."

"I'd like to think we're more than that," Isacsson said. "I'm pretty impressed with the document as it's coming out. And it's not all Ansen. Sure, he did a lot of work setting all this up, and his decision tree was a huge help, but he's not just driving his own vision through. It's all getting debated point by point."

"Speaking of which, you had a nice argument on the conscription debate there, Nils," Dempsey said. "I thought Manfred Koch was going to carry the day until you presented your counter. That was nicely done."

"Thanks. But that's my point. Ansen wasn't even part of that. Sure, he's mixed up in a lot of the debate, both him and Mazur, but he's not forcing the issue anywhere. And I think he and Mazur are enjoying going after each other."

"You got that right," Rivera said, laughing. "Ansen's eyes light up every time Mazur calls out 'Debate' from the floor."

"I'm impressed with the document, too," Cotillard said. "I hope it's not all for nothing."

"I don't think it is, Jacques," Paxton said. "Something else is going on here. There's something we don't know. I keep waiting for the other shoe to drop."

"Well, Ansen better drop it soon, Jane," McNee said. "We've got but two months to go on the document, and then what?"

"I don't know, Donal. I just don't know," Paxton said.

Another meeting was taking place seventy light years away, on Jablonka, in James Allen Westlake's office in the Planetary Governor's Mansion.

"We're picking up some indications that someone's poking about, Georgy," Westlake said.

"Do we know who?" Orlov asked.

"Arlan Andrews, most likely. Or one of his cronies."

"There's still, what, four months of the conference? And then another month or so for the news to propagate."

"Yes. And I worry Andrews will kick off something against us before we can pull the trigger on the Commonwealth."

A Charter For The Commonwealth

"Probably not going to happen," Orlov said. "His position isn't that secure to be able to take any really big action. Not before we announce the Commonwealth. His coalition would likely break up and your father-in-law would be back on top. Andrews isn't going to risk that."

"You're probably right."

"But we're ready in any case. I expect the big blow to come here, because it's the one place Andrews can hit the Fournier-Westlake-Orlov faction the hardest. And with you as the Chairman of the Commonwealth Council, Jablonka is the obvious move. So I've been concentrating firepower here. We'll have thirty-two battleships in-system by the time the Commonwealth is announced. I figure sixteen to defend Jablonka and sixteen to space for Earth."

"Is that enough, Gerry?" Westlake asked.

"Against Earth frigates? Yeah, that's enough. They're practicing maneuvers in divisions of four, so they can act as units rather than as individual ships. Sigurdsen says that's working out really well so far. As a matter of fact, they've discovered something interesting."

"What's that?"

"They practiced transitioning hyperspace together, and some wiseguys on a couple ships decided to try the radio," Orlov said.

"The radio worked?"

"Sort of. Some garbled noise was picked up by the other ship. So the engineers played with it and figured out how to encode it or decode it or something. I'm not a radio guy. But our ships can now communicate while in hyperspace, and Sigurdsen says theirs can't."

"How did no one ever figure that out before?" Westlake asked.

"I had the impression our radios now work in some frequency band no one ever tried before. Everybody knew radio didn't work in hyperspace, so when the technology changed, nobody checked it."

"Does he think that gives him an advantage?"

"Oh, yeah," Orlov said. "He's real excited about it, because apparently the radio signals travel in hyperspace at hyperspace speeds. So he's working up some new tactical possibilities."

"What about Ansen's request?"

"Well, I know why he wants it. At some point he's going to move for the conference to declare the Charter and name itself the Council. He needs something to show them so they know that's not a suicide move. So we put together a little documentary. I sent you a copy."

"I saw it. Did you send it to Ansen?" Westlake asked.

"Yes. He'll have it by the time he needs it."

"All right. Good." Westlake looked out the window, then sighed. "We're getting close. So many variables. So many possibilities."

"But we've got lots of options, too, Jim. And we've got all the likely moves countered. Speaking of which, what have you done about your personal security?"

"We've tightened it up some. There's only so much we can do there. It was already pretty good."

"Well, take care. You're an obvious target for Andrews once this goes down. But you already know that."

The Video

"You have a guest. Patryk Mazur awaits admittance."

"Dacha, admit Patryk Mazur," Kusunoki said.

Mazur came out onto the lanai, where Ansen and Kusunoki waited. "Who all is for dinner tonight?"

"It's just us tonight, Patryk. I need to show you something. I want your feedback before I share it with everyone else," Ansen said.

"OK, fair enough."

"First, though, how do you think it's going right now?"

"I think we maybe have a week's work left. Things have been moving along pretty well. And others have taken up most of the slack. You and I haven't had a decent debate in weeks."

"Our last big one was on the requirements for amendment to the Charter," Ansen said.

"Yes, I was convinced you had set the bar way too high, until you rolled out some of those historical precedents. That was brutal. A ban on the sale and consumption of alcoholic beverages? In a 'free' country?"

"So my eighty percent requirement stood."

"Hell, Gerry, after your presentation, even I agreed with you. Some of the debates since have been pretty epic, too, though. Jane Paxton on civil rights was one we ought to release as a public video."

"Poor Manfred Koch. I don't think he knew what hit him," Kusunoki said.

"Well, leave it to the German to value order over freedom. He came around, though," Mazur said.

"He had to," Ansen said. "She must have had every form of civil rights violation committed by government in the last five hundred years documented in her paper."

"Yes, but it wasn't the gross violations that were the most telling. It was the subtle ones, committed despite solid protections being in place. Asset seizure without conviction. No-knock raids. The use of eminent domain for private purposes. Forty-eight-hour police holds without arraignment or charges filed. Preferential enforcement."

Mazur shook his head. "Awful. Just awful."

"I'm glad she took it upon herself to rewrite the protections of my proposed article on rights and freedoms," Ansen said. "It's much stronger for her work."

"The whole document's stronger for the last six months of work. Every decision that got made, in my opinion, made it a better document."

"I agree," Kusunoki said.

"I agree, too. Even when I didn't at the time. Pride of authorship and all. But looking back on it all now, it's much improved. Really solid."

"Yes," Mazur said. "And now we're getting to the big question. What are we going to do with it?"

"I think that's as good a segue as I'm going to get into what I want to show you, Patryk. Let's move inside."

They all grabbed their drinks and moved to the sitting arrangement in the living room.

"Dacha, close and darken the glass wall."

The glass wall slid out of its pocket in sections and covered the entire opening onto the lanai, then faded to black, darkening the living room.

"Dacha, set living room for display."

The far wall was a pastel color, with a triptych of tropical paintings prominently in the center. All that was revealed now to be a display as they disappeared and the wall went dark.

"Patryk, I'm going to have to ask you to hold what you're about to see confidential for the time being."

"Sure, Gerry. I know how to keep a secret."

Ansen set his comp on the table and began a video to the wall display.

The video opened with a shot of a large ship suspended in space. It had four crew cylinders toward the back, with four large black radiators like fins projecting out at right angles to each other. Along its length, it had ten circumferential belts of a hundred and sixty or so total containers. These ended in the front with eight massive containers arranged around the nose.

As the ship hung there in space, a bronze plaque faded into view against the space at the lower right of the display. It read

A Charter For The Commonwealth

"Commonwealth Space Ship INDEPENDENCE Battleship BB-001.'

Ansen heard Mazur catch his breath.

The video cut to the inside of the ship. The general quarters alarm sounded, and spacers headed to their duty stations at a dead run, sliding down stairway handrails multiple decks at a time. Damage control parties stood by with sealing plates and toolboxes. Engine rooms were manned. The bridge was shown, every console manned, a scene of intense concentration.

"Weapons: MINES" appeared in the upper left corner, as the camera moved along the length of the ship and the containers racked there. The scene shifted to a single container floating in space on the left, with a radar image on the right. The container exploded, seeming to disappear, but on the right the radar image tracked the shot expended by the mine, with a velocity reading alongside.

"Weapons: BEAMS" appeared in the upper right corner, as the camera played across the front of the ship and showed the beam emitters, covered in the prior view, lurking in each of those eight large containers. The view shifted to the aft of the ship, and played across the four large containers there, also with their emitters exposed. The view shifted again to a split display, with a bridge view on the left, and an asteroid hanging in space on the right. "Distance: 1 light-sec, Size: 500 meters." appeared on the bottom of the display. "Fire," the gunnery man said, and pushed the Fire icon. One second later, the asteroid exploded into fragments.

"Weapons: KINETIC" appeared in the upper right corner, and the camera once again played down the containers along the ship's side. This time the ship was spinning, and one of the containers released from the ship and continued along the direction of its tangent motion. The view shifted to a planetary surface, a small island in a large ocean. "Time rate: 1:100" appeared along the bottom of the display. A canister came into view coming straight in from the top of the display, glowing yellow and trailing smoke and debris. It hit the island in a tremendous explosion.

"Weapons: NUCLEAR" appeared in the upper right corner, and the camera focused on a group of sixteen containers mounted on top of the eight large containers in the front of the vessel. A hatch in the corner of one of those containers blew off and a projectile emerged in a blast of air or smoke in the vacuum. The projectile trailed off and down toward the planet. The view switched to a view of the ocean, with a buoy floating in the camera view. "Time rate: 1:100" appeared along the bottom of the display. The projectile appeared in the top of the display, going much slower than the kinetic weapon, but it hit the floating buoy dead-on. The buoy disappeared into a shower of fragments as a water spout shot into the sky. A couple of seconds later, the surface of the water erupted with an explosion from below.

The display went blank, and then a gold-colored logo faded into view in the center of the display. Around the outside ran the legend "COMMONWEALTH SPACE FORCE." Below it, the legend "CSS Independence" faded into view.

And then, across the entire display, more names faded into view, one after the other. CSS Victory, CSS Vengeance, CSS Adventure, CSS Vanguard, CSS Defiance, CSS Triumph, CSS Enterprise, CSS Freedom, CSS Avenger. It went on and on, until the display around the logo was completely covered with them, seventy in all. The Commonwealth Space Force logo in the center seemed to shine, as if a light played across it, and then the entire display faded to black.

The entire video had taken just twenty minutes.

"Dacha, open the glass wall," Kusunoki said quietly.

The glass wall sections returned to clear and retreated back into their pocket. As outside light came into the living room, Mazur was gaping at the blank wall. He turned to Ansen.

"My God, Gerry. How many of those ships exist?"

"All of them. Seventy," Ansen said quietly.

"But, but how?"

"The Orlov Group and the other mining companies began converting big freighters four years ago. In Jablonka, in Bahay, in Calumet, in Kodu – all across the Commonwealth. The beam weapons are mining equipment, pressed into service as ship-to-ship weapons. The nuclear demolitions in the mines and nuclear weapons are mining demolition charges. The kinetic weapons are just containers full of fernico, the densest stuff we can get cheap.

"They've been training up those crews for two years. There are a total of seventeen thousand trained spacers, all employees of the Orlov Group for now, on those seventy battleships, and they're ready for battle. Right now, if it comes to that."

"You knew. The whole conference, you knew. This is what you've

A Charter For The Commonwealth

been building up to. This is why the Charter is not just a hypothetical exercise, why you wanted it all debated so thoroughly. This isn't some rich kid's pipe dream. This is real."

"Patryk, I've known for four years, since before the Westlake Prize was announced. The Westlake Prize was just an excuse to call a constitutional convention. And the three years' delay was to give them time to build up the navy we needed to defend the charter we were going to write. We're at the end of the process now, not the beginning.

"We have a Charter *and* we have a Navy, and now I'll throw your own question back to you. What are we going to do with it?"

Mazur turned back to stare at the blank wall as if there was some answer there. He turned back to Ansen.

"Gerry, I quit smoking decades ago, but, if you could spare one, I could really use one of those cigars."

Ansen retrieved a cigar from the open box on top of the bar, and they all moved back outside. Mazur lit the cigar, drew on it, and exhaled with a sigh.

"I had almost forgotten how good Earth cigars are," Mazur said.

Ansen and Mazur sat there, smoking their cigars, staring out to sea, in silence. Kusunoki, curled up in one of the big armchairs off to the side, watched their faces carefully.

After some minutes, Mazur broke the silence.

"If we were to declare the Commonwealth, Gerry, we need a Council," Mazur said, continuing to stare out to sea.

"The quorum requirement was most carefully drafted, Patryk."

"Ah," Mazur said and nodded.

Minutes passed.

"And the third delegate from each planet?"

Ansen looked over to Kusunoki and nodded.

"The planetary governors," she said quietly. "I could explain why, if you wish."

"No, no. I see it. It's brilliant."

Mazur continued to star out to sea, and more minutes passed.

"The Chairman of the Council, then. That's Westlake?"

"Yes," Kusunoki said.

"And that's the reason for the non-Council ministers. He needs Orlov for defense."

"Correct," Ansen said.

More minutes passed.

"Does Earth have anything that can stand up to that Navy?"

"No," Ansen said.

Mazur nodded. "So the plan is to go to Earth and blow things up until they say 'Uncle.'"

"More or less," Kusunoki said. "We figure to disable things without breaking them first, then give them a list of the things we could break."

"Cause the disruption, but everything repairable. Sign on the dotted line. Or else the next round costs you big money."

"That's right," Kusunoki said.

Mazur nodded. "Smart."

Mazur continued to stare out to sea, and the minutes went by. He finally broke the silence.

"Well, I don't see it, Gerry."

"See what?"

"The hidden flaw. That's what you wanted from me, isn't it? I assume you and Mineko and Westlake and Orlov have been all over this, over the last four years, so I'm not surprised I don't see one." Mazur turned to look directly at Ansen. "But I don't."

"So what's the answer to your question?"

"We declare the Commonwealth, and we fight."

"Will you support me in conference?"

"I'll even make the argument, if you wish. There will be no better time than now, and you and I both know the current situation is not going to last. One caution, though."

"Yes?"

"Some of the Council shouldn't go right back to their planets. The Earth's ruling families have their own cliques and allies. If their planetary governor is allied with the current regime under Arlan Andrews, they could get executed when they get home, whereas if their planetary governor is part of Fournier's group, they're probably OK. I know I can't go back to Kodu right away."

"That's a good point. Where to, then?"

"Just take them back to Jablonka with you. That'll be the capital anyway, right? So they didn't return right home, they're at the capital. So what? No foul there."

138

The Charter Debate

The Charter was complete. After six months of hard work, the conference recessed for four weeks' vacation before reconvening to consider "any remaining business."

Ansen sent the Charter to Westlake via the fast courier ships.

Three weeks later, Westlake and Orlov sat in Westlake's office in the Planetary Governor's Mansion.

"What do you think, Georgy?"

"It's brilliant, Jim. More than that, it's exquisite. They've managed to avoid every historical mistake in governance I can think of."

"I guess that's what you get if you put a liberal sprinkling of history professors in the conference."

"Apparently so. What about you? What do you think?"

"Oh, I agree with you. I guess I'm in a bit of a state of shock. I can't find a single thing I would change. And there's a lot of things in there I didn't think of."

"Ansen also requested a list of planets that conferees shouldn't return to right away. He thinks they should come here to Jablonka, since it's the capital."

"Oh, I agree. Kodu, for one. That's Andrews' son-in-law. There's maybe a dozen planets where it's definitely unsafe for them to go back right away, until things get sorted out. I'll send him a list."

"And I guess I should book passage from there to here for them as well."

"Makes sense to me. And I'll get a reply to Ansen. Then we can start drawing up letters to our families on Earth."

Mehta banged the gavel three times.

"The conference will come to order."

Conversations died down and everyone took their seats. On the Monday after four weeks of vacation, things were going slower this morning than usual.

"The chair will now consider any unfinished business."

"Here," Mazur called out.

"Mr. Mazur."

Mazur walked up to one of the two lecterns in the well and looked up at Mehta.

"You have the floor, Mr. Mazur."

"Thank you, Madam Chairman.

"Madam Chairman, distinguished colleagues.

"I move we modify the Charter to name ourselves the Council and declare the Commonwealth in effect."

"Second!" Guadalupe Rivera screamed out over the roar that erupted among the delegates.

"Debate!" a dozen delegates shouted.

"Counter!" Gerald Ansen shouted.

Mehta let the general bedlam continue for about five minutes before gaveling for order.

"The conference will be in order."

It took another couple of minutes for things to die down enough for her to have much success.

"The conference will be in order. Thank you. Mr. Mazur, your motion has been seconded, and there is a call for debate and counter. How would you proceed?"

"I would make an opening statement, Madam Chairman, and then yield the floor to debate and counter. I would also reserve my right to a closing statement."

"Very well. Mr. Mazur, your opening statement."

"Thank you, Madam Chairman."

Mazur straightened his papers on the lectern and took a drink of water before beginning.

"Madam Chairman, distinguished colleagues.

"We have for six months met in conference to consider the matter of how the colonies might rule themselves once the break with Earth comes. For we know this break is inevitable. Historically inevitable. Sociologically inevitable. Economically inevitable. There is no precedent in history for a stable colonial relationship. Were this one such, it would, in human history, be the first.

"We also know, absent something like the structure detailed with care in this Charter, the costs in blood and treasure of that break are unknown and unknowable, and further the governance that emerges after that break has terrible odds of producing anything like the sort of situation we would all prefer. The likelihood of a technology-driven tyranny dreary enough to rival the most ghastly historical precedent is high.

"We know these things to be true. It is why we are here. We have labored these six months to produce this Charter. Further, we labored the prior three years in correspondence to prepare for this conference. More, most of us have labored all our lives to develop the knowledge and understanding that prepared us for this task. For me, personally, it has been the labor of over half a century to arrive at this point, right here, right now.

"And now we can grasp that architecture of freedom we have designed with our own hands and minds, and bear it forward for our planets, for our people, for our children, to a bright future.

"Or we can simply go home.

"I am not prepared to do that. I am not prepared to walk away from what is our best chance at a glorious future of freedom.

"If not us, my friends, then who?

"If not now, when?"

Mazur organized his papers during the applause from some delegates, buzzing conversation from others. He turned to Mehta.

"Madam Chairman, I yield and reserve."

Mazur stepped down and returned to his seat.

"Thank you, Mr. Mazur. There were multiple calls for debate. I'll give you a few minutes to decide if you can pick one as your speaker, or if you will need multiple speakers. Everyone who called debate, please meet over here."

Mehta pointed to the well on her right. Ansen already stood at the lectern to her left for counter. A dozen delegates, almost twenty percent of the conference, met in the corner and held a sometimes animated conversation for several minutes. Gradually most of them returned to their seats, leaving only Roman Chrzanowski and Jane Paxton.

"Madam Chairman."

"Mr. Chrzanowski."

"Madam Chairman, we believe two speakers will be able to cover our points in debate, myself and Ms. Paxton. I will speak first."

"Very well, Mr. Chrzanowski. Your opening statement."

"Thank you, Madam Chairman."

Paxton returned to her seat for the moment, and Chrzanowski advanced to the lectern.

"Madam Chairman, distinguished colleagues.

"My objection to Mr. Mazur's proposal is not an objection to his ideas. It is not an objection to his words. My objection is that his speech – indeed, the Charter itself – is only ideas, only words. And words and ideas will not be enough when the Earth navy shows up to lay claim to what they think is rightfully theirs.

"We are sixty-six people. Even Doma's police force would have little trouble rounding us up in short order if it came to that. And Earth's Navy has hundreds of warships. We have no means to defend against that, no countervailing forces to deploy. They would snuff out our fledgling commonwealth like a candle.

"We have a dream, yes. But without the means to defend that dream, to defend that Charter, we are better off continuing to work toward that dream than losing it entirely."

Chrzanowski nodded to Mehta.

"Thank you, Mr. Chrzanowski. Mr. Ansen, your opening statement."

"Thank you, Madam Chairman. With your indulgence, Madam Chairman, my opening statement is in the form of a video."

"Is there an objection, Mr. Chrzanowski?"

"No objection, Madam Chairman."

"You may proceed, Mr. Ansen."

"Thank you, Madam Chairman."

Ansen nodded to Kusunoki, who entered commands into her comp. The room lights went down to half, and the video Ansen had shown Mazur five weeks before played out on the large display at the front of the room. Mehta watched the video on the display built into the chairman's podium.

There were some reactions from the delegates to various parts of the video, but nothing like the reaction to the last frame, as ship name after ship name appeared on the screen. As the screen faded and the lights came up, the conference was abuzz with conversation.

Mehta let this carry on for several minutes before she gaveled for order. She looked to Ansen, and he nodded.

"The conference will come to order. Thank you, Mr. Ansen. Mr.

A Charter For The Commonwealth

Chrzanowski, the floor is open for debate."

"Thank you, Madam Chairman. Mr. Ansen, I have to ask you, how many of those ships, of that group of names at the end, how many of those exist?"

"All of them. All seventy of them."

The conference dissolved into disorder again. Mehta let the conversations carry on for a couple of minutes before gaveling for order.

"Mr. Chrzanowski, the floor is still open for debate."

"Thank you, Madam Chairman. Mr. Ansen, I am at a loss. We, the Commonwealth – our side, if you will – have a navy of seventy battleships?"

"Yes, Mr. Chrzanowski. The Orlov Group and other mining companies have been purchasing large freighters and converting them to battleships, in systems across the Commonwealth, for four years. Their crews, for the time being all Orlov Group employees, have been training for two years. Those activities and this conference, which the Orlov Group sponsored, were timed to conclude simultaneously."

Mehta let animated discussion in the audience go for a couple of minutes before gaveling for order. She nodded to Chrzanowski.

"Mr. Ansen, why would Stepan Orlov, of all people, want to fund what amounts to a revolution against himself and the other ruling families of Earth?"

"I don't know anything about Stepan Orlov, Mr. Chrzanowski. What I do know is that his son, Georgy Orlov, who is based on Jablonka and has been for fifteen years, has funded this navy and this conference. I also know that the younger Orlov and Jablonka Planetary Governor Westlake are very much aware the current colonial relationship with Earth is not stable, and will likely end in violence and tyranny if steps are not taken.

"As to motives, it is much easier to run a profitable business under a classical liberal regime than under a totalitarian one. Or perhaps it is simpler than that. Perhaps our esteemed colleagues in the universities of Earth have done a better job of educating these young men in classical liberal Enlightenment values than their parents ever expected, or even desired."

"Back to my original topic. Mr. Anson, is it not true the Earth has many more than seventy warships?"

"That is true, Mr. Chrzanowski. Earth has on the order of three hundred frigates, light warships used primarily for the enforcement of commerce rules against unarmed freighters. The Earth Navy has nothing that can stand up to a Commonwealth battleship, even with a heavy advantage in numbers."

Chrzanowski looked to his supporters in the audience, back to Ansen, and considered for several seconds.

"Madam Chairman, I withdraw my objection to the proposal."

The audience reaction was mixed to that, though the applause well outweighed the grumbling.

"Ms. Paxton."

Jane Paxton walked up to the empty lectern as Chrzanowski returned to his seat.

"Ms. Paxton, your opening statement."

"Thank you, Madam Chairman.

"Madam Chairman, distinguished colleagues.

"My concern with this proposal is one of propriety and authority.

"Let us assume for the moment we adopt this measure, and even, with the use of our newly-revealed navy, we prevail. By what measure are we anything other than one ruling clique replacing another? What is our authority? What is our right?

"Clearly, many people will be better off under our planned structure. Just as surely, some will be worse off. There is seldom any change in the affairs of men that is one hundred percent positive. What right then do we sixty-six have to select one system over the other for the governance of our fellow men?

"Yes, yes, we believe this is a better structure, granting more rights and freedoms to more people, and it better comports with our Enlightenment values. But parse that sentence again. '*We* believe.' '*Our* Enlightenment values.'

"And to what extent are we even sticking to our Enlightenment values, to our own Charter, if we abrogate its powers to ourselves, by declaring ourselves to be the Council in violation of the Charter itself? As merely one example, the Charter requires the Council to be made up of three delegates from each planet, not two.

"Further, what administrative experience to run such a government do we sixty-six have? Academics all. And given how popular our Enlightenment ideals are even within our own academic milieu, most

144

of us have never even headed our own departments."

Amid the ensuing chuckles, Paxton nodded to Mehta.

"Mr. Ansen, your opening statement."

"Thank you, Madam Chairman."

"Madam Chairman, distinguished colleagues.

"Mr. Mazur's proposal is we modify the Charter to name ourselves the transitional Council. That action would not thus be outside the Charter, but internal to it. Such transitional language is often required in such an instance.

"With regard to three delegates from each planet as the Charter specifies for the Council, rather than the two delegates each planet has here at this conference, I agree. But there is already one delegate named and in place for each Commonwealth planet. The planetary governors have been named – by Earth, granted – as the authority on each planet under the current regime. Adding the members of this conference to the existing authority of the thirty-three planetary governors, we arrive at the Charter-specified Council of ninety-nine.

"The Commonwealth can thus be seen not as a replacement of the current governance structure with another, but as an outgrowth from and enhancement of the current governance structure.

"Finally, the admitted weakness of this body in administrative background is much bolstered by naming to the Council the planetary governors, administrators all."

Ansen nodded to Mehta.

"Ms. Paxton, the floor is open for debate."

"Thank you, Madam Chairman. Mr. Ansen, do you seriously propose to put the planetary governors, the very symbols of Earth's domination of the colony planets, on the Commonwealth Council?"

"Of course. Ms. Paxton, transitions are always the most troublesome time for endeavors such as ours. The planetary governors already command the police forces, which not only maintain the regime but protect against all the common crimes – murder, theft, and the like. Those police are generally recruited locally. Why would we not still want such police protections from locally recruited citizens?"

"And police suppression of civil rights, Mr. Ansen?"

"Is now illegal under the Charter, Ms. Paxton. My argument has always been not with the administrators who enforce Earth's decrees, but with those decrees themselves. We all will swear new oaths, as required by the Charter, to preserve, protect, and defend the people and planets of the Commonwealth."

"And if a planetary governor refuses such oath, Mr. Ansen?"

"Why then, he cannot be seated, Ms. Paxton."

"And if they swear such oath, and, forsworn, attempt to undermine the Charter and return the Commonwealth to Earth domination, Mr. Ansen?"

"Then they will be outvoted in Council, Ms. Paxton."

"Madam Chairman, I maintain my objection absent enabling language for the original proposal."

"Thank you, Ms. Paxton, Mr. Ansen. Mr. Mazur, your closing statement."

Paxton returned to her seat and Mazur took the lectern.

"Thank you, Madam Chairman.

"Madam Chairman, distinguished colleagues.

"We have a Charter, as fine a structure for enlightened governance as the finest Enlightenment minds of these thirty-three planets can construct. We have a Navy, the most powerful navy in space, to defend that Charter and those planets. And so I repeat my questions to you from earlier.

"If not us, my friends, then who?

"If not now, when?"

Mazur grabbed up his notes and returned to his seat.

"Thank you, Mr. Mazur. Mr. Mazur, Mr. Chrzanowski, Ms. Paxton, and Mr. Ansen, could you approach the chair, please?"

The four speakers on the proposal came up to the chairman's podium and they had an off-record conversation. The four speakers then returned to their seats, and Mehta addressed the conference.

"My fellow delegates.

"The proposal before us is of such moment it deserves consideration and debate appropriate to its consequence. I am therefore exercising the chairman's prerogative to restructure the proceedings somewhat on this matter.

"We will stand in recess until Wednesday morning. For the rest of today and all of tomorrow, I would urge the delegates to discuss these matters among yourselves. Seek out today's speakers for any additional information you require. Work on enabling language for the proposal discussed here today. Such language might be included in a new article at the end of the agreed document, titled Transition Process or some such.

"And on Wednesday morning, we will begin to hear motions and debates on the enabling language and such other proposals as you might make.

"I am also reminded that this conference's deliberations are confidential, and that in particular encompasses the contents of the video we saw today and certain conclusions one can draw from it.

"In the meantime, Mr. Mazur's motion of today remains tabled. Perhaps a vote on it will be the final approval vote required once all the enabling language and transitional measures are acted upon.

"Mr. Mazur, Mr. Chrzanowski, Ms. Paxton, Mr. Ansen, do I hear any objections?"

"No objection, Madam Chairman."

"We are in recess until Wednesday morning."

The Council

It took over two weeks to debate proposed language, consider all amendments, and pass the individual steps required to come to a final vote. It was Thursday morning of the second last week of the Westlake Conference before Patryk Mazur's proposal came back up for a vote.

But Gerald Ansen had something he wanted to do first.

"Are there any unfinished items before proceeding to Mr. Mazur's original proposal?"

"Madam Chairman, I have one item. It is a letter, just arrived, to this conference from James Allen Westlake VI, His Excellency, the Planetary Governor of Jablonka. I propose to read it to the conference."

"Do I hear an objection? No objection being heard, you may proceed, Mr. Ansen."

"Thank you, Madam Chairman.

"I should perhaps mention to my distinguished colleagues, with the indulgence of the chair I sent a copy of the Charter as passed prior to the vacation break to Mr. Westlake on Jablonka six weeks ago. This letter is his response by return courier mail.

"My Dear Professor Ansen:

"Thank you for sending me a copy of the Charter in its current form in time for me to remark on it prior to the closing of the conference.

"As you and I both know, and as we have discussed, the current relationship between the Earth and its colonies is not stable. The prospects for a peaceful transition, or for a stable subsequent colony government based on the Enlightenment principles we both hold dear, were not good. It is for that reason I asked you, four years ago, to design a classical liberal government for Earth's colonies.

"You wisely saw the need to draw on the best Enlightenment minds available across Earth's colonies, to bring together the expertise and wisdom required to produce the best result. You proposed the Westlake Conference, and I was happy to sponsor it and secure funding for it, in the hope you would be successful.

"I am pleased to be able to tell you that you and your colleagues have exceeded every expectation, every hope, every dream I have had for this project. I am confident this document will lead to a brighter future not just for the citizens of the colonies, but on the longer term for all mankind.

"Please pass on my highest regards and heartfelt gratitude to your distinguished colleagues for their efforts in producing what I believe will be a treasured document for generations.

"Know that I remain gratefully yours,

"James Allen Westlake VI."

Ansen left the lectern to return to his seat, but Mehta stopped him.

"Mr. Ansen, a point of personal curiosity. Did Mr. Westlake originally approach you to begin this whole project?"

"Yes, Madam Chairman. Mr. Westlake invited, on his own initiative, Ms. Kusunoki and me to meet with him, and at that meeting he asked us to design a classical liberal government based on Enlightenment principles for the colonies. As his letter noted, it was we who said this was a job for a constitutional convention, and proposed the Westlake Conference."

"Remarkable. Thank you, Mr. Ansen. We now move on to the last item of business. Mr. Mazur."

Patryk Mazur walked up to the lectern.

"Thank you, Madam Chairman.

"Madam Chairman, distinguished colleagues.

"As previously agreed, this is a motion in substitution of the tabled motion. I move this conference pass the proposal before you, amending the Charter as previously agreed, passing the Charter in its final form, and seating the Council as specified."

"Second," Guadalupe Rivera called.

"We have a motion and a second. Do I hear any objection? No objection being heard, we are voting on the motion. Ayes? Nays? The Ayes have it. The motion passes. I declare the Westlake Conference closed."

Mehta pounded the gavel and the delegates erupted into cheering.

Ansen walked up to the conference table that stood this morning in the well between the two lecterns and lifted off a black velvet cover to reveal a large document of the final language of the Charter, indelibly printed on archival paper. Kusunoki came up and signed it under "For Jablonka" and Ansen signed under her. The delegates lined up to apply their signatures to the document as Ansen, Kusunoki, Mazur, and Mehta watched. There were eight columns, of eight signatures each, and, centered under the others at the bottom, as the host planet, the Doma delegates' signatures.

When all the delegates had signed, Ansen brought out from under the table a large flat metal box with a plate glass lid. He set it on the table next to the document, opened it, and placed the document inside. He then closed the box, capturing the document.

Ansen and Mazur picked up the box by the two sides, walked it back to the chairman's podium, and set it vertically on the floor leaning against the podium.

Mehta went back to the chairman's chair, sat down, and started gaveling for order. Once everyone was seated and the conversation had died down, Mehta announced:

"As Chairman Pro Tem of the Council, a quorum being present, I declare the Council of the Commonwealth of Free Planets in session."

Mehta banged the gavel and another huge cheer went up, with much applause. Some of the delegates were weeping openly. It was twenty minutes before Mehta would even attempt to establish order.

The first agenda of the Council was simple. Take the oath of office, elect a Chairman, elect a Chairman Pro Tem, and agree on the wording of a press release announcing the formation of the Commonwealth of Free Planets and distributing its Charter.

The Council elected James Allen Westlake VI as Chairman and confirmed Sania Mehta as Chairman Pro Tem. A wording of the press release was agreed on, and the Council agreed to delay the publication of the press release until Friday two weeks hence, and to maintain their confidence until then, to meet Ansen's promise to Westlake. The delegates from Doma would publish the press release from Doma on that day.

And, as promised, Ansen sent a letter to Westlake informing him of events.

First Blood

"Sir, as you requested, I've been looking into Fournier, Westlake, and Orlov, looking for anything unusual in their business dealings," Andy Hasper said.

"Good. What did you find?" Arlan Andrews asked.

"It may be nothing, sir, and it was four years back. But Orlov Group bought some really large freighters, our biggest design, along with a lot of mining equipment. Containers, beam cutters, and nuclear demolitions."

"That doesn't sound unusual, Andy."

"They were really large orders, though, sir. Eighty freighters, and tens of thousands of containers, hundreds of beam cutters, and thousands of nuclear demolitions. It took the manufacturers two years of overtime shifts to make them all."

"OK, I agree. That is unusual."

"That's not all, sir. They were slow getting the freighters into service. And we still aren't seeing the kind traffic with them one would expect with that many ships. You can sort of figure out travel and loading times and the like, and calculate from that how often they should be showing up here. And it's maybe a quarter of what it should be."

"Something's going on. And those ships still show up here?"

"Yes, sir. Not as often as you'd expect, but they do come through."

"We need to inspect one of those ships and see what's going on. Order the Navy to seize and board one of those freighters and go through it with a fine-tooth comb. I want to know what they're up to."

"Yes, sir."

"Approaching hyperspace transition point, sir."

"Whenever you're ready, Mr. Asnip."

"Beginning hyperspace transition."

The klaxon sounded, followed by the four bells of the hyperspace warning.

"Hyperspace transition now, sir."

Captain Heller had reduced his safety margins after the first trip, and *Stardust* transitioned into normal space only about five percent farther from Earth than the published system periphery. Oconnell sent their arrival announcement, and Asnip was about to flip ship to get underway toward Earth when they were hailed.

"Sir, I have ENS *Moses Lambert* hailing. You need to hear this."

Without waiting, Oconnell switched the recorded reception to the speakers.

"ENS *Moses Lambert* here. *Stardust*, maintain position and prepare to be boarded."

"Oh, I don't think so," Heller said. "Mr. Asnip, engines at one hundred percent. Mr. Oconnell, sound general quarters. Mr. Scott, blow the aft beam covers and bring up the emitters."

Instead of the all-clear the crew was expecting, the general quarters alarm sounded. They had maintained periodic drills on their transits, and as the gravity came up the crew ran for their posts.

"Mr. Stodden, what have you got?"

"Three ESN frigates at one-fifty degrees mark ten, sir. Range one quarter light-second. They're accelerating hard, sir. They'll range us in minutes."

"Mr. Asnip, come to thirty degrees minus ten. Let's show them our after aspect."

Another radio reception played over the speakers.

"What the hell are you up to, Heller? You can't outrun me. Shut her down or we'll open fire."

"Stand ready, Mr. Scott."

"Targeted and ranged, sir."

"Sir, they're opening rapid fire."

"You may fire, Mr. Scott."

"Firing four. Firing four. Firing four."

"All three ESN frigates exploded, sir. We still have incoming projectiles."

"Mr. Asnip, try to avoid them."

"They fired a broad pattern, sir. There are hundreds of them. I can't dodge them all."

"Do your best, Mr. Asnip."

The first projectile to hit *Stardust* hit her in the number four radiator. She started streaming coolant.

"Hit on Radiator Four, sir. We're losing coolant," Greg Yetter said. The loadmaster was using his outside cameras to monitor for damage.

"Radiator Control says they're on it, sir," Bryan Jones said.

"Pressure dropping in Radiator Four," Seaman 1st James Yount said. "She's been holed."

"Shut it down," Petty Officer 1st Lindsay Harwood said.

"Shutting down the coolant pump to Radiator Four," Seaman 1st Jennifer Lowenthal said. "Radiator Four flow rate dropping. Radiator Four flow rate zero. Closing inlet valve on Radiator Four. Radiator Four pressure dropping. Closing outlet valve on Radiator Four. Radiator Four isolated."

And then the world exploded.

The second projectile to hit *Stardust* hit her in Beam Emitter 10. The round plowed through the emitter dish and deep into her internals.

"Hit on Beam Emitter 10, sir. She's on fire," Yetter said.

"Jettison Beam Emitter 10, Mr. Yetter."

Yetter pushed the Jettison icon for Beam Emitter 10, and the dozens of explosive bolts that held it in place blew off. The massive 24'x24'x80' unit slid off the back of *Stardust* under the .6 gravity acceleration and fell behind.

"Mr. Scott, target and range that beam emitter. Fire when you're ready. We don't want to leave it behind."

The third projectile to hit *Stardust* hit her in Cylinder Two. It came through the deck below Jennifer Lowenthal's station chair and passed vertically through her body before punching through the next three decks above. At ten thousand feet per second, the hydrostatic pressure literally blew Lowenthal apart, and the concussion of the shock wave as the shell passed through the compartment knocked everyone else unconscious.

Seaman 1st Toby Cobb and Seaman 2nd Paul Clithero heard the impact and the air whistle from their GQ station and came racing down the corridor and into the compartment. Clithero kicked debris out of the way and set the patch plate over the ragged hole in the deck. The flexible plate deformed to match the bent deck plate and Cobb sprayed sealant around the seam. The sealant sucked into the seam and Cobb kept spraying until it sealed up.

They looked up from their work and for the first time noticed the compartment. Five ratings were down. Blood and bone, muscle and organs were splattered all over the compartment, dripping from the ceiling and running down the walls and consoles.

"What the fuck?" Clithero looked down at the debris he had kicked aside to set the patch. It was a human arm raggedly torn off at the shoulder.

Clithero wretched and then threw up in his suit helmet. He staggered out into the hallway, slipping on the bloody floor. As senior, Cobb should report, but Clithero saw he was down on his hands and knees, vomiting helplessly. Clithero tried to raise Damage Control on his helmet radio and couldn't, then realized his mike was blocked. He sucked vomit off and out of the mike and spat it aside.

"Damage Control. Seaman Clithero. Cylinder Two, Deck One sealed. Medics to Radiator Control. At least one dead, five down."

"We have three ESN frigates incoming, sir, at ninety mark ten range three light seconds, and three more incoming at two seventy minus ten range two light seconds," Stodden said.

"Mr. Asnip, begin spinning the ship. Don't unfold cylinders or shut down the engines for the moment, just start us spinning. Twenty-five percent spin."

"Yes, sir."

Stardust started spinning with the cylinders folded, adding a small side gravity.

"We're at twenty-five percent, sir."

"Mr. Asnip, bring engines to zero."

The 'down' gravity suddenly disappeared, leaving only the side gravity.

"Engines at zero, sir."

"Mr. Scott, blow the forward emitter covers and bring up the emitters."

Scott pushed the icon on his display to eject the covers and started initiation on the front emitters. The eight covers sailed straight out away from *Stardust*.

"Mr. Yetter, jettison the cargo."

"All of it?"

"All the fernico. Just keep weapons and supplies. Do it."

"Yes, sir." Yetter pushed the master cargo jettison icon on his display.

Cargo latches released, sending the top layer of containers sailing out from the spinning *Stardust*, then the next layer released, and the next layer, and the next layer. Only the weapons and stores containers of the innermost layer remained.

"Cargo jettisoned, sir."

"Cease spin, Mr. Asnip. Status, Mr. Stodden."

"Range now two light-seconds on group one, one light-second on group two."

"When your spin is at zero, Mr. Asnip, bring us to ninety mark ten."

"Spin at zero. Coming to ninety mark ten."

"Mr. Scott, when you have targets, you are free to fire on both groups."

"Coming into angle. Targeting. Ranging. Firing Three. Firing Eight. Firing Three. Firing Eight. Firing Three. Firing Eight."

"All targets destroyed," Stodden said. "Those last couple just lit up the debris."

"Anything else out there to worry about, Mr. Stodden?"

"No, it looks like that was it, sir."

"Mr. Oconnell, send Black Earth message via corporate relay on Earth."

"Sending Black Earth message, sir."

"Damage Control, are we hyperspace capable?"

"Yes, sir," Jones said. "We're down one radiator, but we know that's OK."

"Mr. Asnip, bring us around and make hyperspace transition when you're ready. Make course for Jablonka."

"Yes, sir. Hyperspace transition in five minutes."

The hyperspace warning sounded. Five minutes later, *Stardust* disappeared from normal space.

"One of those freighters came in-system, sir," Andy Hasper said.

"Did they get a look at it?" Arlan Andrews asked.

"No, sir. They tried to stop it, but it got away."

"Didn't they shoot at it?"

"Yes, sir, they did. But it shot back with something we don't understand. That freighter took out nine of our frigates."

"A Q-ship! That's what Orlov's doing. He's building Q-ships."

"Yes, sir. Apparently so. Do you want them to try again?"

"No. We'll show them they can't just waltz in here and shoot up the place. Start gathering our navy power. Call ships back. Get some of those ones that are sitting around all the time up to snuff. Let's pull some power together."

"Yes, sir. Maybe some of the mothballed ships as well?"

"Yes. Excellent. But don't bother any of Orlov's ships again. We already know what's going on. He's screwed up this time. He's tipped his hand. Q-ships run by amateurs don't stand a chance against real warships run by professionals."

"They did take out nine of our frigates, sir."

"Yes, but that's because our people went spacing in there all fat, dumb, and happy. They weren't expecting anything. Ask Admiral Bruneau to stop by. I have some instructions for him."

A Charter For The Commonwealth

Letters

James Allen Westlake received the press release before anyone else outside of the Doma system, it having been sent to him by Gerald Ansen immediately after it passed. It was three weeks since Ansen sent it. Westlake had requested a two-week delay, which meant the press release from Doma was already one week along on its way to Earth, Jablonka, and the other star systems of the Commonwealth.

PRESS RELEASE

Nadezhda, Doma – The Council of the Commonwealth of Free Planets has announced the enactment of the Charter of the Commonwealth of Free Planets and the creation of the Commonwealth, a confederation of the thirty-three planetary systems in Earth's first round of colonization.

The Charter lays out the structure and powers of the new government as well as the rights and freedoms guaranteed to the Commonwealth's citizens and member planets.

The Council is to be composed of three delegates from each of the thirty-three member planets. The initial delegates to the Council are the thirty-three existing planetary governors plus an additional two Commonwealth citizens from each member planet. The initial Chairman of the Council is James Allen Westlake, the Planetary Governor of Jablonka.

The Charter was enacted and signed in Nadezhda, the planetary capital of the Doma system.

Attachments: 1) List of the thirty-three member systems of the Commonwealth. 2) The text of the Charter of the Commonwealth of Free Planets.

Westlake had, over the past month, composed letters to his father, his father-in-law, Claude Fournier, and the thirty-two other planetary governors of the Commonwealth systems. He reread those letters in the light of the press release and they did not require any changes.

Georgy Orlov had also composed a letter to his father, Stepan

157

Orlov. Given the short timeframe they knew they would be under once Ansen's letter came, Orlov had given his letter to Westlake for transmission.

Westlake queued all thirty-five mails in his outbox and hit Send.

My Dearest Father:

You will be receiving news of me in the next day or two that will raise questions in your mind about my actions and my motives. I write this letter so that, as always, things will be clear between us.

We often talked in my youth about Earth's colonies, and their likely future. It was my interest in the colonies, I am sure, that motivated you and Claude to arrange my posting to Jablonka.

Suzette and I have loved our time here. Your grandchildren were born here and have prospered here. While Earth's rule over the colonies is absolute, I have endeavored throughout my time here to be an enlightened despot, eschewing the more aggressive measures by which some other planetary governors have fulfilled their duties.

Jablonka has thrived under that leadership over the last fourteen years. While not being the most populous of Earth's colonies, it is now the most prosperous, and produces the greatest income for Earth. In such manner have I fulfilled my duties.

At the same time, our earlier conversations have troubled me. We both know the current situation cannot last. The type of people that populate Earth's colonies are, by and large, the sort you and I admire, the sort who would rather scrounge for scraps in freedom than dine in chains. A blow-up was coming, with what violence and disruption we could only guess.

And so, after ten years of contemplation and study, four years ago I set in motion a series of events which have culminated in the news you will receive shortly. I saw the opportunity, and the confluence of people, resources, and circumstance that made it possible, and I acted.

You know me not to be impulsive, though the news you will receive may make me look so. And while the current clique in control on Earth will no doubt respond poorly to the news, they will ultimately find the colonies are prepared for their countermoves. Trust me when I say Earth cannot prevail.

What is important to Earth is its trade with its colonies. What is important to the people of the colonies is their sovereignty over themselves. These are not conflicting goals. Attempting to maintain the *status quo* would inevitably end in violence and disruption that would put everything at risk. I have endeavored instead to steer a better course forward for us all.

With love and respect, I remain, as always, yours.

James Allen Westlake VI

My Dear Colleague:

For over a hundred and twenty years, the Earth has asserted sovereignty and exercised administrative control over the thirty-three planets of its first wave of colonization.

That period is coming to an end.

We have all seen it coming. As the colonies have grown larger, they have also grown more self-sufficient. More, over the last twenty years, the population of the colonies has grown more restive. The colonies no longer need or want Earth's administrative control.

Our options going forward are to become ever more repressive, building up more and more pressure to an ultimate explosion that would consume us all, or to seek another way forward.

The primary value of the colonies to Earth is in trade. The Earth does not need either sovereignty or administrative control of the colonies to engage in and profit from that trade. Indeed, maintaining that sovereignty and exercising that administrative control is a cost to Earth, one that will increase rapidly as things come to a head.

Happily, we do not need to carry on down that path. The thirty-three planets of Earth's first wave of colonization have now set up their own administrative entity, the Commonwealth of Free Planets.

All the planetary governors have been included in the Council of this Commonwealth, its legislative body. There are also roles for us either on our own planets or as Cabinet Ministers of the Commonwealth.

I urge you to join me in welcoming this transition to a new administrative regime on our planets, one that can be stable over the long term and be a positive force for trade, prosperity, and growth for the Earth and its colonies.

I remain yours,

James Allen Westlake VI

Planetary Governor of Jablonka

After Westlake told Georgy Orlov that evening that he had received Ansen's message and sent out the letters, Orlov called Jarl Sigurdsen. Sigurdsen then sent out a large number of queued mails as well.

Seventy in all.

AARs

"Seaman Yount noted Radiator Four was losing pressure and stated it was holed. Is that right, Petty Officer Harwood?" Senior Chief Abby Swogger asked.

"That's correct, Senior Chief," Petty Officer 1st Lindsay Harwood said.

"And you did what?"

"I ordered it shut down, Senior Chief."

"And did Seaman Lowenthal shut it down?"

"Yes, Senior Chief."

"Did Seaman Lowenthal shut it down in a timely way as compared to drills?"

"Yes, Senior Chief. I believe she was faster than drills."

"And then what happened?"

"And then I woke up in sick bay, Senior Chief."

"Was that immediately after shutting down Radiator Four?"

"Yes, Senior Chief. Lowenthal had just reported Radiator Four isolated. I knew the engines were at 100%, and I didn't even have time to order people to watch our temperatures on the other radiators."

"What did you do when you heard the impact, Seaman Clithero?" Swogger asked.

"Cobb – that's Seaman Toby Cobb – and I ran down the corridor to Radiator Control, went in to Radiator Control, and sealed the hole, Senior Chief," Seaman 2nd Paul Clithero said.

"Did you note the state of the compartment when you entered it?"

"No, Senior Chief. We were focused on patching the hole."

"When did you notice the state of the compartment?"

"Once the hole was patched, Cobb and I looked around, Senior Chief. That's when we saw the compartment."

"What did you do then, Seaman Clithero?"

"I threw up in my helmet, Senior Chief. Then I went out into the corridor."

"When did you notice Seaman Cobb had not reported?"

"I looked back when I got into the corridor, Senior Chief, and I saw Seaman Cobb was incapacitated."

"How was he incapacitated?"

"He was on his hands and knees vomiting in his helmet, Senior Chief."

"And that's when you reported for your team?"

"No, Senior Chief. I tried to report, but my microphone was blocked."

"What was blocking your microphone?"

"Vomit, Senior Chief."

"And what did you do then, Seaman Clithero?"

"I cleared my microphone and reported for the team, Senior Chief."

"How did you clear your microphone? Did you remove your helmet?"

"No, Senior Chief. Damage control parties must remain suited up during general quarters in case there's another projectile."

"Then how did you clear your microphone, Seaman Clithero?"

"I sucked the vomit out of the microphone to clear it, Senior Chief. Then I reported in."

"How many incoming projectiles were you tracking from the Earth Space Navy frigates, Mr. Stodden?" Bryan Jones asked.

"Approximately two hundred, sir. I couldn't track them all," Karl Stodden said.

"And these were fired from the ESN frigates over what period of time, Mr. Stodden?"

"Over the course of a minute or so, sir."

"So you would say the ESN frigates have a rate of fire on their projectile weapon of about one round per second, is that right?"

"At least, sir."

"And of those two hundred projectiles, how many struck *Stardust*, Mr. Stodden?"

"I tracked four, sir."

"Four? I thought there were three impacts."

"No, sir. I believe if you check you'll find we took a projectile in one of the stores containers. It hit the same time as the one hit Beam

Weapon 10, sir. It sounded like one impact, but it was two."

"The rest of the approximately two hundred projectiles missed *Stardust*, Mr. Stodden?"

"No, sir. *Stardust* missed them."

"Explain."

"Mr. Asnip moved the ship away from the path of most of the projectiles, and positioned *Stardust* in a gap in the incoming fire."

"So *Stardust* dodged the densest area of projectile fire?"

"Yes, sir."

"If *Stardust* had not dodged, how many impacts might we have taken, Mr. Stodden? Do you have an idea?"

"I can't be sure, sir, but ten to fifteen hits would have been the likely range."

"Based on what you saw on the radar?"

"Yes, sir. I saw them go zipping by, sir."

"I've reviewed all the interviews Senior Chief Swogger conducted with ratings, sir, and I conducted the officer interviews. I also viewed bridge, radar, and control systems records from the battle," Bryan Jones said.

"Very good. And what did you learn, XO?" Captain Marc Heller asked.

"First is that Seaman 1st Jennifer Lowenthal beat all drill records in shutting down Radiator Four, sir. And it's a good thing she did. The projectile that came in through Radiator Control killed her and knocked all the other ratings unconscious. There was no one on those consoles for almost twenty minutes, sir."

"In which time we would have lost coolant and been stuck."

"Yes, sir."

"What else?"

"The damage control parties reacted completely by instinct, sir. They didn't even look around the compartment until the leak was sealed. And it's a good thing they didn't. The scene was ghastly, sir. Both seamen vomited inside their helmets, one being completely incapacitated. The junior member of the team was only able to report after he sucked the vomit out of his microphone to clear it, sir."

"But their quick action sealed the leak and his report got medics and a relief crew into Radiator Control."

"Yes, sir. Thirty-six seconds on the seal."

"Outstanding. What else have you got for me?"

"Mr. Asnip dodged a field of approximately two hundred projectiles to take just four hits."

"Four hits?"

"Yes, sir. Mr. Stodden said he tracked four hits, and on an exterior camera review we found a hit in one of the storage containers. The point being that Mr. Asnip dodged the main field of the projectiles. Mr. Stodden estimated ten to fifteen hits had Mr. Asnip not dodged the central mass."

"Sounds like Mr. Asnip was on top of his game."

"Yes, sir. At the same time, I think he blames himself for the hits we did take. For Seaman Lowenthal's death. I wonder if you might talk to him, sir."

"I'll do that, XO. So, do you have recommendations?"

"Yes, sir. One is that standard stores on departure should include one full charge of coolant for the radiator system.

"Another is that the ship be modified to include backflow valves and hydraulic fuses to shut off radiators automatically in the case of a puncture.

"My third recommendation is that damage control microphones be reoriented so the openings are on the bottom rather than the top, so they can shed the, um, occasional fluid while remaining operational.

"Finally, we should consider armor plate on Deck One to reduce penetration of those projectiles. Give us one armored aspect to show the enemy."

"All right, XO. Good job. Write up those recommendations and make them part of your report."

"Yes, sir."

"And ask Mr. Asnip to see me at his opportunity."

"Yes, sir."

Reaction To The Charter

When the press release from Doma got to Jablonka, the editors of the two biggest newsfeeds called the planetary governor's office to inquire as to whether it was OK to publish it. The press liaison in the planetary governor's office said, "Of course, it's OK to publish it. If you read it, you know Jablonka now has freedom of the press, as well as all the other freedoms called out in the Charter."

The newsfeeds ran with the press release, and also reported Planetary Governor Westlake's office had confirmed all the civil rights called out in the Charter were now guaranteed on Jablonka.

The press liaison of the planetary governor's office also gave them some news. The planetary governor had reviewed all the convictions of people currently being held in jail for any crime inconsistent with the civil rights now guaranteed by the Charter. Several dozen people's convictions were being overturned and they would be released within the next week.

Those sort of specifics of the way in which the Charter would affect people's lives seemed to hit much more of a nerve than the legalistic wording of the document itself.

The news hit the newsfeeds early Saturday morning, and by midday crowds had gathered in the Jezgra City Park and on the quad of the campus of the University of Jablonka. The two crowds joined forces in the city park at some point during the early afternoon. Various speakers took to the microphone in the band shell to address the crowd, and the whole thing turned into a party that ran late into the night.

Less public and less well noticed changes were also happening in orbit. Jablonka space traffic controllers stood amazed at their consoles when thirty-two freighters in the Jablonka system started squawking military transponder signals.

OGS *Star Tripper* was an Orlov freighter in the Pahaadon system. Jarl Sigurdsen's mail came in to her captain, Douglas Baird. He was given the crypto key and directed to open a previous, encrypted mail that contained his new orders. Following those orders, a number of things happened.

The entire crew individually swore an oath to "preserve, protect, and defend the Charter of the Commonwealth of Free Planets."

The officers of the *Star Tripper* received their commissions and rankings in the Commonwealth Space Force.

The ship's safe was opened, and two sealed packages withdrawn.

The first package was opened, and officers and enlisted crew were distributed new rank badges for their work uniforms. Dress uniforms would have to wait.

The second package was opened, and it resulted in a little ceremony on the bridge. The composition plaque on the back wall of the bridge that declared 'OGS Star Tripper, The Orlov Group' was replaced with a bronze plaque announcing 'Commonwealth Space Ship RELIANT, Battleship BB-021.'

Already spinning in high orbit about the planet, *Star Tripper* blew her forward and aft emitter covers.

Finally, *Star Tripper* changed her transponder settings from 'Star Tripper, Orlov Group Freighter' to 'CSS Reliant, Commonwealth Battleship.'

"Well, there's Westlake's play," said Michael Jacobus, head of the Earth Special Police on Bahay, as he handed back printouts of Westlake's letter from Jablonka and the Commonwealth press release from Doma.

"Apparently so. It's a bold move," said Richard Mcenroe, Planetary Governor of Bahay.

"And a stupid one. What's he going to do when the ESN shows up?"

"First, one thing Jim Westlake has never been is stupid. Second, I had a curious call from Jim Polaski today."

"The head of Bahay Space Traffic Control?" Jacobus asked.

"Yes. He said the two ESN frigates that are pretty much always stationed here for enforcing the commerce regulations left the system. They filed a spacing plan for Earth."

"Without waiting for their replacements?"

"That's right," Mcenroe said. "That was yesterday. And he said another curious thing happened today. An Orlov Group freighter in orbit changed its transponder code. It's now squawking it's the CSS *Courageous*. Polaski wanted to know if I knew what was going on."

"CSS?"

"Commonwealth Space Ship. And it's squawking its ship type as 'Battleship.'"

"Battleship? Earth's navy doesn't have any battleships," Jacobus said.

"No. But apparently Mr. Westlake's Commonwealth navy does."

"I wonder how many of them he has?"

"I did a little search through newsfeed archives," Mcenroe said. "The Orlov Group and two other mining concerns active in the thirty-three first-wave colonies purchased eighty of the biggest freighters Earth makes four years ago. Fifteen hundred feet long. Seems like that would make a pretty good platform for a battleship. And four years is a long time for mounting weapons and such if your hull and propulsion are all complete."

"*Eighty* battleships?"

"Don't know. Could be. And four years ago, Westlake changed the name of his police force from Earth Special Police to Jablonka Protective Service. That was the same week as Orlov's freighter order, now that I think of it."

"The same week?" Jacobus asked.

"Yes. Now, let me run a couple of other things past you. Who's Westlake's father-in-law?"

"I don't know."

"His wife's maiden name is Suzette Fournier," Mcenroe said.

"*Claude* Fournier?"

"Yes. And Georgy Orlov, who runs his father's colonial mining interests out of Jablonka? His sister Anastasiya is the wife of the planetary governor of Doma, where this Commonwealth Charter was signed. And the name of the planetary governor of Doma is –"

"Edmond Fournier," Jacobus said in a whisper.

"Got it in one."

"My God, is Fournier finally moving against Andrews?"

"Don't know. Could be. The Fournier, Westlake, and Orlov families are all close, on Earth and out in the colonies. My point, though, is there is much going on here I don't yet understand. And I didn't get to where I am by leaping without looking."

"So you're going to wait and see what happens?"

"Sure. It's not like I need to make any decisions yet. We just keep doing what we're doing. Only one thing I think might be smart to do, and that is to rename your police force the Bahay Protective Service."

"You think we should?"

"Sure, why not? Depending on which way the wind blows, having 'Earth Special Police' stenciled on your building in big letters might not be so smart with a Commonwealth battleship holding the high orbitals, eh?"

Claude Fournier, Stepan Orlov, and James Allen Westlake V were on a video conference call on Earth.

"I am assuming we all got correspondence from Jim Westlake on Jablonka, is that right?" Fournier asked.

"I did," Westlake said.

"I got correspondence from Georgy, who's also on Jablonka, but I suspect it amounts to the same thing," Orlov said.

"And we've all seen the press release from Doma?"

Westlake and Orlov both nodded.

"So what do we make of it all?" Fournier asked.

"Well, our kids – and I include Suzette in that – are clearly on the right side of history. We three have discussed this before. At some point, the colonies are going to go their own way, and the best move at that point is to make sure we have a friendly enough relationship with them we can continue trading with them. It seems they think now is the time," Westlake said.

"And Georgy is obviously in there with them. Putting Jim and Georgy both on Jablonka together might have been a mistake in retrospect," Orlov said.

"I got a letter from Edmond, too," Fournier said. "He just heard about this whole thing when the press release issued on Doma. He's pretty upset about it, that they did it on Doma without even talking to him about it. He's afraid of reprisals."

Fournier waved a hand, as if to brush everything aside, before continuing.

"Be that as it may, we are where we are. The question now is what do we do about it. Andrews is chairman at the moment, and he will be until his term is up, absent a no-confidence consensus. I don't think that's possible right now."

"It may be, if he overreacts and steps in it as badly as he could," Westlake said. "He's not a deep thinker, and he's not exactly known for his restraint. Jim seems to think the colonies are in a position to force the issue, and Earth won't be able to counter them."

"Georgy was more explicit," Orlov said. "They have a navy, and he's convinced they can prevail over the ESN. He wasn't very specific on details, but Georgy tends if anything to understate such things. And I will mention one other thing. Jarl Sigurdsen is his VP of operations out there."

"*Admiral* Jarl Sigurdsen?" Fournier asked.

"Yes," Orlov said. "And in addition to being a damn fine admiral in his own right, he knows all of ESN doctrine. Bruneau is going to have a hard time with him."

"So what I hear emerging as a consensus is that Andrews is going to overreact and probably do something incredibly stupid, and then Sigurdsen is going to hand Bruneau his head," Fournier said.

"Probably," Westlake said.

"I agree," Orlov said.

"All right. So we're going to have to let Andrews play out his hand. At some point his position is going to become so untenable I will be able to force a no-confidence. We'll just have to bide our time and watch for our opportunity."

"Agreed," Westlake and Orlov both said.

"That's what they're up to. They're making a play to take the colonies for themselves," Arlan Andrews said.

"That's what it looks like, sir. The younger Westlake is named here as the Chairman of the Council. The chief executive, I guess," Andy Hasper said.

"Oh, they're all in on it. The younger Orlov. Fournier's daughter. Fournier's son, too. This damned charter thing was signed on Doma."

"And Fournier's son is married to Orlov's daughter."

"Oh, yes. It all fits a pattern now," Andrews said. "What the hell are they thinking? They're going to pit some fucking Q-ships against the ESN? Good luck with that."

"Maybe they think you'll treat it as a fait accompli, sir."

"That's not going to happen. No, we're going to teach Fournier,

Westlake, and Orlov a lesson they're never going to forget."

"What do you want to do, sir?" Hasper asked.

"Tell Bruneau I want him to get together what ships he has here and space for Doma."

"He's going to want to wait for more ships, sir. They're just starting to come in from the closer colonies."

"Navy people always want more ships," Andrews said. "It's part of their DNA. You tell him he can wait a week, then whatever he has, he has. We'll send anything that comes in later to Doma to meet him there."

"All right, sir. And his orders for Doma?"

"Burn it down. Bomb the cities. Destroy Orlov's mining interests there. Lay waste to the system. Leave Fournier nothing."

"Are you sure, sir?" Hasper asked.

"Yes, dammit! Fournier wants to fuck around? OK, fine. He fucked around with the wrong guy."

"Yes, sir."

"And then get in touch with your assets on Jablonka. Young Westlake? I want that little prick dead."

Jablonka

As the news of the Charter spread across the Commonwealth, Gerald Ansen, Mineko Kusunoki, Patryk Mazur, and twenty-three other members of the Council were in transit to Jablonka. Ansen and Kusunoki were once again aboard the *Jewel of Space*, and Ansen once more had his smoking lounge across the hall.

They had actually left after the press release had been published. Passenger ships between systems did not leave every day, or even every week. Interstellar travel was expensive, and the number of passengers willing and able to pay such fares was limited.

As a result, they didn't get to Jablonka until eight weeks after the press release was published.

News of their impending arrival reached Jablonka five weeks before they did, on the high-speed courier ships that delivered interstellar mail. Those same ships had carried the news of the Charter to Earth in four weeks, and Arlan Andrews' orders back to Jablonka in another three.

Richard Paolinelli considered the mail he had just received from Earth. It had a return address he knew led nowhere, but he knew who it was from. The message itself was cryptic, but he knew what it said.

Kill Westlake? How the hell was he supposed to pull that off and get away with it? It was a truism that any political figure could be assassinated as long as the assassin didn't care whether or not he got away, but Paolinelli did care.

It didn't help that Westlake had become an insanely popular figure. The news from Doma of the Charter, and Westlake's whole-hearted endorsement of its civil rights clauses, had occurred almost a month ago. People who had had to worry their whole lives about what they said, or what they printed or published, had become sort of giddy with the freedom to say or print or publish whatever the hell they wanted. Westlake had always had a light hand compared to some planetary governors, but that just made him even more popular. In the view of many, he had been conspiring all along to break away from Earth and make Jablonka free.

Which was all well and good, but it didn't help Paolinelli do his job. And of course the Charter and Commonwealth nonsense was the whole reason for doing the job in the first place, he had no doubt of that. His orders came from Earth, and the colonies breaking away from Earth would not be a popular concept in some quarters there, that's for sure.

Whatever. A job is a job.

He went back to considering how he was going to pull this off.

The newspaper said there was going to be a rally at the shuttleport to welcome back the members of the Council from Doma. Maybe he could do the old switcheroo play.

The shuttle down from the *Jewel of Space* touched down on the farthest shuttlepad from the terminal building of Jablonka spaceport. This was to accommodate the crowd that had come out to welcome the return home of Gerald Ansen and Mineko Kusunoki as well as the arrival of another two dozen members of the Commonwealth Council.

The Planetary Governor, James Allen Westlake VI, and several other dignitaries were waiting on the next shuttlepad closer to welcome them home. Perhaps ten thousand people stood between the shuttleport building and the barricades separating the crowd from the dignitaries. There was a microphone set up so Westlake could address the crowd. A small passenger shuttle for the dignitaries and the ever-present ambulance when Westlake was out and about stood on the next pad to the side.

The big passenger shuttle from the liner came slowly down out of the sky and landed on the far shuttlepad. The hatch opened and Ansen appeared in the doorway and waved. A cheer went up from the crowd. Ansen started down the stairs, followed by Kusunoki and the other Council members. They walked from the far shuttle pad to the pad where Westlake and the dignitaries waited.

Ansen walked up to Westlake and shook his hand, as did Kusunoki. Ansen then introduced each of the Council members to Westlake in turn. Westlake's aide said each Council member's name over the microphone as Westlake shook their hand, and the crowd cheered each name.

When the introductions were done, Westlake addressed the crowd.

A Charter For The Commonwealth

Ansen was standing behind Westlake slightly to Westlake's left, with Kusunoki to Ansen's left. She held his arm, as she often did when they were out. Just after Westlake started speaking, Kusunoki tightened her grip on Ansen's arm once, then twice more, not as hard.

As most couples who've been married a while, they had their signals. Kusunoki's were mostly non-verbal. The one hard grab was "I don't like this," and two short grabs were, "Look at that."

Ansen scanned the crowd, and he saw it. One young man in a spaceport uniform standing in the second row of the crowd, behind the barricades about ten yards distant. The problem was, his expression was all wrong. He cheered whenever everyone else did, but it wasn't real.

As Ansen watched, a hand with a gun reached out of the crowd and lifted toward Westlake. Ansen threw his arms around Westlake and spun one hundred and eighty degrees as gunshots rang out across the spaceport.

Paolinelli had gotten to the front of the crowd. He wanted to be in the second row. He was standing right behind and just to the right of a man in the front row. Once Westlake started talking and he was a stationary target, he reached his hand out between the two men in front of him and opened fire.

Westlake and Ansen went down, whereupon Paolinelli dropped the gun on the pavement and grabbed the man in front of him, dragging him to the ground.

"I've got him, I've got him," Paolinelli yelled as security men rushed forward.

Ansen and Westlake both went down and the crowd shrieked. Some people started running for the terminal building, while others stayed, transfixed by the scene. There was shouting from the shooter's location. Medical men rushed out of the ambulance twenty meters away, two of them carrying equipment and four of them carrying a litter.

When they got to the scene, Westlake and Kusunoki were on their knees over the prone Ansen. He was laying on his chest, and had three bullet holes in the back of his jacket. The EMTs cut through his shirt and jacket up the middle of his back, applied a stop-it to each of the bullet holes and activated them, then rolled Ansen on to the litter and ran for the back door of the ambulance.

Kusunoki was right with them, and jumped aboard as the ambulance spooled up. The doors auto-closed and the ambulance veritably leapt off the ground and shot across the spaceport for University of Jablonka Medical Center.

Ansen was awake as they connected an IV with a pint of blood to his right arm. Kusunoki was on Ansen's left.

Ansen looked up at Kusunoki and whispered, "Do not grieve, my Love. I'm very happy, and I've had a wonderful time."

And then he died.

When the ambulance got to UJ Medical Center, Kusunoki got off the ambulance shuttle on the roof, took the elevator down to street level, and hailed a cab. She took it to the gate of the Planetary Governor's Mansion, and asked to see Westlake.

"I'm sorry, ma'am, he's not seeing anybody right now."

"Tell him it's Mrs. Ansen."

"Oh! Oh, yes, ma'am. Just one moment."

The gate guard returned in just seconds.

"This man will take you there, ma'am."

Another guard led her behind the guard shack to an electric cart. He handed her aboard and then drove her across the grounds, into a cart entrance, and to a stand of elevators in the basement. He parked the cart there, handed her out, and then led her into the elevator.

At the proper floor, he waved her out of the elevator.

"This way, ma'am."

He led her down the hall to a large set of double doors she recognized. Knocking once, he let her into the room and closed the door behind her.

Westlake looked up from his desk, which had several other men around it talking animatedly. He got up and came to her.

"Professor Kusunoki, how is Professor Ansen?"

"He died in the ambulance on the way to the hospital."

"I am so sorry. Clearly I was the target. He saved my life."

"Yes, but the reason I'm here is you have the wrong man."

"What?"

"The man arrested at the spaceport is the wrong man. The shooter was behind him, the man who dragged him to the ground."

"Are you sure?"

"Positive. I signaled Ansen that something was wrong, that the fellow in the spaceport uniform looked wrong. He saw it, and we were looking right at him as he raised the gun. Ansen didn't have time to do anything else but put you behind him. The guy he dragged to the ground didn't do anything."

"Detective Hartman."

One of the men walked up.

"We have the wrong guy. It was the guy in the spaceport uniform who dragged down our suspect. He was the real shooter."

Richard Hartman looked at Kusunoki, back to Westlake.

"Are you sure, sir?"

"Test his hands for gunpowder residue. You should be able to tell whether he recently fired a gun or not. And find that guy in the spaceport uniform. I want that guy. And anybody who drags his feet on this is going to be busted down to guarding bus stations."

"Yes, sir. We're on it."

"We need to do this by the Charter. Get me warrants to sign."

Spaceport security cameras showed Paolinelli getting on the people mover in to Jablonka. An electric bus system that ran in its own traffic lanes, it made stops at several stations on its way to the center of Jablonka. There was also a ring route of the bus system.

Security cameras showed Paolinelli transferring from the shuttleport bus to the ring route bus, and exiting the ring route bus two stops later.

JPS officers flooded into that neighborhood, asking everyone whether they had seen this person, and showing a still from one of the security cameras. Between the change of name from Earth Special Police to the Jablonka Protective Service and Westlake's embrace of the charter four weeks before, people were no longer afraid of the police.

They got a break. Someone had seen Paolinelli get in a cab two blocks away and around the corner from the bus stop. They had noted it because he was in a spaceport uniform.

And the cab company had a record of the trip.

Four hours after the assassination, Richard Paolinelli was arrested for the murder of Ansen and the attempted murder of Westlake.

Randy Upton, the fellow Paolinelli had dragged to the ground, did in fact test negative for gunpowder residue on his hands, and he was released from custody.

Once Paolinelli was arrested, the forensics team went to work. It was very difficult to break into modern electronic devices, but it was not impossible. Not if you had a lot of computing capacity and time.

Using the search warrants, they also got his bank data and everything else they could find on Jablonka about Richard Paolinelli.

Hartman was able to brief Westlake on the initial findings the next morning.

"It was Earth," Hartman said.

"Are you sure?" Westlake asked.

"Oh, yes. We have records of the bank transfers, and we can sync them up to other fishy happenings over the past ten years. He seems to live pretty well for someone who has not had any record of income since he got here ten years ago. From Earth, by the way."

"And? You have more than that, surely."

"Yes. We are busting our way – slowly, mind you – into some encrypted communications. I think what's more telling than the contents is the timing. He received an encrypted communication two days ago. First one in about six months."

"Does the timing for that work out?"

"Oh, yes. We know when the Charter press release reached Earth. And we know which courier ship Paolinelli's encrypted mail came in on. There's about a 36-hour window there, from the news of the Charter arriving on Earth to the departure of the courier ship from Earth to Jablonka."

Mike Skibbe, the military liaison, walked into Westlake's office.

"Sir, we've just received communications from *Stardust*. She's one of Mr. Orlov's freighter conversions, and she just made her hyperspace transition into Jablonka. They jumped her. The ESN, that is. There was a battle, and *Stardust* took some hits, had some casualties. Here's the captain's AAR, sir."

Admiral Sigurdsen and Westlake made the trip to inform Jennifer

A Charter For The Commonwealth

Lowenthal's parents of her death.

"You don't have to do this, sir," Sigurdsen said.

"On the contrary, Admiral. Ultimately, I won't be able to do it for everybody, and so, for her, I must."

Sigurdsen looked at Westlake a long minute.

"I understand completely, sir."

It was hard. It was always hard. They stayed for a couple of hours, and listened to the sobbing parents' stories of their beloved daughter, the Commonwealth Space Force's first death in action.

Patryk Mazur stopped by to visit Mineko Kusunoki that day. Kusunoki was dressed all in white, the traditional color of mourning in Japan. She let him in and they took seats in the living room.

"I just wanted to tell you how sorry I am about Gerry," Mazur said.

"Thank you. I will tell you he felt complete, as if the Charter was something he had prepared all his life to do, and he had completed his task. It is a tremendous blessing to me to know that. We always thought he would die before me, but to have him die before completing his life's work would have been a tragedy."

"And he died protecting Westlake. No small thing."

"It is a huge thing," Kusunoki said. "Mr. Westlake is a father, with a wife and children. What a tragedy that would have been. And Mr. Westlake understands what we tried to do, and has the administrative experience to succeed in leading the Commonwealth. He is the best person to carry Gerry's work forward. In some sense, Gerry's work was done, but Mr. Westlake's real task is just beginning."

Mazur looked down at his hands. He didn't know what to say. Kusunoki seemed already at peace with Ansen's death, where for Mazur it was very difficult. Granted he had not seen Ansen for fifty years, but for the last year they had both been more alive and engaged than in years, and he felt the loss keenly.

"Well, I will be staying at the Jezgra Suites Hotel downtown. If you want to get in touch with me, or if you need anything –"

"But you were invited to stay here, Patryk."

"But Gerry is gone."

"And your staying at the Jezgra Suites Hotel will not bring him back."

"I just worried about what people would think. About your

reputation."

Kusunoki laughed.

"Gerry and I never cared what people thought. Or rather, he cared that they not think us too conventional. That was always his concern."

"Ha! He had little to worry about there."

"Indeed. Patryk, there is absolutely no sense in you being alone and lonely downtown and me being alone and lonely here. I am not quite the group conversationalist Gerry was, but you may be surprised how well I can hold my own in a one-to-one conversation."

"If you're sure...."

"I am sure, Patryk. You are always welcome here."

Mazur moved his things into Kusunoki's guest room that same afternoon. That evening they sat in the living room and watched Westlake address the Commonwealth on video.

"My fellow Commonwealth citizens:

"Yesterday, an assassin tried to kill me, but Gerald Ansen knowingly stepped into the path of the assassin's bullets. Gerald Ansen – the Architect of the Commonwealth, the Drafter of the Charter – died defending me from this cowardly attack.

"Last night we captured the assassin, and this morning I was briefed on the status of the investigation. The one thing that is sure at this point is that the assassin was paid by, and operating under the orders of, the Earth government.

"That briefing was interrupted by the news that the *Stardust*, a Commonwealth ship, was the victim of an unprovoked attack by the Earth Space Navy on entering the Earth system. She was struck several times, and one of our spacers, Jennifer Lowenthal, was killed in the attack. Jennifer was only twenty-eight years old. I visited her parents this afternoon to give them that terrible news and to hear their stories of their remarkable daughter.

"It is clear the Earth does not wish the Commonwealth to survive, does not wish the colonies to be out from under its domination, does not want the citizens of the Commonwealth to enjoy the freedoms protected by Gerald Ansen's Charter.

"I am sorry to give Earth some bad news. The Commonwealth will survive, and if Earth desires to throw itself against the rocks of our determination, their ruin will be a shipwreck on the shore of history."

Countermoves

Hopalong Ginsberg was caught between a rock and a hard place. If he did as he was told, and he was caught, he would be executed. Attorney-client privilege wouldn't protect him. Not on Earth. But if he didn't do as he'd been told, he'd be guilty of standing aside rather than prevent an act of mass murder.

Nobility won out over personal fear, and he sent the message.

It took two weeks to ensure every ship of the task force was topped off on stores and reaction mass, and to effect more permanent repairs to the *Stardust*, now under her CSF name, the CSS *Independence*. There was no way Admiral Sigurdsen could not take her with him for the attack on Earth. She had earned her battle honors.

In fact, he decided to fly his flag on the *Independence*. Was it the correct thing to do? He wasn't sure, but he was sure it was the right thing to do. Of such simple things are legends made, on such simple things do traditions grow.

Sigurdsen had with him detailed instructions from higher, strategic goals, tactical plans, and even the text of a treaty the Commonwealth would accept.

Sixteen ships in four divisions spaced for Earth the week after Ansen's death:

- the *Independence*, the *Victory*, the *Vengeance*, and the *Vanguard*;
- the *Challenge*, the *Endeavor*, the *Enterprise*, and the *Adventure*;
- the *Charter*, the *Freedom*, the *Liberty*, and the *Citizenship*;
- the *Triumph*, the *Defiance*, the *Vigilance*, and the *Endurance*.

There were no cargo containers, there were no beam emitter covers, there were no fake transponder codes. The Commonwealth Space Force wasn't hiding from anybody anymore.

Before they left, each crew member on every ship was given a photograph of Jennifer Lowenthal, a photograph of Gerald Ansen, and a copy of the Charter they had sworn to defend.

It was eight weeks transit to Earth, and the ships would be in radio contact with each other all the way.

The Destruction of Doma

A week after the news of Gerald Ansen's murder and the ESN's attack on the *Stardust* arrived in Doma, Planetary Governor Edmond Fournier was meeting with Kim Sommer, his chief of staff.

"This message came in to me personally, anonymously," Fournier told Sommer, and handed him a printout.

Sommer read the printout and whistled.

"Anonymously? That's not easy to do."

"I know. I can't decide whether that gives it more credibility or less. So now what do I do?"

"But it's from Earth?" Sommer asked.

"Last hop, anyway. It came in on the courier ship from Earth."

Sommer looked at the message again: "ESN has orders NOT to accept surrender. Evacuate your cities NOW."

"Would Andrews do that? Ignore a surrender? Bomb cities?" Sommer asked.

"Over this Charter business? I don't know. Maybe. He's not completely rational where my father is concerned. Maybe he thinks the charter was our doing, since it was signed here and the press release issued from here."

"But you looked into that, right? Doma was just the nicest place to call the conference. I mean, if everybody has to travel to get together anyway, why not here?"

"I understand," Fournier said. "But Andrews may not. He's been getting more and more paranoid."

Fournier sighed.

"I can't ignore it," Fournier said. "If Andrews is that crazy – and I'm not sure he isn't – it would be too catastrophic to think about if I ignored this. Get plans together, quickly, and let's get moving. And let's plan on getting everybody into the forests, not out in the open."

"Plans? I don't even know where to start."

"Well, food and water is the biggest one. We don't really need shelter in this climate. Pick the hiding places. Access to fresh water is an important selection criteria. Then collect all the non-perishable food and drink you can and get it to the hiding places. Then let's start moving people. And let's get going on it. I'm not sure how long we have."

The next two weeks were a madhouse on Doma as everyone was to be moved out of the three big cities of Nadezhda, Vera, and Istina. Each of the cities had lush tropical forests with fresh water streams flowing down from the mountains in the twenty to forty mile range from town that was considered optimal.

Under Planetary Governor Fournier's emergency order, all non-perishable food items were packaged up in containers and trucked to the sites, where the containers were dropped off in open areas within the forest. The populace ate the perishable food in the meantime.

When all the food was moved, the next task was to move fifteen million people from the cities out into the woods. Most people went without trouble on the assumption Fournier, who had been a good planetary governor, knew what he was doing.

The holdouts stopped being holdouts and became enthusiastic volunteers when the ESN dropped out of hyperspace.

"Captain, we have a large group of hyperspace transitions, one-thirty-five mark forty on the planet, and thirty light-minutes out. It looks like seventy or more of those ESN frigates and ten larger vessels," Lieutenant Jon Glenn reported from the sensors console.

"Thirty light minutes out?" asked Captain Dave Mann, captain of the CSS *Invincible*.

"Yes, Sir. It looks like they're making for Doma-5."

"They're going after the mining operations there."

"That looks like it, Sir."

"All right. Keep an eye on them. Mr. Blackard."

"Yes, Sir," Ensign David Blackard said.

"Transmit a message to Doma Space Traffic Control. Warn them about the ESN fleet. They probably already know, but let's be sure."

"Yes, Sir."

"Mr. Weese, let's fold cylinder and get under way. Southern system periphery, closest approach. Those frigates are faster than we are, and I don't want to be racing them on short notice."

"Yes, Sir," Lieutenant Derek Weese said. "Sounding maneuvering alarm."

The klaxon blared, then three bells sounded.

"Halting spin.

"Spin at zero. Folding cylinders.

"Cylinders confirm locks. Engaging engines.

"Engines at eighty percent, making for southern system periphery at closest approach. Steady on zero minus ninety on the planet. Securing from maneuvering."

The speakers sounded two bells.

"Flip us over in time to hit zero velocity at the system periphery, Mr. Weese. I want to watch what happens from a safe distance before we abandon the system."

"Yes, Sir. Plotting for zero velocity at system periphery. Approximately eighty hours to mid-course flip."

"Mr. Glenn, keep an eye that none of them slip over the system periphery and into hyperspace. I don't want any of them dropping out of hyperspace in front of us."

"Yes, Sir."

Almost four days passed before the ESN fleet arrived at Doma-5c.

"Confirmed, Sir. The ESN is firing on the mining operations on Doma-5c," Glenn said.

"What are they using, Mr. Glenn?"

"Looks like nukes from here, Sir."

"Did anyone get away?"

"Yes, Sir. Two ships spaced from the mining operations in the other direction three days back. ESN didn't send anyone after them."

"All right. Let's see what they do next."

"Yes, Sir."

It was just a couple hours later when Glenn reported again.

"The ESN has set course for Doma, Sir."

"Across the system? That'll take them more than a week. They should have gone back out and hypered around."

"It's about the same either way, Sir."

A week out from Doma, the *Invincible* reached the system periphery.

"We're at the system periphery, Sir. Zero velocity relative to the star."

"Well done, Mr. Weese. Let's spin the ship. We might as well be comfortable while we wait."

"Sir? My sensors will have better resolution if we're not spinning."

"Understood, Mr. Glenn. Let us know when they get close to Doma and we'll stop spin."

"Yes, Sir. Thank you, Sir."

"What kind of communications are you picking up, Mr. Blackard?"

"Doma sent out a surrender, Sir. It's repeating."

"And the ESN fleet?"

"They haven't responded, Sir."

"Boy, I don't like the sound of that. Mr. Blackard, Mr. Glenn, make sure you're recording everything."

"Yes, Sir."

"They're getting close to the planet, Sir," Glenn said.

"All right. Mr. Weese, halt spin."

"Halting spin."

The gravity gradually went to zero g.

"Spin at zero."

Admiral Philippe Bruneau had had his chief of staff quietly run a selective infrared scan of the surface of Doma. The cities were quiet, shut down, cold on the infrared. But there was a large thermal bloom outside each of the cities, a thermal bloom centered in the mid-90s Fahrenheit.

Hoppy Ginsberg must have sent Bruneau's message to Fournier. Bruneau had certainly dragged his feet long enough getting to the planet. His orders had said to burn it down, to leave nothing. No 'thing.' His orders didn't say anything about killing civilians. They said nothing about people at all.

It was a fine point, but an important one. Leave it to a paranoid bastard like Arlan Andrews to have agents within Bruneau's own fleet, within his own staff. If he refused to carry out Andrews' orders, he would probably be shot and the orders carried out anyway. And, given the sort of people Andrews hired, they would probably bomb those thermal blooms as well.

It wasn't much, but what he could do, he had done.

Edmond Fournier stood on a rocky hill in the woods twenty-five miles north of Nadezhda. He could see the city clearly from here. There the Planetary Governor's Mansion, there the spaceport, there the city park. The homes, the shops, the churches, the schools.

A faint whistling noise got his attention. He looked up and he saw hundreds of projectiles coming down out of the sky. He watched, sickened but helpless, as they impacted across the city, smashing homes, crashing into streets and shops and parks and schools indiscriminately across the whole city.

It was three minutes before the noise got to his location, sounding like distant thunder.

And then, the faint whistling noise again, but this one was different. He looked up, saw more projectiles, but this wave was different. Fewer, but larger, projectiles. He watched them come down, but they did not impact. Short of the ground they exploded in huge white snowflakes blanketing the city, and wherever the white hit, the fires started.

The initial projectiles had shattered buildings and created debris, and the incendiaries set it on fire. Fournier watched in horror as the fires grew and grew, until a firestorm developed, all the fires contributing to the updraft, sucking in more and more air, generating more and more heat.

It built and built, that blast furnace of destruction, consuming everything. It was so hot steel buildings twisted and bent and ultimately collapsed as the temper went out of the steel and they could no longer hold their own weight. Concrete cracked and failed, and those buildings, too, collapsed.

It took several days for the fires to go out. When they had, there was nothing left.

Where Nadezhda had been, there was only ashes.

"Oh, God," Glenn cried out in despair.

"What is it, Mr. Glenn?"

Glenn turned to Captain Mann with tears in his eyes.

"They've firebombed the cities, Sir. Nadezhda, Vera, Istina. They're all on fire. Huge fires. It's like the whole city is just one big fire."

The bridge crew collectively made a muffled cry like a wounded animal. All the crew had had shore leave on Nadezhda, and if there was a more beautiful place in human space, with more wonderful people, Mann hadn't seen it.

"Make sure you record everything, and save the recordings, Mr. Glenn. For the war crimes trials."

"War crimes trials, Sir?"

"Hopefully, Mr. Glenn, we'll get the chance to kill the bastards outright. But sometimes you have to settle for second best."

Invincible could not make it to Jablonka before the Earth Fleet could, even at one hundred percent on the engines. But the system's mail relays, hovering on the system periphery, were undamaged, and *Invincible* transmitted her sensor recordings to the mail relays for transmission to the courier ships that connected human space together. Those ships never entered the system periphery. They dropped out of hyperspace, collected and delivered the mail via high-speed transmission to and from the relays, and transitioned right out again.

The news of Doma's destruction would take just three weeks to reach Jablonka, and four weeks to reach Earth.

Reaction To Doma

Westlake and Orlov were in Westlake's office in the Planetary Governor's Mansion. Westlake sat and stared at his hands, clasped between his knees.

"You knew Andrews was going to do something, that this wasn't going to be all daisies," Orlov said.

"I know, I know. I'll be all right. It's just getting to be a bit much. Ansen shot and killed right in front of me. Visiting Lowenthal's parents. And now Doma. I could never have imagined Andrews would pull something like this."

"Captain Mann's report said they were evacuating the cities well before the ESN showed up. Somebody on Earth tipped them off."

"I wonder if Edmond got everybody out. If Edmond and Anastasiya are OK," Westlake said.

"No way to know yet. Hopefully my sister and our mutual brother-in-law were smart enough not to go down with the ship. So the question is, What do we do now?"

"Relief efforts, obviously. Assuming they got out, we have fifteen million people living off the land."

"Well, not quite. They apparently didn't bomb the farms. That would be hard to do anyway. So there's plenty of beef and chicken, and lots of fruits and vegetables. With that climate, they have three growing seasons. And the cities are all located near fresh water. Probably the biggest things they need are trucks and fuel, to make sure they can move all the food to where it needs to be. Next priority is all the infrastructure items to get back up and going again. Construction equipment, generators, hospital equipment. All that sort of thing."

"How do you rebuild a whole city?"

Orlov shrugged.

"One brick at a time, the same way you built it the first time."

Westlake took a deep breath and let it out slowly.

"What do you think the ESN is going to do now? Are they going to hit any other planets we can't defend?" Westlake asked.

"I don't think so. Doma is where the charter was signed, and so it stuck out. And Jablonka is where you are so it sticks out. No other planet really stands out enough from the rest to be a target. And any other planet Andrews hits, the family with the charter on that planet will turn against him, hard."

"So you think they're coming here."

"Yes," Orlov said. "It's either that or go back to Earth. But their plan was to have you gone, so Jablonka would have been leaderless on the short term, making it an easier target. So I think they're coming here. I hope they're coming here, because we're ready for them."

"Mann's report said they had seventy-some frigates and ten bigger ships, and another dozen frigates arrived in ones and twos before they left the system."

"That's fine. Most of those bigger ships are going to be freighters, smaller freighters that can keep up with Bruneau's combat elements. If they knew they were going to destroy Doma's infrastructure, they knew they couldn't restock and refuel, so they had to bring all that with them. They may have a couple of larger combat units, old stuff they pulled out of mothballs."

"And you're not worried we can handle them if they attack us here?" Westlake asked.

"No. At least, Admiral Sigurdsen isn't."

"But the ESN is likely to get here while Sigurdsen is still on Earth. Is Admiral Holcomb going to be able to handle them?"

"Sigurdsen has complete confidence in Admiral Holcomb," Orlov said. "Brian is another former ESN admiral – rear admiral, I think – and he was Sigurdsen's chief of staff back in the day. When he retired from the ESN, he followed Sigurdsen here. So we're in good shape if and when the ESN shows up here."

"All right. I guess I better get relief efforts organized for Doma. Trucks and fuel, you said?"

"And then hospital equipment, and then construction supplies. Oh, and probably a couple thousand military-type mess tent setups, with all the cooking appliances and such. That's before the hospital equipment, so you can feed everybody."

"Got it. I'll have to see what we can put together. You have some freighters I can use?"

"We have those extra ten we bought and didn't convert. I'm not sending any of them to Earth until this is all straightened out. They look just like our battleships. And they'll take two thousand containers apiece, easy. Three thousand in a pinch."

"Good. We're going to need them. And soon. It's two months for them to get to Doma, even if we run them flat out. We need to get things started heading in their direction as soon as we can."

"Sir, we've done some experimentation with the system periphery. We basically took some older freighters, hooked them up with automated controls, and then ran them into hyperspace unmanned. They were programmed to transition back out of hyperspace after a delay, and we ran them further and further into the system periphery. We measured stresses on the hull, and we kept increasing the distance until they broke up. So we think we know what we can get away with. If we run one of the battleships in partway, and measure the stresses, we can compare that to the curve we have and figure out the maximum we're willing to press it," Captain Steven Taylor said.

"If we can hyperspace transition closer in, why is the published system periphery where it is?" Admiral Brian Holcomb asked.

"The problem is the system periphery isn't constant, Sir. It changes over time, and no one knows why. But it changes slowly, over a period of years. What we're talking about is where the system periphery is right now, and for the next few months."

"How much closer are we talking about?"

"About twenty percent. Maybe twenty-five."

"Excellent. I was afraid it wouldn't be enough to make a difference. That will definitely make a difference. What's the next step?"

"We need to have one of the battleships do a test run, Sir. Maybe ten percent less at first. To get some hull stress data," Taylor said.

"Ask the captains for volunteers. See who you get."

"Captain Benjamin Olsen of the *Intrepid* heard about what we were doing. He already volunteered, Sir."

"All right. Darryl, cut orders detaching *Intrepid* for the experiments, please."

"Yes, Sir," said Captain Darryl Hadfield, Holcomb's chief of staff.

Admiral Holcomb, Captain Hadfield, and Captain Katelyn Walker were giving a videoconference briefing to the captains of the four divisions of Commonwealth battleships tasked with protecting Jablonka.

"Good morning, Captains," Admiral Holcomb said. "We expect the ESN fleet to be here in the next two to three weeks. You've all heard what this particular fleet did to Doma, and we want to give them the proper reward for a war crime of that magnitude. We have a plan, and I think it's a good one. Captain Walker is a particularly devious person, and she's proved it yet again with this plan. With that introduction, I'll let her go ahead and brief you up on it. Go ahead, Captain."

"Thank you, Sir. This plan depends on the fact the Earth fleet has to make transition at or outside the published system periphery. That will likely be either due north or due south of Jablonka, as the point of closest approach of the system periphery to the planet. Anything else increases their spacing time to Jablonka, and Earth's rather rudimentary doctrine is to make their hyperspace transition at that point. I suspect that is because the ESN has never faced a real space-based military threat before.

"Admiral Bruneau also tends to be pretty doctrinaire in his approach to problems, which gives us more reason to anticipate a hyperspace transition at zero mark ninety or zero minus ninety at the published system periphery. That was also his approach in Doma, where he made transition at zero mark ninety on Doma-5c, their initial target.

"Our Plan Alpha assumes their transition at one of those two points, probably at zero minus ninety because that is closer to the line between the Jablonka and Doma systems. We also have several contingency plans in case they make their hyperspace transition somewhere else.

"Basically, they have to make their hyperspace transition *somewhere*. Thanks to Captain Olsen and the *Intrepid*, however, we know we can currently make hyperspace transitions twenty-five percent closer to Jablonka than the published system periphery, and they don't know that. Which means, for an entire day, they will be trapped in our hyperspace volume.

"And, thanks to a couple of radio operators who didn't know any better, we can now communicate in hyperspace, and they can't.

"Okay. That's the background. Now let's look at the details...."

"How'd the briefing go, Sir?" asked Commander Brian Livingston, executive officer of the *Intrepid*.

"Well, I hate to sound overconfident, Brian, but this looks like it's going to be shooting fish in a barrel," Captain Benjamin Olsen said.

The ESN Home Fleet

When Admiral Jarl Sigurdsen's ships reached Earth, they held in hyperspace, taking positions three-quarter light-seconds out from the normal hyperspace transition points on the system periphery above and below the planet. Dropping out of hyperspace into a hostile system without first looking to see what was going on was not in Sigurdsen's plans.

"All divisions report in position, Sir," Lieutenant Commander Nancy Ganka said. "*Independence* and *Challenge* divisions reporting at zero minus ninety, system periphery plus three-quarter light-seconds, and *Charter* and *Triumph* divisions reporting at zero mark ninety, system periphery plus three-quarter light seconds."

"Are the *Star Maiden* and *Star Princess* in position as well?" Sigurdsen asked.

"Yes, Sir. They are reporting system periphery plus ten percent, at zero minus ninety and zero plus ninety respectively."

"All right, Ms. Ganka. Option Peekaboo. Send the order."

"Transmitting, Sir."

Star Maiden sat outside the normal transition point, waiting for orders. She and *Star Princess* were unconverted freighters, carrying three thousand containers of extra provisions for the fleet. But what they also were was an extra set of eyes and ears.

"Orders, Sir," Lieutenant Hans Starmans said. "Option Peekaboo."

"Thank you, Mr. Starmans," Captain Jack Batchelder said. "Hyperspace transition when ready, Ms. Whalen."

"Yes, Sir. Hyperspace transition now," Lieutenant Patricia Whalen said.

"Stand by on sensors, Ms. Schulte."

"I'm recording, Sir," Ensign Barbara Schulte said.

"Hyperspace transition complete," Whalen said.

"Twenty ESN frigates sitting on zero minus ninety on the planet, Sir. System periphery plus one-quarter light-second. I have clean scan," Schulte said.

"Hyperspace transition, Ms. Whalen. Take us out of here."

"Hyperspace transition now."

"Hyperspace transition complete."

"Transmit Ms. Schulte's scans, Mr. Starmans."

"Transmitting, Sir."

On the north side of the system, Star Princess had done the same.

"Sir, *Star Maiden* and *Star Princess* both report a detachment of twenty Earth frigates watching the standard hyperspace transition points at zero mark ninety and zero minus ninety, above and below the planet. Those frigates are at the system periphery plus one-quarter light-second, pointing through the transition point toward Earth," Ganka said.

"Somebody's idea of a mousetrap," Sigurdsen said. "That's why you go look-see first before you go blundering in."

"Yes, Sir. Kind of stupid if you ask me," Kirby said.

"The ESN isn't used to fighting a real navy. We've got to be careful, though. People learn fast when they're getting shot at. Ms. Ganka, transmit orders to *Independence* and *Charter* divisions. Option Flasher."

The twenty ESN frigates had seen a large freighter transition well behind them, and then transition back out, but couldn't make heads or tails of its actions.

"Maybe they botched the navigation on their transition, and figured they would take another shot rather than spend an extra couple days getting to Earth," one captain mused to another.

"We have scans from *Star Maiden*, Sir," Ensign James Oconnell said aboard *Independence*. "Transferring to gunnery console."

"Mr. Scott?" Captain Marc Heller prompted.

"I have the scans, Sir. Twenty ESN frigates maintaining station at zero minus ninety plus one-quarter light-second. They are in our range from here," Lieutenant Shell Scott said.

"Mr. Asnip?"

"Rotating ship to firing position, Sir. Standing by for hyperspace transition."

A Charter For The Commonwealth

"*Independence* division ready for transition, Sir. Reported to the Flag. *Challenge* division has also reported ready," Oconnell said.

"Let's wait and see what the Admiral wants to do," Heller said.

"We have orders from the Flag, Sir. *Independence* division, Option Flasher."

"All right. Orders to *Independence* division, Mr. Oconnell: Option Flasher, Firing Plan Alpha, guns free, fire at will."

"Transmitted, Sir."

"Orders to *Independence* division: Transition on the mark. Count it down, Mr. Oconnell."

"Hyperspace transition in four, three, two, one, now."

"Hyperspace transition now," Asnip said.

"Targeting. Ranging. Firing eight. Firing eight. Firing eight," Scott said.

"Targets destroyed," Lieutenant Karl Stodden reported from the sensor console.

"Call it out, Mr. Oconnell."

"Hyperspace transition in four, three, two, one, now."

"Hyperspace transition now," Asnip said. "Hyperspace transition complete."

"All units report hyperspace transition complete, Sir."

"Well, that was nicely done, everyone," Heller said. "Mr. Oconnell, report to the Flag."

"*Independence* and *Charter* both report all twenty ESN frigates on station destroyed, Sir," Ganka said.

"All right. Let's post some eyes and ears and see what they do about it. Option Watchtower, Ms. Ganka. Send the order."

"Transmitting Option Watchtower, Sir."

"Orders, Sir," Starmans said. "Option Watchtower."

"Thank you, Mr. Starmans," Captain Batchelder said. "Hyperspace transition when ready, Ms. Whalen."

"Yes, Sir. Hyperspace transition now," Whalen said. "Hyperspace transition complete."

"Maintain watch on sensors, Ms. Schulte."

"Maintaining watch on sensors, Sir. Whole lotta nothin' out there at the moment."

"What do you think they'll do, Sir," asked Captain Morgen Kirby, Sigurdsen's chief of staff.

"I'm not sure, Morgen. They'll probably come out after us. That would be normal doctrine. We can't be sure who's really in charge here right now. Admiral Bruneau might be here, or he might be away. At Jablonka, for instance. And we can't be sure how much the navy is calling the shots and how much the civilian leadership is calling the shots. That's always been a problem for the ESN."

"What if they don't come out after us, Sir?"

"Then we'll have to go in after them. We can't earn our bacon sitting out here."

"Did the amount of activity in the system look normal to you, Sir?" Kirby asked.

"From the little look we got? Hard to tell. It was certainly not usual to have twenty frigates watching the standard transition point. There are a few freighters and passenger liners in transit to the hyperspace transition points on the system periphery. That looked normal. As for traffic around the planet itself, there's a lot of clutter there. It's hard to tell much from way out here."

"Shit!" ESN Vice Admiral Courtney Ballard said. "So much for Mr. Andrews' 'great idea.' Did he really think Jarl fucking Sigurdsen was going to transition in here all fat, dumb, and happy?"

"What was going on with the freighters that transitioned in, then transitioned out?" ESN Rear Admiral Robert Amsler asked.

"When it happens both above and below the system in exactly the same way, at exactly the same time, that is not a coincidence. I think they transitioned that far out so they could safely see what was going on at the transition point and then go into hyperspace and tell the battleships what they saw. Which means they've figured out some way for their ships to communicate in hyperspace. Which means we are seriously screwed if we go out there after them. Which Andrews will probably order anyway.

"Civilian control of the military is all well and good as long as they let us do our goddamn job. There went a full third of what forces I had left after Bruneau took half the fleet with him. Now I have to defend this system with eighty ships."

"That's still a ten-to-one advantage in ships, though," Amsler said.

A Charter For The Commonwealth

"You think so? Why would you think Jarl Sigurdsen would show all his forces if he didn't need to? Best guess is he has double that strength. Now you're looking at five-to-one odds. We jumped just one of those damned battleships four months back with nine frigates, and even caught by surprise it killed them all like it was swatting flies. Worse. Swatting a fly usually takes two tries.

"But Andrews has some cockamamie idea those battleships are nothing more than Q-ships crewed by amateurs. I guess you could call them Q-ships if you want, but Sigurdsen's been retired over ten years. We have no way of knowing how long he's been training his people, but I know damn well he didn't space with green crews."

ESN Captain Doug Harrell walked into the Command Center from Communications.

"Orders from higher, Ma'am." Harrell said, and handed her a printout.

"What'd I tell you? 'You are to gather your forces and engage the enemy.' Shit."

"Sir, we have a group of ships leaving orbit and heading this way," Schulte said.

"How many ships? Can you tell at this distance, Ms. Schulte?" Captain Batchelder said.

"Looks like seventy or eighty, Sir."

"Are any ships heading north?"

"No, Sir. Everything is headed zero minus ninety from the planet. I guess if there were some headed out zero plus ninety, I might not be able to see them."

"Understood. Let's transition and report. Whenever you're ready, Ms. Whalen."

"They're coming out to meet us. This has to be some civilian's idea," Sigurdsen said.

"Looks like just the southern approach, Sir," Kirby said.

"He doesn't want to divide his forces, Morgen. That's smart. For being such a stupid move overall, that is."

"What do you want to do, Sir? They'll be four more days getting out here."

"Let's order *Star Maiden* back to her watch position, and have her report in every twenty-four hours or whenever something changes significantly. Jack Batchelder is smart enough to be able to run with those orders."

"Hyperspace transition, Sir. It's *Star Maiden*. Receiving message. They say no change, Sir. Scans transferring. Scans transferred," Ganka said.

Sigurdsen looked at the scans on his display.

"No new orders, Ms. Ganka. They can return to station."

"Transmitted, Sir. Hyperspace transition. *Star Maiden* back on station."

"Hyperspace transition, Sir. It's *Star Maiden*. Receiving message. They say ESN force made their flip early, Sir. Scans transferring. Scans transferred," Ganka said.

Sigurdsen looked at the scans on his display.

"They're not coming all the way out. They're going to stay well inside the system periphery. I think somebody over there with a brain is doing the best he can within his orders."

"So we're still going to have to go in after them," Kirby said.

"That's what it looks like. Let's send *Star Maiden* back, then get the *Charter* and *Triumph* divisions over here. They've concentrated their forces, and we should probably do the same."

"What about us joining *Charter* and *Triumph* divisions on the north approaches and coming in on the planet while the ESN is sitting over here?"

"No, that's not going to work," Sigurdsen said. "They're faster than we are, and they would be back covering the planet before we could get there. I don't want a straight-up battle well inside the system periphery against that force. Eighty frigates can throw over five thousand rounds of projectiles a minute. Even if we burned them all, none of us would survive the projectile storm. No, we have to do something they're not expecting, catch them by surprise. So let's get everybody together."

"Yes, Sir. Go ahead, Ms. Ganka."

"Transmitted, Ma'am. Hyperspace transition. *Star Maiden* back on station. Acknowledgments received from *Charter* and *Triumph* divisions. They're on the way. *Triumph* reports they figure twelve hours to space around the system periphery and come back in to here, all in hyperspace."

"Hyperspace transition, Sir. It's *Star Maiden*. Receiving message. They say ESN force is spreading out in a big arc, Sir, like the top of an umbrella, with the concave side toward Earth. Scans transferring. Scans transferred," Ganka said.

Sigurdsen looked at the scans on his display.

"It looks like they're going to come to a stop about twenty percent short of the system periphery. They know we have to come in after them. We didn't come all this way to just sit out here."

"So now what do we do?" Kirby asked.

"Ms. Ganka, send *Star Maiden* back to station with instructions to return with scans as soon as the ESN ships come to zero velocity. Morgen, ask Commander Tibbs to meet with us in my ready room as soon as he can."

"Yes, Sir."

"Reporting as ordered, Sir," said Commander Scott Tibbs, the hyperspace specialist on Sigurdsen's staff.

"Thanks, Scotty. Have a seat," Sigurdsen said.

Scott sat down across from Sigurdsen and Kirby.

"The ENS fleet has taken up a position about twenty percent inside the system periphery, with all their guns pointed out toward our necessary line of approach. I want to hyperspace transition in behind them and catch them by surprise. Tell me why that's a bad idea."

"Generally speaking, Sir, that's a terrible idea. There's a reason it's called the system periphery, and hyperspace transitions within a system are a really bad idea. Ships blow up, break apart, all that sort of thing. It's like they just get pulled apart at the seams.

"That having been said, in specific cases it's less of a bad idea than it might be. The actual operational system periphery is not a hard and fast line. System boundaries are conservatively stated, because that whole ship breaking up thing is so unpleasant, and further they shift over time. We don't know why they shift over time, but there's a theory it has to do with the positions of large planets."

"Explain," Sigurdsen said.

"Well, the biggest difference between wide open space and a solar system is the presence of mass, and the only effect of the presence of mass that extends out as far as the system periphery is gravity. So the theory is the system periphery is determined by gravitation. Now, if you have some really big planet, like Earth-5 or Earth-6, maybe that bulges the operational system periphery out farther wherever they are than wherever they aren't.

"When you have a published system periphery, it better be far enough out to cover the maximum extent of where ships break up and other bad things happen. So the published system periphery has to cover all the variation, which is likely due to those big planets being around, on the same side of the system as you are. But right now, the gas giants Earth-5 and Earth-6 are on the other side of the system from the populated planet, Earth-3.

"That's the theory, anyway. If it's true, we can hyperspace transition that close with few if any problems."

"And if it's not true?" Sigurdsen asked.

"All the ships could break up."

"What's your opinion?"

"I think the theory is correct, but I wouldn't risk a fleet on it to find out."

"What about a single ship?"

"That would be a hard call for me, Sir."

"All right, Commander. Thank you for the briefing."

"How long does it take an ESN frigate to flip ship?" Kirby asked.

"In an emergency? Twenty seconds," Sigurdsen said.

"And how fast can a Commonwealth battleship hyperspace transition?"

"Nine seconds."

"There's three transitions there. In and out and in," Kirby said.

"But the first doesn't count, right? Because they don't start reacting until the first transition happens. And there's command delay. Maybe three or four seconds to issue the command, another two or three to transmit, and another two or three to implement. Call it seven to ten seconds more."

"So we have nine to twelve seconds? That's it?"

"Until they fire, yes, but we'll be way out of their range. Three-quarters of a light-second is over a day at ten thousand feet per second. We also have a total of a hundred and twenty-eight guns and only eighty targets," Sigurdsen said.

"Yeah, there's that."

The video conference was just ending.

"Everyone have your assignments? Everyone clear?" Sigurdsen asked.

After the general acknowledgements, Sigurdsen said, "All right. And good luck, Captain Hamill."

Captain John Hamill's *Defiance* would test the hyperspace limit.

Star Maiden returned with scans of the ESN position, the Commonwealth ships took up positions in hyperspace, and targets were allocated.

"Whenever you're ready, *Defiance*. All ships stand by for transition immediately on *Defiance*'s return. Guns free."

Aboard the ENS *Dexter Guptill*, Rear Admiral Robert Head waited for any sign of his enemy. He was well back from the system periphery, had his forces concentrated, and had them arrayed across a wide circular section of a sphere two light-seconds across.

"Hyperspace transition one eighty mark zero!" Lieutenant Commander Brandon Bowers screamed from the sensor console.

"All ships! Flip ship!"

CSS *Defiance* transitioned out of hyperspace three-quarters of a light-second behind the ESN formation, hovered nine seconds, and transitioned right back out again. Nine seconds later all sixteen of the Commonwealth battleships transitioned out of hyperspace.

The ESN ships were halfway through their flip, which made them even more vulnerable to the Commonwealth's fire, as they were broadside to the beams and easier to hit.

Each Commonwealth battleship fired three times – a total of three hundred and eighty-four beams – at the eighty ESN frigates.

None survived.

On Earth that evening, Vice Admiral Courtney Ballard got slowly and thoroughly drunk looking through the scrapbooks and mementos of her navy career.

At a little after 2:00 AM, she picked up her service pistol and shot herself in the head.

Regime Changes

The Commonwealth fleet spaced for Earth unopposed.

"Sir, I'm downloading mail and newsfeeds from the relays. There's something here you really need to see," Lieutenant Commander Nancy Ganka said over the intercom.

"Route it to me here, Ms. Ganka," Admiral Jarl Sigurdsen said back over the intercom from his briefing room on the flag deck of the *Independence*.

"Yes, Sir."

"You wanted to see me, Sir?" Captain Morgen Kirby asked.

"Yes, Morgen. Have a seat. Ms. Ganka just downloaded our mail. There was an 'All Ships' notice from the *Invincible* in there that the ESN firebombed the cities of Nadezhda, Vera, and Istina on Doma from orbit."

"My God."

"The planetary governor was attempting to evacuate the cities, but *Invincible* wasn't sure how far they had gotten. There's no information on casualties."

"It could be in the millions," Kirby said.

"Yes, it could. As I say, there's no information on casualties – they were observing from the system periphery – but the three cities were completely destroyed in huge draft-fed firestorms. *Invincible* withdrew from the system because they were overwhelmingly outnumbered. The ESN ignored Doma's surrender transmission."

"Those bastards. It makes me want to show them what a planetary bombardment looks like, up close and personal."

"Me, too," Sigurdsen said. "But this fleet is not going to commit any war crimes. Earth has earned its reputation now, let it live with it. I have no desire to share it with them. We need to talk to our captains about it, and make sure we stay focused on our goals. Let's let Admiral Holcomb show them the errors of their ways."

"You think they're going to go to Jablonka, Sir?"

"Yes. And they'll find more than one Commonwealth battleship waiting for them there. That'll just have to be good enough."

"Understood, Sir."

"All divisions reporting in position, Sir," Ganka said.

"Transmit the message, Ms. Ganka," Sigurdsen said.

"Transmitting, Sir."

"So we go to Phase One if they don't accept the demands, Sir?" Kirby asked.

"Yes. They're fools if they don't accept them. We could demand surrender of the planet at this point, but all we're asking is they acknowledge the Commonwealth and sign the treaty."

"And turn over Andrews for trial."

"I added that," Sigurdsen said. "Arlan Andrews is a war criminal. The attempted assassination of Westlake could – I say, could – be argued to be an attack on a valid military target, since he's commander-in-chief. But ignoring a surrender message and firebombing the cities of Doma is a war crime he has to answer for."

"He's not going to accept their terms," Fournier said.

"Of course not. They're demanding we turn him over," Orlov said.

"What the hell was he thinking, bombing Doma after a surrender?" Westlake asked.

"I don't know. And we still don't know how many people were killed. We still don't even know if Edmond or Anastasiya survived," Fournier said.

"How badly are we going to get hurt if they start bombing the planet?" Orlov asked.

"We could get hurt badly. And we aren't even in a moral position to complain about it, after that bastard Andrews bombed Doma after a surrender transmission. We aren't surrendering, and so they can keep up military activities," Fournier said.

"Do we have enough to move against Andrews yet?" Westlake asked.

"Not yet. Soon, I think," Fournier said.

"They're basically not responding at all, Sir," Ganka said.

"Ignore us and we'll go away, huh?" Sigurdsen asked.

A Charter For The Commonwealth

"Apparently that's what they think, Sir," Kirby said.

"All right, on to the next step. I want to try one more thing before we go to Phase One. I have a special target. Transmit these orders."

Sigurdsen keyed a file off his console to Kirby.

"Is this for *Independence*, Sir?" Kirby asked.

"No. This one's for *Vengeance*."

"Orders incoming from the Flag, Ma'am," Ensign Shira Tomboulian said. "Sending to your display."

Captain Pamela Wright, captain of the *Vengeance*, looked at her orders.

"Wow. Five hits on one target. I think Admiral Sigurdsen doesn't like somebody," Wright said.

The bridge crew chuckled. Wright had a wicked-dark sense of humor, and the bridge crew often found themselves laughing. That was not to say, however, that you ever took Captain Wright lightly. The crew had a saying: '*Vengeance* is mine, sayeth the Captain.'

"All right, Ms. Teller. What's our time to arrival within the target cone?"

"I make it twenty-five minutes, Ma'am," Lieutenant Wendy Teller said from the sensor console.

"All right, Chief Gants. Stand by your guns."

"Standing by, Ma'am," Chief Petty Officer Robert Gants said from the gunnery console. Unlike most of the young officers in the new Commonwealth Space Force, Gants was a grizzled veteran of the merchant marine, and had been spacing freighters for thirty years. He also had a daughter about the same age as Jennifer Lowenthal.

"We will have five minutes within the target cone, Ma'am," Teller said. "Coming up in three minutes."

"Chief Gants, make it sixty seconds into the target cone, then thirty-second intervals."

"Yes, Ma'am. Thirty-second intervals programmed in."

Teller counted it down.

"Target cone in ten seconds. Five seconds. Begin target cone. Ten seconds in. Twenty seconds in. Thirty seconds in."

Gants touched the picture of Jennifer Lowenthal on his console – "This one's for you, honey," he said – and pushed the Launch icon.

"First munition away.

"Second munition away.

"Third munition away.

"Fourth munition away.

"Fifth munition away. Firing sequence complete, Ma'am."

Before the Commonwealth fleet had left Earth, James Allen Westlake, the Chairman of the Commonwealth Council, had given Sigurdsen the coordinates on Earth of Arlan Andrews' estate in upstate New York. Andrews spent most of his time there, pulling the strings of the puppet planetary government. He also had a serious underground shelter there, which he would take to if there were real trouble. Westlake knew all this before he left Earth, and family sources had recently confirmed it was still Andrews' lair and retreat.

The five twenty-ton nuclear demolitions came down out of the cloudy sky at thirty-second intervals. The first one came through the roof of the big stone house, with a delayed detonation taking place after it had penetrated to the basement. It blew out all the windows, and blew the wood floors, furnishings, and roof out the top of the stone walls, after which the stone walls crumpled and collapsed.

Each successive detonation went off deeper and deeper into the crater they were building within the house's footprint. The fourth one penetrated into the underground bunker. The fifth one blew the remnants of the concrete bunker out of the hole.

"Repeat our demands now, Ms. Ganka. Let's see if we've managed to change the regime down there enough for reason to see the light," Sigurdsen said.

"Transmitting now, Sir."

"I think the Commonwealth fleet has successfully managed to remove Mr. Andrews as a problem," Fournier said with some satisfaction.

"Are we going to be able to solve this now, before the Commonwealth fleet gets down to business?" Orlov asked.

"Yes. I'm getting calls from people who are not sure Admiral Sigurdsen doesn't have their home address as well and would like to see this process come to an end. Quickly. I just tell them to call the

Secretary General."

"Has the Secretary General called you yet?" Westlake asked.

"No, but he will once the consensus becomes apparent."

There was an attention tone and Fournier looked away from the camera.

"Ah. There he is now. I'll call you back."

"Sir, the Earth Secretary General has transmitted Earth's acceptance of your terms. He wants to know where you want to have the signing of the treaty. He also notes that Mr. Arlan Andrews has passed away, and cannot be produced for trial on war crimes charges," Ganka said.

"I like the way he phrased that. I guess Mr. Andrews must have been home when *Vengeance* came calling," Sigurdsen said.

"Well, that's satisfying," Kirby said. "What about the signing of the treaty, Sir? Here aboard *Independence*, wouldn't you think?"

"I think that would be appropriate, considering. I certainly am not going down there. Not after Doma. I don't trust the bastards."

"But will he trust us to come up here?"

"He's a puppet," Sigurdsen said. "He'll do what the families tell him to do. Unless I miss my guess, Claude Fournier is calling the shots now. So yes, the Secretary General will come up here. We'll send a shuttle down to get him."

"Your message, Sir?" Ganka asked.

Sigurdsen typed rapidly on his console.

"Transmit that, Ms. Ganka."

"Transmitting, Sir."

One of *Independence*'s shuttles made the run down to Earth to pick up the Secretary General, V. R. Konner, in New York City and bring him up to the *Independence* for the signing of the treaty whereby Earth recognized the Commonwealth of Free Planets as an independent polity and abandoned all claims of sovereignty over its systems. In the treaty both parties agreed they would allow mutual free trade and accord safe passage to the others' ships across human space.

The Earth and the *Independence* sent out 'All Ships' messages to their respective navies announcing the treaty, announcing the halt of hostilities, and recalling all their ships to their own systems.

What the Commonwealth would call the War Of Independence, and the Earth would call the Insurrection, was over.

But the news would take some time to propagate.

The ESN Expeditionary Fleet

Sixteen Commonwealth battleships waited in hyperspace. On the northern approaches of Jablonka it was:
- the *Pioneer*, the *Pathfinder*, the *Explorer*, and the *Trailblazer*;
- the *Dominant*, the *Gallant*, the *Brilliant*, and the *Luminant*.
On the southern approaches it was:
- the *Peacekeeper*, the *Equalizer*, the *Empower*, and the *Endanger*;
- the *Thunder*, the *Specter*, the *Encounter*, and the *Troublemaker*.
Admiral Holcomb flew his flag on the *Thunder*.

"We're all in position for them whenever they decide to show up, Sir," said Captain Darryl Hadfield, Admiral Holcomb's chief of staff. "We have two divisions here on the southern approaches waiting in hyperspace, and two divisions waiting in hyperspace on the northern approaches. And we have eyes in normal space at system periphery plus twenty percent."

"Excellent," Admiral Brian Holcomb said. "I was worried about hovering around in hyperspace so long, and Captain Taylor said, 'Why? We spend weeks in hyperspace in transit.' And he's right. It just seems weird to be sitting in hyperspace and not going anywhere."

"It is counterintuitive, Sir. It's the space equivalent of crouching behind concealment."

"The problem always was, you didn't know when to jump up and yell 'Gotcha!' But now we can communicate in hyperspace, so we just hunker down here and wait for the call."

"All right," Admiral Holcomb said to the video conference of his captains. "They could show up any time in the next two weeks. We need to be ready to space on half an hour's notice. We're going to want the divisions on the other side from the attackers to maneuver around the system in hyperspace so we can consolidate our forces. That'll take time, but I want the ESN ships to build up speed headed into the system, which they have to burn off, then build up speed again in the other direction to get out, so we've got the time.

"They're going to be accelerating in, with all the guns on their lighter units pointing with their bows. Since the ship velocity and the projectile velocity add up, we want to get them turned around. Then the ship velocity will actually subtract from the projectile velocity. So we'll hit them from behind first, and get them to turn around before we bring in the other two divisions.

"We also want to hit their heavier units first. Some of those are combat units and some are fleet auxiliaries. Those bigger combat units have full-sphere coverage on their offensive weapons, so we need to take them out right off. Rather than taking time to figure out which is which, we'll take out all the heavy units, both combat units and auxiliaries. If it's big, shoot it first. That also leaves them trapped here, because Doma to Jablonka is a long haul, and without reaction mass and supplies they aren't going anywhere.

"That's the rationale behind Firing Plan Gamma. Half our guns in the first attack should be at the big stuff. That's thirty-two beams spread across ten units for the first two divisions. The other half will all be on individual lighter units. The second two divisions will hit the lighter units.

"Any questions?"

The ESN ships from Doma, which could not communicate while in hyperspace, dropped out of hyperspace on the northern approaches of Jablonka over the course of several hours. There were now a total of one hundred frigates, three light cruisers, a heavy cruiser, and six fleet freighters in the fleet. They organized themselves into their formation.

"Well, we're here," said Rear Admiral Michael Antoniewicz, Admiral Bruneau's chief of staff, on the flag bridge of the heavy cruiser ENS *Fury of Space*.

"Yes. And I don't expect they'll be stupid enough to come out after us," Admiral Philippe Bruneau said.

"I expect not, Sir. Which means we have to go in after them."

"We didn't come all this way to sit out here and wave. Still, it bothers me we don't see our opponent. I would think there would be a large concentration of warships here at the capital."

"Maybe they figured we wouldn't go straight to the capital, we wouldn't go for a straight-up fight," Antoniewicz said.

"Westlake is here. He's the one organizing this little party. They had to know Andrews would send us here to deal with him."

Bruneau looked at the scans, which showed one small craft sitting well out from the system periphery.

"I also don't like this guy sitting out here. And where did his friend go? There were two when we got here," Bruneau said.

"We're pulling newsfeeds and mail right now, Sir. We'll see if that tells us anything."

"You're going to love this. The newsfeeds are full of news about the trial of an Earth agent who made an assassination attempt on Westlake sixteen weeks ago," Antoniewicz said.

Bruneau shook his head.

"Mr. Andrews just can't leave any stone unturned in antagonizing someone, can he?" Bruneau asked.

"Oh, it gets worse, Sir. The assassin missed Westlake, and instead shot and killed a Professor Gerald Ansen, who wrote the Charter of the Commonwealth they're all excited about. He actually saw the attempt coming, and put himself between the assassin and Westlake as the assassin fired."

"And now he's a martyr, and Westlake is still in place."

"You got it, Sir," Antoniewicz said. "And they call Andrews, you, and the ESN war criminals for the destruction of Doma."

Bruneau closed his eyes and sighed. That one hurt, mostly because, he supposed, it was largely true.

"They've been organizing big relief efforts to Doma out of Jablonka, and that may be where their battleships went. They converted freighters to build them, and they are still capable of carrying freight.

"The other thing we got was mail. Andrews apparently has a spy ring here. They sent a mail "To Any ESN Ships" that documented four divisions of battleships under Admiral Holcomb leaving here, one division at a time, over the last three weeks."

"Brian Holcomb?" Bruneau asked.

"Yes."

"Wonderful."

Antoniewicz looked at Bruneau quizzically.

"Holcomb was Sigurdsen's chief of staff before they both retired."

"That could be bad."

"Tell me something I don't know," Bruneau said. "Well, let's get us under way. And make sure the cruisers are at combat stations. He'll try to come in behind us if he can. The sooner we can get off the system periphery and away from the possibility of him jumping us from hyperspace, the better I'll like it."

Holcomb's *Thunder* and *Peacekeeper* divisions were making their best speed around the system in hyperspace to join the *Pioneer* and *Dominant* divisions on Jablonka's northern approaches.

"It's going to be about eight hours to get into place, Sir," Hadfield said.

"That's OK," Holcomb said. "He'll be well within the system periphery by then, he'll think, but only a quarter of the way across our little extra cushion. That'll be about perfect, actually. It'll take him another eight hours to stop and eight more hours to get out."

"Unless he decides if we can do it, he can do it, Sir."

"But he doesn't know we're not doing something different. We could have some new hyperspace technology, and if he tries to hyperspace transition, all his ships will break up. And the deeper he gets, the more likely he is to think that."

"Good point."

"I think what we want to do on the way is spell our first-shift crews so they're fresh when the action starts. Let everybody get some food and sleep."

"I'll pass that around as a suggestion, Sir."

"This is kind of eerie," Bruneau said.

"I know what you mean. But we are seeing some action around those four big ships in orbit. They're the same type as the Commonwealth battleships," Antoniewicz said.

"Yes, or they're freighters. If they were battleships, you'd think they'd want to keep the big, bad war criminals away from the planet."

"Well, something's going to happen sooner or later."

"That's what I'm afraid of. Make sure the gunners on the cruisers aren't sloughing off as we get deeper."

"OK, here are the latest scans, Sir," Hadfield said.

"Is everybody in position?" Holcomb asked.

A Charter For The Commonwealth

"Yes, Sir."

"Well, let's kick this off, then."

Peacekeeper, *Equalizer*, *Empower*, and *Endanger* dropped out of hyperspace at one thirty five mark zero on the ESN formation, behind the ESN ships and to starboard, while *Thunder*, *Specter*, *Encounter*, and *Troublemaker* dropped out of hyperspace at two hundred twenty five mark zero on the ESN formation, behind the ESN ships and to port, at a distance of three-quarter light-seconds.

"Flip ships and engage the enemy," Bruneau said.

The Commonwealth battleships poured fire into the ESN fleet. All ten of the larger ESN vessels took multiple hits in the first few seconds of fire, and several of them exploded. The smaller ships were also disappearing as the second console gunnery officer had control of half the forward guns on each Commonwealth ship and was free to fire at the smaller ships.

Admiral Philippe Bruneau had just enough time to appreciate that he would have no more nightmares of being trapped in a burning house before ENS *Fury of Space* broke up and then exploded.

Ten seconds after the *Thunder* and *Peacekeeper* divisions, with the ESN ships flipping back against their velocity and their command structure gone, *Pioneer*, *Pathfinder*, *Explorer*, and *Trailblazer* made hyperspace transition at zero mark forty five on the ESN ships, ahead and above their velocity vector, and *Dominant*, *Gallant*, *Brilliant*, and *Luminant* made hyperspace transition at zero minus forty five on the ESN ships, in front and below their velocity vector, at a distance of three-quarter light-seconds. The angles were picked carefully so no Commonwealth ships would be in the line of another's fire.

In fifteen more seconds it was over. There had never been any time for anyone to surrender.

The Earth Expeditionary Fleet, which had firebombed Doma at Arlan Andrews' orders, had been destroyed to the last man.

Celebrations

It was late Saturday morning in Jezgra when the news came in from Admiral Holcomb's fleet that the Earth Space Navy that had firebombed Doma had been destroyed in Jablonka space. There would be no invasion, no firebombing of Jezgra.

The Chairman's office made the news public immediately. When the news hit the newsfeeds, crowds spilled out into the streets and the parks and the party was on.

"I told you they had nothing that could match our firepower," Orlov said. "We designed our navy to fight another navy, they designed their navy to enforce the commerce rules against unarmed freighters. Against unarmed freighters they would have done fine."

"That's pretty harsh."

"Not really. Their doctrine was built around projectile weapons, with their time-of-flight issues. They simply weren't prepared for light-speed weapons. Or for our ability to maneuver and communicate in hyperspace."

"It could be different at Earth. There we're the attacking force, and they're the defending force," Westlake said.

"They still don't have anything with the reach or speed of the beam cutters, and they don't know how to coordinate maneuvers by communicating with each other in hyperspace."

"You know they're going to, though. Assuming we win at Earth, they will rebuild their navy, and this time they're going to build it to fight another navy. Including all your bells and whistles."

"Yup," Orlov said. "And we're going to have to stay ahead of them, which will not be a big deal, because we'll be a free society and they still won't be. I'm not worried, Jim."

"I wish I had your optimism, Georgy."

"No, you don't. One of us has to run the brakes while the other runs the throttle, or we never would have gotten this far."

Mike Skibbe, the military liaison, came in.

"Sorry to interrupt, sir. High-priority message for your eyes only."

A Charter For The Commonwealth

He handed the message, which was in a sealed envelope from the communications center, to Westlake. Westlake opened the envelope and took out the message. He read it twice, and when he looked up at Georgy his eyes were full of tears.

"Sigurdsen defeated the Earth Home Fleet. They didn't have to bomb the planet. Earth has signed the treaty and recognized the Commonwealth. It's over. We won."

Westlake handed the message to Orlov, who read it carefully.

"Well, they mostly didn't have to bomb the planet. That was smart to give Arlan Andrews' home address to Sigurdsen."

"He was a war criminal. His life was forfeit."

"And removing him simplified Earth's power structure."

Westlake nodded. He reached out and Orlov handed back the message. Westlake wrote 'For Immediate Release. JAW' on the message, and handed it back to Skibbe.

"Can you drop this with the press office for me, Mike?"

"Of course, sir."

When the news of the defeat of the Earth Home Fleet and the signing of the peace treaty hit the street, the party really kicked into high gear. Planetary Governor Westlake sent an entire refrigerator truck full of beer down to Jezgra City Park, and the Jablonka Protective Service served free beer to everyone.

If anyone thought it was weird for the police to be serving free beer in the city park, no one mentioned it. It became a tradition that was repeated every Treaty Day, as this day would come to be known.

There was one more bit of good news that miracle Saturday. Westlake and Orlov received mail from Edmond and Anastasiya Fournier. They had just gotten the radio connection to the Doma mail relays back up and running. Not only had Edmond and Anastasiya survived, but they had gotten everyone out of the cities. There had been no mass casualties in the firebombing of Doma.

The Westlakes and the Orlovs had dinner together that evening, and gave thanks for the survival of their relatives and the other millions of people on Doma. After dinner, they all went out to the park, and Westlake and Orlov took their turn serving free beer.

Edmond Fournier never did find out who sent him advance warning of the ESN's orders, but Claude Fournier did. To his shock, Hopalong Ginsberg received a small, elegant Thank You card containing the number of a private Swiss bank account and personally signed by Messrs. Claude Fournier, Stepan Orlov, and James Allen Westlake V.

Planning The Future

"Now that we won the war, I feel like the dog who was always chasing ground cars. I caught it, now what do I do with it?" Westlake asked.

Orlov laughed.

"We need to do several things at once, I think," Orlov said. "You need to fill out the Cabinet. We need to build a fleet base with training and headquarters facilities and all that. We need to start designing a real navy, with keel-out designs. We need to build a capital complex for the Council. You know, Council chamber, offices for Council members and their staffs, offices for the Cabinet ministers and their staffs."

"And continue the relief of Doma."

"And continue the relief of Doma."

"On the Cabinet, I have some ideas," Westlake said. "I'm waiting to hear from the other planetary governors, hear what their plans are."

"Don't be surprised if a couple of them decide to split off and become a little duchy of their own."

"That wouldn't be wise. I think we're going to be stationing a couple of battleships at each of the potential problem colonies for a while, just as a reminder."

"That's smart," Orlov said. "You can probably get away with one at every colony whose planetary governor can count to eleven with his shoes on. Mcenroe on Bahay, for example."

"Yeah, he's OK. There's probably two dozen planetary governors, now the issue is decided, who will get with the program. They didn't get to where they are, for the most part, by being stupid. As for the fleet base, it should probably be here to keep the command loop short. Somewhere close to Jezgra."

"I have a couple hundred square miles on the coast twenty miles south of downtown you can have. I'm not using it, and I can't think of a better purpose for it."

"That would be perfect," Westlake said. "Jablonka Fleet Base. Who do we have design it?"

"Let Jarl Sigurdsen run it all. Design the base, design the training, all that. I mean he would have lots of help, but he would be the administrator for the whole effort. I think I'll make him Chief of Naval Operations and ask Rick Ewald to be Chief of Naval Research. Rick likes all the engineering side of things."

"Which brings us to keel-out designs."

"I bet there's a bunch of retirees around who wish they could have stayed in their jobs with the big shipbuilders. We can ask around. Have them train some of the younger people." Orlov thought a few seconds. "Oh, wait, even better. Ask University of Jablonka to put some naval engineering curricula together, and we can get the retirees to teach a whole new generation of naval engineers."

"That sounds really good."

"What about money for all this?"

"That's waiting for a Finance Minister," Westlake said. "I'm talking to Shelly Stewart this afternoon. But when Earth ceded sovereignty, they also ceded the ability to tax. We'll have more money than we know what to do with on all the colony planets. The Council has to pass a head tax, but there's plenty of money."

"Shelly Stewart. President of the Jablonka Branch of the Bank of Earth? She's a really good choice. She knows where all the levers and buttons are."

"That's what I figure. We need to stop the flow of funds to Earth, which is our right under the treaty, but it's going to take someone who knows what they all are to pull that together."

"So what else did we have?" Orlov asked. "Oh, yeah. A capital complex, or government center. Whatever you call it."

"Commonwealth Center. The Planetary Governor's Mansion has a huge estate, fifty square miles, which is no longer needed. We'll build it here. This part can stay Jablonka's government center, and then we'll build Commonwealth Center on the north end, up the coast."

"That's right. You also need to start a planetary government. An electoral republic?"

"Sure," Westlake said. "I asked the Council members who are staying here until the dust settles to design one for me as a project. They've been working on it since they got back four months ago. They're trying to make a model constitution for planetary government that any of the other colonies could use as well. Not something

A Charter For The Commonwealth

Jablonka dependent."

"That sounds good." Orlov clapped his hands. "All right. Since we solved all the world's problems this morning, what say we get some lunch?"

The Relief of Doma

Stargazer made its hyperspace transition on the system periphery at zero mark ninety on Doma, north of the planet. It was fourteen weeks since the ESN had firebombed Doma's cities, and, space travel and communication being as slow as they were, it was only now the first relief was arriving.

Before starting in toward the planet, *Stargazer* pulled mail and newsfeeds from the mail relay. When she had left Jablonka eight weeks before, it had been fifteen weeks since the murder of Ansen, there was no news yet from Admiral Sigurdsen's fleet at Earth, and Admiral Holcomb was waiting for the arrival of an ESN fleet at Jablonka.

There was no way Captain Scott Huggins was going to start in toward the planet before he found out what had happened during *Stargazer*'s two months in hyperspace.

"All hands, this is the captain. We have pulled the mail and newsfeeds before starting in toward the planet. I have some news you all want to hear.

"First, the ESN fleet that firebombed Doma's cities has attacked Jablonka. Admiral Holcomb's fleet engaged them and destroyed them. Every one of the bastards who bombed Doma is dead."

A cheer went up in the ship. Huggins waited.

"Second, Admiral Sigurdsen's fleet defeated the ESN Home Fleet at Earth in two separate battles."

Another cheer.

"Third, the Earth government has signed a treaty recognizing the Commonwealth of Free Planets and given up its claims to the colonies. We're free of them."

That cheer was loudest of all.

"All right, so that's the news. I've also been in touch with the planetary governor on Doma, and they're really glad to see us. It's been fourteen weeks since the bombings, and they need a lot of what we brought. It's going to take us another week to get there, but then we're going to help these poor people get back on their feet.

"I've opened up the newsfeeds to the crew, and I know everybody wants to read all about all that's gone on, but we still have a ship to run. So read the news on your off-shift so we don't run into a planet or something, OK?

"Captain out."

Stargazer took a week to make Doma orbit. The two big cargo shuttles on its bows separated and each grabbed eight of the big containers off her racks for the trip down to the planet. A dozen big cargo shuttles also met *Stargazer* in orbit. Each grabbed eight containers and headed down to the planet.

Even so, it would take days to unload the more than three thousand containers aboard *Stargazer*.

As they started to unload *Stargazer*, the *Starhunter* reported in from the system periphery and began its trip to Doma orbit.

There were several big paved areas alongside highways that ran between the coastal cities of Nadezhda, Vera, and Istina, and between the cities and the farms located in the interior. Rest areas and the like.

The first shuttle loads got set down in these areas. Coming down on the pavement, the shuttles set the first loads of containers, in a block four wide and two high. Doma men standing by opened the lower four containers and climbed behind the wheels of large semi-tractor trucks with refrigerated trailers. The upper four containers were tanks, filled with diesel fuel. They fueled the trucks up and ran them out of the containers, to start making food runs between the farms and the camps of people outside the cities.

After several trips of the shuttles, with over four hundred trucks delivered, the loads changed. Now four-wide-by-two-high blocks of containers were all diesel fuel tanks, to add to the supplies already emplaced.

The next round of deliveries were hundreds of "mess kits," containers that each contained a complete mess tent, with the tent, the appliances and utensils, pots and pans, tables and benches. Every three of these also had one container that was a huge cylinder of LP gas. These the shuttles brought down in four-by-four blocks, and they dropped each layer of four – three mess kits and a propane cylinder –

in a different spot in and around the cities.

One thing Doma wasn't lacking was manpower, and large teams of men set to each container to set up the kitchen mess tents. These were set up around and within the burned cities, usually in the parks, and would function as meal locations now and as the reconstruction work proceeded.

The next round of supplies were hospital tents and sanitary tents, which were a block of bathrooms integrated to a small chemical treatment plant. These came down organized in pairs, in four-by-four blocks, and the cargo shuttles dropped a pair at each location of three mess tents. The hospital tent container included a stationary generator that was shared among the hospital, mess, and sanitary tents.

"That's it for us, sir," Huggins said. "Our focus was the food supply and processing, hospital and sanitation. I'm not sure what *Starhunter* has aboard, as they were loading her when we left."

"You've been a big help, Captain Huggins," Planetary Governor Edmond Fournier said. "It'll be nice to have a hot meal again. I can't thank you enough."

"You're very welcome, sir. And now we're off back to Jablonka to see what we can bring for you next time."

"All right, Captain. And maybe next time we'll be organized enough down here to give your crew some decent shore leave. Until then, good spacing to you."

Starhunter was loaded down with almost four thousand containers, but it was all light cargo. Processed food – pasta, cereal, canned goods, flour, sugar, salt, cooking oil, spices. Clothing, mostly heavy work clothing that would stand up to a beating as the reconstruction proceeded. Laundry facilities in the form of a laundry tent for each mess tent complex. Containerized water purification plants, and containers of pipe and plumbing supplies. A centralized administrative center for the planetary government, in the form of a dozen tents for offices to coordinate the effort. A communications and administrative container for each mess tent complex. It went on and on.

Jablonka had long been a supplier to small colonies getting started, and its manufacturers were working twenty-four-by-seven to meet the needs of rebuilding an entire planet.

After eight weeks of relief effort, with a freighter of supplies arriving every week from Jablonka, they were finally around the bend on the humanitarian crisis. It was time for reconstruction to start.

"Sir, we just had fourteen large ships make hyperspace transition on the southern approaches. They're requesting permission to enter Doma space," said Don Meaker, Edmond Fournier's chief of staff.

"Did they identify themselves?" Fournier asked.

"Yes, sir, but – Well, they say they're from Earth, sir. Twelve freighters of construction supplies and two passenger liners full of construction crews."

"Give them permission, Don. The ships we don't want are the ones that don't ask permission."

"Yes, sir."

"Yes, sir, we're here to help anyway we can," David DeLorme said.

"You're the commander?" Edmond Fournier said.

"I suppose you could say that, sir. I'm a Senior Project Manager in Earth's Major Projects Agency. I manage big construction projects for a living."

"What have you got aboard, Mr. DeLorme?"

"Construction equipment, sir. We have gravel crushers, heavy quarry equipment, dump trucks, bulldozers, cement mixers, cranes both large and small, all that sort of thing. We also brought a hundred million board feet of lumber or so, several thousand containers of structural steel, thousands of containers of cement, rebar, shingling, rivets and rivet guns, nails and nail guns, large stationary generators – pretty much anything you need to build without any local infrastructure, sir. Oh, and four thousand construction crew in the liners. They hot-bunked it on the way here to get them all in."

"That's incredible, Mr. DeLorme. Well, we can sure use you. So do you want to start on one city, or spread your effort across all three at once?"

"Oh, we'll have to start all three at once, sir. To have enough room."

"Enough room?"

"I'm sorry, sir. I should have mentioned. This is just the first shipment."

All the colonies together didn't approach Earth's massive economic output. While simply keeping everyone on Doma alive was for Jablonka a major relief effort, rebuilding Doma's cities was for the Earth a medium-sized remote construction project. Whole fleets full of supplies and personnel continued to arrive, and those supplies and personnel poured into Doma's cities.

Another Regime Change

Richard Mcenroe, His Excellency the Planetary Governor of Bahay, was sitting out on the balcony of the Planetary Governor's Mansion with Michael Jacobus, the head of the Bahay Protective Service, looking out over the Kabisera City Park.

"What do you think, Michael?" Mcenroe asked.

"About the proposed planetary constitution?" Jacobus asked.

"Well, Jim Westlake doesn't call it proposed. He doesn't even say it's recommended. He just calls it an option for member planets that is consistent with the Commonwealth Charter."

"I understand. It still seems a bit heavy-handed to me."

"We can't forget it was Jim Westlake and all the people he recruited to his cause – Georgy Orlov, Gerald Ansen, our own Jane Paxton, and this entire navy he just pulled out of his hat – that freed us from Earth. The amount of money Earth was pulling out of the colonies is staggering. We can cut the tax burden in half and still have more money than we know what to do with. So I'm willing to cut Westlake quite a bit of slack. And we can still come up with something else. It just has to be compatible with the Charter. The civil rights provisions, mostly."

"Of course, it's just – I don't know. I guess I should be grateful. When Earth came down with new stuff it was all mandatory. And now I'm grousing about suggestions."

Mcenroe laughed.

"That's my take. I have a pretty free hand from here, but I think I'm just going to go along with Westlake's suggestion. He's been right all down the line so far, and that's no small thing, considering what he's pulled off."

"What happens to us, then?"

"Bahay still needs a police force, and it still needs a chief of police or whatever we call it. As for me, at the Commonwealth level, I'm a member of the Council for the time being. I could be in the Bahay legislature, or run for the executive or whatever. We've been pretty light-handed here, and I think people will remember that. I'm pretty young to retire, but I could do that, too. Or go into business or something. Lots of choices. And nobody from Earth can tell me I can't."

"So you think you're going to sign the suggested planetary constitution?" Jacobus asked.

"Yes. The transition language in there is such that, as Planetary Governor and Member of the Council, I can sign it and have our other two Council Members sign it, and then it starts the election cycle. You know, I could make a big celebration out of it. We should do that, don't you think?"

"Have a big party?"

"Sure," Mcenroe said. "We do it in the park. I sign the document, Jane Paxton signs the document, whoever the other guy is –"

"Anderson Lail."

"Anderson Lail, that's right. He signs the document, then we have a big party. Constitution Day. I'll even do the beer truck thing Jim Westlake did. You should consider it, too."

"You mean, have the police passing out the beer, like they did in Jablonka?"

"Yeah. Why not? Start a tradition. New beginnings are a good time for new traditions."

Jane Paxton and Anderson Lail both received hand-delivered invitations to dine with Robert Mcenroe that evening. Both told the driver who dropped around with the invitation that they would come. And at the appointed hour, the driver reappeared to pick them up.

Jane Paxton was handed into the rear of the car by the driver. Anderson Lail was already seated in the back. They had not seen each other since they had gotten back from the Westlake Conference nearly six months ago.

"What's this all about, Andy?" Paxton asked.

"I have no idea. I received an invitation to dinner. That's all I know," Lail said.

"Do we get arrested or does he give us a medal?"

"My internal odds maker puts it at fifty-fifty."

Paxton laughed.

A Charter For The Commonwealth

They were shown through the Planetary Governor's Mansion to a large stone patio in the back. From the hill it was on, it looked out over Kabisera City Park. There was a single table there, set with three chairs. Mcenroe was on the patio, smoking a cigarette and looking out over the park. At the noise from the doors, he turned and walked forward to meet his guests.

"Welcome, welcome. Ms. Paxton. Mr. Lail."

They each shook his hand, somewhat in a daze, and mumbled something in return. He laughed and waved them to be seated.

"Would you care for a drink? Or a smoke?"

Paxton and Lail both demurred.

Mcenroe turned to his major domo.

"Thirty minutes, Patrick."

"Yes, sir."

Mcenroe turned to his guests.

"I'm sorry if I've caught you off guard, but I needed to ask you something. Did you both receive copies of Mr. Westlake's suggested planetary constitution?"

"Yes," Paxton said. Lail nodded.

"What do you think of it?"

Paxton and Lail both looked at each other, turned back to Mcenroe.

"OK, maybe it's unfair to put the question that way, open-ended, given the history. Let me put it this way. I am disposed to sign it, and I wondered if either of you knew any reasons why we shouldn't."

Paxton and Lail both had a bit of a stunned look. Paxton shook herself out of it first.

"No, I have no reason not to sign it. I think it would be wonderful."

"I agree," Lail said. "It's built on the work we did on Doma."

The mention of Doma cast a cloud for a moment.

"I want to say that what the Earth did to Doma was a war crime and I hope Arlan Andrews burns in hell," Mcenroe said.

"Really?" Paxton asked.

"Oh, yes. You knew you didn't like Earth policies. You didn't know that I didn't like them, either, but I had no choice but to implement them, as reasonably as I could. Being under Arlan Andrews' thumb the last ten years has not been easy."

That was a new perspective for Paxton, whose world view was undergoing some serious re-alignment.

"Bear in mind that no one in human space was free to make his own decisions for the last ten years except Arlan Andrews. My hands were often tied. And I knew he had spies and operatives here. My life would be forfeit if I didn't do as I was told. What leeway I had, I used, but there was always a danger in pushing too far."

"That is, um, illuminating," Lail said. "I had no idea."

"Yes, well, that's all gone now. We are free to make our own decisions. What I would like to do is to sign the planetary constitution, without changes, for Bahay. This weekend. Saturday at noon. Right out there."

Mcenroe waved out at the park.

"Then we can all have a big party."

Mcenroe looked back and forth between them.

"What do you think?"

Saturday was a beautiful spring day in the Kabisera City Park. There was a stage set up under an awning at one end of the long main lawn. Large video displays framed the stage, and were replicated at intervals down either side of the lawn. The crowd started to gather at 10:00, and by noon at least ten thousand people were present.

Anderson Lail started with a short speech about the Charter and the civil rights it granted. Robert Mcenroe followed with a short speech about the future of Bahay. Finally, Jane Paxton gave the short version of the sort of stemwinder she was famous for.

When Paxton sat back down at the table, on the other side of Mcenroe from Lail, Michael Jacobus brought out a large document and set it in front of Mcenroe. The video zoomed up to show Mcenroe sign the document with a flourish. The document was moved over, and Lail countersigned, and then it was moved to Paxton, and she countersigned. When Paxton signed the document, a cheer went up from the crowd.

Mcenroe, Lail, and Paxton all stood and shook hands.

Jacobus went up to the microphone.

"Happy Constitution Day, everybody. In the dozen booths you see on each side of the lawn, the Bahay Protective Service is now serving free beer. Let's party!"

Yet Another Regime Change

On Kodu, His Excellency Daniel Sparks, the Planetary Governor, had other ideas. He was also talking to the head of his police force, Mark Hunter.

"What gives Westlake the right to turn everything topsy-turvy like this? He's got his own damned planet, he can do with it as he wishes, but he should leave me and my planet alone," Sparks said.

"He thinks he's the head of all the planets now, the ones that matter. He's the Chairman of the Commonwealth Council," Hunter said.

"Just words. He's not here, and I am."

"Are you forgetting about the two Commonwealth battleships in orbit?"

"No, I'm not forgetting. They don't belong here. I never signed up for this Commonwealth nonsense." Sparks stalked back in the other direction. "Do you think I can order them out of the system?"

"You can try, but I don't think they're going to leave. And with them holding the orbitals, there's nothing I can do about them."

"What are they going to do? Bomb the planet? I don't think so. You saw what the uproar was over the Doma thing. I think they had it coming, personally. But there's no way they're going to bomb the planet."

"Are you forgetting what happened to your father-in-law?" Hunter asked.

"That was a damned shame. Murdered him, right in his own home. He understood what we were trying to do out here. I always liked him. Never any of this namby-pamby stuff. Not like Fournier and his crew."

"Well, Fournier and his crew are back in charge on Earth. Even if the Commonwealth didn't exist, we'd be under that bunch again."

"Yes, I know. And they gave me no end of grief last time about the simple measures that were necessary to maintain order." Sparks stalked back across his office. "Shit. What am I supposed to do now?"

"I don't know. I will tell you all the Commonwealth news has really got people riled up. And the news that Bahay and a bunch of the other planets have adopted the new planetary constitution has made it even worse. I'm going to have trouble keeping the lid on if this keeps heating up."

"No, you won't. We'll do whatever we have to do to keep order."

"And those battleships in orbit?" Hunter asked.

"They're all show. They're not going to do anything."

Aboard the CSS *Intolerant*, Captain James Scorse was reviewing his options. *Intolerant* and *Adamant* were here to protect Commonwealth citizens' rights under the Charter, but his options were all pretty big sticks.

"Russ, do we have any of the dummy rounds for the directed aerial munitions?" Scorse asked Commander Russell Sellick, his executive officer.

"The practice rounds, Sir?"

"Yes."

"Yes, Sir, we've got 'em. Thinking about a little demonstration?"

Scorse sighed. "I may have to. If Dan Sparks has two functioning brain cells, I think he must have them under lock and key to keep from wearing them out."

Sellick chuckled. "He does seem just a might thick on this one, Sir."

"We are monitoring their police communications in the capital, in Linn, are we not?"

"Yes, Sir. And recording."

"Good. If this starts to get out of hand, I want to know about it soon enough to do something about it."

"Sir, I think we have a situation developing in Linn," Sellick said. "There is a pro-constitution movement calling for a rally in the city park on Saturday afternoon, and Sparks has declared the rally illegal. He says they will do whatever they need to do to keep the park clear of protesters. And police superintendent Mark Hunter has rescinded all leave and days off for Saturday. He'll have one hundred percent of his police force on duty that day."

"Dammit. Just when I thought this might not boil over," Captain Scorse said. "I'm going to need to talk to Sparks. He can't make a rally illegal. That's black-and-white against the Charter."

"What if he doesn't take your call, Sir?"

"I'll think of something."

"Sir, Captain Scorse of the CSS *Intolerant* wants to talk to you," said Mike Piskos, Planetary Governor Sparks' chief of staff.

"Tell him to go fuck himself. And get his goddamn ships out of my system."

"Yes, sir."

"Captain, I have a response from Planetary Governor Sparks. He says to, um, perform a biologically impossible autoerotic act and also to get your ships out of his system," Lieutenant Jason Weiser said from his comm console.

"Tell him to look out his office window. Ms. Modesitt, you may launch when ready."

"We're in the cone, Captain. Launching. Munition away," Lieutenant Lori Modesitt said from her gunnery console.

"Uh, sir? Captain Scorse said to look out your office window," Piskos said.

"What the hell is he talking about?"

Sparks walked over to the windows. There was a two-thousand-acre park behind the Planetary Governor's Mansion, three square miles that was walled off from the city, for his use alone. Down the slope from him was a twenty-acre pond, shaped like a dogbone, with a Japanese-style arched concrete bridge across the narrow portion, joining the formal gardens on this side to the less formal meadows and woodlands on the other.

As he looked out the window, a dummy munition from *Intolerant* hit the bridge square in the center, passing right through the deck, shattering the bridge, and raising a geyser of water. The remains of the bridge collapsed into the hole as much of the water in the pond was pushed out in two great waves that rushed over its banks at either end.

"Shit!" Sparks said as he jumped back from the windows. "Is this guy a fucking maniac?"

"Sir, Captain Scorse wonders if you would like to speak to him now," Piskos said.

"You're goddamn right I wanna speak to him."

"Putting you through, sir."

"What the hell is your problem, Scorse? You just bombed a populated area in a major city."

"I put a dummy round into an empty area to get your attention, Mr. Sparks. You are not allowed to ban or disrupt a peaceful rally under the civil rights clauses of the Charter."

"What are you gonna do about it, Scorse? Bomb the cops? They'll be in close, clearing out illegal protesters. You can't use any of your weapons there. You'll kill thousands."

"No, Mr. Sparks. I won't bomb people carrying out illegal orders. I'll bomb the person who gave them. If you persist, I'll put one into your office, and it'll be a twenty-ton nuke."

"You're bluffing."

"Mr. Sparks, please listen carefully. It's very important that you understand this. I have five hundred crew on these two warships who all swore a personal oath to preserve, protect, and defend the Charter of the Commonwealth of Free Planets, as did I. That includes its civil rights clauses. We will do whatever we need to do to stop you from violating those rights. Anything whatsoever."

"I don't believe you. There's no way Westlake gave you those orders. You're way outside your authority."

"Mr. Sparks, consider the math. The Commonwealth has seventy battleships and thirty-three planets. That means, were there two battleships deployed to every planet, there would only be four battleships remaining for all patrols, repairs, refitting – for every other purpose.

"The obvious conclusion is there are not two battleships deployed to every Commonwealth planet. But there are two deployed here, and that's because Mr. Westlake anticipated your reluctance to honor and protect the civil rights every Commonwealth citizen enjoys under the Charter.

"I can assure you, Mr. Sparks, I am well within the orders Mr. Westlake issued to *Intolerant* and *Adamant*, and which I discussed with him personally before leaving on this assignment. I guess he's willing to treat your life and your civil rights with the same casual disdain with which you treat everyone else's.

A Charter For The Commonwealth

"But know this for a fact: If you attempt to suppress the civil rights of the Commonwealth citizens on Kodu, I will use whatever means, up to and including the use of deadly force against you personally, to stop you."

The air went out of Sparks as he listened to Scorse's little speech. He had more than a little experience judging people's personalities, and Scorse was a straight arrow, the sort of person who would never be able to lie very well, and Sparks knew he wasn't lying now. Scorse also came across to Sparks as the sort of person who kept his promises.

All of which meant he was well and truly screwed. If he couldn't suppress the demonstrations, they would grow until it was impossible to keep them from overturning his regime. And then his life would be forfeit to the crowd. But if he attempted to suppress the demonstrations, Scorse would do the job for them.

"What am I to do, Captain? If I cannot take the measures I think are necessary to keep order on the planet, I cannot even guarantee my own safety or that of my administrators. Would you leave us to the mob?"

"No, Mr. Sparks, I would not leave you unprotected or at risk. I have been authorized to offer you, your administrators, and your families, should you decide to step down and return to Earth, amnesty and free passage home."

Sparks considered, and Scorse noted his hesitation.

"You've had a long run here, Excellency, and done well for yourself and your family. Maybe it's time now to pursue other opportunities for the future. I would be happy to arrange safe and comfortable transportation."

Kodu was a major business hub. Passenger traffic was still down due to the uncertainties associated with the War Of Independence, and the local office of a passenger carrier was more than happy to book a first-class charter from Kodu to Earth.

Scorse arranged the evacuation of the planetary governor, his associates like Piskos and Hunter, and all their families to the passenger ship. When they departed for Earth, he was more than a little relieved.

On the chance such a thing could be arranged, administrators from

Jablonka had been brought along on the *Intolerant* and *Adamant*, including a senior police captain looking for a career move. They transferred down to the planet and began to clean up the mess.

The demonstration in the park on Saturday came just as the news hit the newsfeeds that His Excellency Daniel Sparks, Planetary Governor of Kodu, had resigned. When Commander Sellick of the *Intolerant* announced to the crowd that Sparks had also signed the planetary constitution for Kodu on his way out – as a condition of his passage, though Sellick didn't mention that – and Kodu's other two members of the Commonwealth Council, safely on Jablonka, had already countersigned it, the planned angry demonstration became a jubilant party. The newly christened Kodu Protective Service served free beer.

After the bridge and the pond were repaired, the two-thousand-acre gardens behind the Planetary Governor's Mansion were named Liberty Park and opened to the public.

Building the Future

Defense Minister Georgy Orlov and Admiral Jarl Sigurdsen were giving Council Chairman James Westlake a tour of the building site for the Jablonka Fleet Base of the Commonwealth Space Force. They were standing on a small foothill at the south end of the large construction site. Across the site they could see Jezgra in the distance beyond.

"This is impressive," Westlake said. "I really like the space, the layout, everything."

"Thank you, sir," Sigurdsen said. "We spent quite a bit of time on trying to get it right."

"It shows. It's marvelous," Westlake said.

Westlake turned around. Behind him, three large houses were being built.

"And these?"

"Houses for the three commanders: the Chief of Naval Research, the Chief of Naval Operations, and the Jablonka Planetary Commander," Orlov said, pointing to them one at a time. "They look out over the base. They're built for entertaining VIP guests. And with the house staff and all, they take all the burden off the top commanders so they can go home and really relax. Not be bothered with the trivia of running a household or any of that."

"Great idea. I like it."

"I copied it from West Point, the old United States Military Academy on Earth. It's a military museum now. We were there on a field trip from school once, remember? Same setup, looking out over the parade ground. I always thought it was a good idea."

Westlake nodded, turned back toward the much larger construction projects on the plain.

"The thing about the construction is we actually had to lay out the organization of the CSF before we could plan the buildings. The construction actually mirrors the structure of the organization," Orlov said.

"And that over there?" Westlake pointed to a large construction project well off to one side, separated from the rest of the site.

"Jablonka Military Hospital. Military people get wounds and illnesses civilian doctors may never see. We want our own hospital facilities to make sure those issues get the proper attention."

Westlake nodded and turned his attention back to the main site.

"This is perfect. I know you've been saying you were happy with the plans, and you were making good progress, but this is amazing. You're both to be congratulated."

Westlake turned and shook the hands of Orlov and Sigurdsen in turn.

"Thank you, sir."

Construction Project Manager Ann Lowenstein was showing Westlake and Orlov around the construction site for Commonwealth Center, the seat of government for the Commonwealth. Much like with Jablonka Fleet Base, Commonwealth Center reflected the structure of the organization it was intended to house.

"Off to the west side there, sir, is the Chairman's Residence, on that hill on the coast. Its rear side faces out to the beach and the sea beyond. You can see it's in a private setting of woods and meadows, a couple of hundred acres.

"There's a tunnel running east below the grounds, connecting the Residence to the executive office building there. That high-rise tower will hold the Chairman's Office and the Cabinet offices and their staffs. Continuing east, that low, domed structure holds the Council Chambers, and east of the Council Chambers is a matching high-rise tower for the Council's offices and staff.

"North of the Council Chambers, that high-rise tower contains one hundred and fifty suites for the Council when in session and any VIP guests. There are four possible views: north up the wild coastline, east to the mountains, south overlooking the city, and west looking out to sea. Each suite has two of those views.

"And there's plenty of room left on the site for expanding the executive offices with another tower north of that one, or for expanding the Council offices with another tower north of that one."

"It's a nice plan, well thought out and with room for the future. And your progress is breathtaking, Ms. Lowenstein."

"Thank you, sir. It's an aggressive schedule, but we're actually managing to hold on to it with our fingernails. There's a couple places we may even be ahead of the game."

"We won't keep you any longer, Ms. Lowenstein. Thank you for your time."

"No problem, sir. Oh, and ask Mrs. Westlake for me. What color does she want the master bedroom?"

Lowenstein winked and Westlake laughed. All the interior design was complete already.

Westlake and Orlov waved goodbye and got back in the ground car for the trip across Government Park, past the planetary government offices, to the Commonwealth government's temporary quarters in the Jezgra Gardens Hotel downtown.

"I still liked your old office better," Orlov said.

"Of course. But it wouldn't be fair not to let the planetary government into their own offices. We're the new guys, after all," Westlake said.

"Oh, I know, I know."

"And the view from here isn't bad."

Westlake had taken the whole top floor for his residence and office. The interconnected set of suites worked well for that, and the security, with a private elevator stop and elevator lobby, worked well for his purposes. It even worked out for the family. The kids were fifteen and seventeen now and thought being downtown was more exciting.

"True, true. Even so, I'll be happy when we move. When is that again?"

"Two more years, if Ms. Lowenstein keeps to the schedule," Westlake said with exaggerated patience. "It's been four years since the signing of the Charter, and three and a half years since the treaty with Earth."

"Time flies, I guess. And I have no doubt Ms. Lowenstein will keep to schedule. I know I wouldn't want to cross her."

"I don't think I would, either, to be honest."

There was a polite knock on the door, and Westlake's long-time retainer entered.

"Excuse me, sir. I thought you would like to know. The *Starcruiser* has made hyperspace transition and announced their arrival from

Doma. Your niece and her husband are aboard."

"Claudette and Fernando?"

"Yes, sir."

"Do we know their arrival time?"

"Saturday afternoon, sir."

"Excellent. Let Suzette know, if you would, Henson. Oh, and would you make sure a guest suite is available for them?"

"Of course, sir."

The butler left, and Westlake turned back to Orlov.

"An unannounced visit from our mutual niece. That's unusual."

"That sounds like a mission, not a visit. I wonder what's up."

"Time will tell."

A Request From Doma

"Hi, Uncle Jim, Aunt Suzette," Claudette Sandoval nee Fournier said as she was shown into the living room of the Westlakes' suite on the penthouse floor of the Commonwealth government headquarters.

She gave them both a hug.

"I want to introduce my husband, Fernando Sandoval."

"Pleased to meet you, sir. Ma'am."

"We're sorry we couldn't make your wedding, dear," Suzette said.

"At interstellar distances? Don't be silly."

Westlake recalled she had brought Sandoval – from another wealthy Earth family typically on the Fournier side of things – back to Doma with her when she finished university. That would have been, what, three years ago now? She had not been present for the bombing of Doma. She was twenty-four, he thought. Yes, that's right. Edmond was seven years older than Suzette, and he and Suzette were a bit older when they had children.

"Yes, but you came here over interstellar distances, and that raises curiosity," Westlake said.

"Uncle Jim, we need to talk. We hoped we could get you and Uncle Georgy together in the same place for a while."

"Georgy and Shufen are coming for dinner. We should have plenty of time."

As a family tradition, no business was discussed over family dinner. After dinner, everyone retired to the living room with after-dinner drinks. Suzette even forgave Westlake the occasional cigar at such times, especially if he sat in the chair below the ventilation system inlet. Georgy smiled as Westlake made a beeline for that chair, and Suzette sighed, as everyone headed into the living room.

"So what's this all about then, Claudette? Not that we don't enjoy your visit, mind you, but something's up," Westlake said once he had his cigar going.

"Doma wants to disappear."

"Disappear?" Orlov asked. "The planet? The whole system? That would be quite a trick."

"No, we're serious. We want to disappear. We came to ask you to write us out of your history. Say Earth destroyed the whole planet, and that was it. Gone."

"Earth has to be part of such a scheme, too, if it has any hope of working."

"Francois went to see Grandfather."

That made a difference. Francois was two years older than Claudette, and was Claude Fournier's oldest grandchild. He had also gone to university on Earth, and he had had quite a bit of contact with his grandfather. They got along tremendously well. It was a smart move to let him handle the Earth side of this request.

"That's a remarkable request," Orlov said.

"No, it's not. You didn't see it. You think you know, but you can't. My Nadezhda – my beautiful Nadezhda that I left behind to go to university. When I returned it was five hundred square miles of ash and debris. From the city center, you couldn't even see anything else. It was bleak and barren and lifeless all the way to the horizon, everywhere you looked. Nothing grew. Nothing stood. It was a scene straight out of hell. My Nadezhda!"

Claudette was in tears now.

"And we don't want it to happen again."

"It won't happen again," Westlake said quietly.

"Are you sure, Uncle? Are you absolutely sure? That when one of Andrews' assholes takes over on Earth next time, they won't do something like it again? Because we're not. And we don't want to take that chance."

There was silence for a moment, then Westlake turned to Orlov.

"What do you think, Georgy? Can we pull it off?"

"Earth might be able to say Doma was totally destroyed. Doma's in Commonwealth territory, a hundred and thirty light-years from Earth. It's not like they're just going to go spacing by one day. But it's less than seventy light-years from here, and closer still to several other Commonwealth planets. The problem with the Commonwealth saying it was completely destroyed is it's not that hard for somebody to go check."

"We have to do something!" Claudette said.

Orlov had a sudden thought.

A Charter For The Commonwealth

"You know, it might be easier to say Doma never existed at all."

"But people know it existed, Georgy. It's in all the records."

"Digital records?" Orlov snapped his fingers. "Oops. Gone."

"I can't do that, Georgy. The only time I could do something like that is if it's a military secrecy requirement."

Orlov was nodding his head. "Exactly right."

"So tell me how this is a military secrecy requirement."

"You know Admiral Sigurdsen has all the technical people we cajoled away from retirement – or from Earth – working on new keel-out warship designs?"

"Yes, of course."

"And you know we are going to have to have a major shipyard to build them all?"

"Yes."

"And you know how much I've been worried about where we put that shipyard because of secrecy concerns?"

"Yes. And if we put it on Doma, you're saying I have an excuse to hide the whole planet."

"Exactly."

"But people have been there, Georgy. Lots of people. People have relatives there."

"What percent have been there do you think, Jim? Of the whole Commonwealth population? I don't think it's one percent. I don't think it's even close to one percent. Interstellar travel is too expensive. And those who have relatives there are even fewer."

"But if Earth says they destroyed it –"

"Lies. We cleaned their clocks in three head-to-head space battles. They're just trying to claim some sort of victory."

"But *we* said Earth bombed it."

"Are you sure, Jim? Check those digital records. Oops."

"But people will remember we said it."

"War-time propaganda. To get people mad at Earth and supporting the Commonwealth. Besides, if you think it really existed, where is it, eh? Look up the coordinates, right? In digital records? Oops."

"The archives people will have a fit."

"Buy them off. They're underpaid. Fire the ones who complain. Better yet, ship them to Doma. Really nice place, I've heard. And they'll need archivists, too, I imagine."

"Somebody who's been there is going to go to the newsfeeds with it. It'll be a big conspiracy."

"Conspiracy theories are great. Nobody believes them but crazies. You can hide anything in a conspiracy theory. As for the legitimate news organizations, ask them not to cover it. Military secrecy. Dammit, Jim, we need that shipyard. And this is perfect."

"What about Doma, though? Claudette, will people on Doma sign up to be the Commonwealth's naval shipyards?"

"As long as we can remain hidden. And that will give us foreign trade, which was one issue we were worried about. Some things are just easier to buy."

Westlake sat and smoked his cigar, staring across the room, eyes unfocused. Claudette was going to say something, but Georgy lifted one hand on the arm of his chair, and she subsided.

"What about the treaty with Earth, Georgy? It specifies thirty-three planets."

"Not if you and Claude Fournier both agree it doesn't. Sign a new one, pitch the old one."

"Do you think Claude will go along on his end?"

"Are you kidding? Claude is going to love this. He can say Arlan Andrews' faction destroyed an entire planet, in a huge war crime, because that's just the kind of bastards they are. They've sullied Earth's reputation in history forever. He'll keep them out of control for thirty years."

Westlake nodded, sat a while longer.

"What about the Charter, Georgy? The Doma representatives signed the Charter."

"When did you last look at the actual Charter, Jim?"

The Yards

Fernando and Claudette Sandoval stayed on Jablonka several months, which allowed several cycles of mail between and among Jablonka, Doma, and Earth. The night before they were to leave, the three couples once again had dinner together. Once again, business waited until after dinner.

"We've certainly enjoyed your visit, Claudette. Fernando. We'll miss you," Westlake said.

"We'll miss you, too, Uncle. All of you," Claudette said. "And we really appreciate your help in carrying out our mission to hide Doma."

"It will disappear into the mists of history. By the time your grandfather loses control on Earth, it will be gone. You will be safe."

"Will it really work, though? Can it work?" Suzette asked.

"I think so," Orlov said. "Earth has removed the mail relays from Doma, so it's cut off from the general mail system. Anything sent to Doma will get a 'no such address' response. We'll put in a dedicated link for military use only.

"Earth has also pulled all their people out of the reconstruction project, which is so far along at this point your people are the main drivers anyway. You two are going back with a trio of understaffed battleships, two of which will remain on Doma for any travel back and forth. Some of their crews have volunteered to move to Doma, so they will be the core of the crews for those ships. No ships from here will ever make the trip again."

"A lot of our ship engineering and construction people will be making the trip with you," Westlake said. "Most of them couldn't afford to retire to Doma before. Now they'll move there, help you build the shipbuilding industry, and then retire there.

"What about the names? Is that decided?"

"Yes, we're going to call the planet The Yards, as Uncle Georgy suggested," Claudette said.

"'Where did that ship come from?' 'From the yards.' 'Where's that?' 'It's a secret,'" Orlov said. "It's perfect."

"And more to the point for me, 'What's this large defense

expenditure?' 'It's for the yards.' I agree. It's perfect," Westlake said. "What about the cities?"

"We're renaming them as well. In case anyone trips over us, so we won't be associated with Doma. Nadezhda, Vera, and Istina will become Phoenix, Athens, and Carthage."

"The Phoenix rose from its own ashes. Poetic," Westlake said.

"You want us to do what?" Senior Archivist John Nicoli asked.

"Edit the archives to remove all references to Doma," Westlake said.

"Edit the archives? Are you serious?"

"Yes. I want all references removed. If Doma is the subject of the article, remove the whole article. If Doma appears in a list of planets, remove Doma from the list."

"But I can't do that."

"You don't have a way to fix errors in the archive? Corrupted files and the like?"

"Yes, of course. But –"

"Mention of Doma is a corruption of the archives. It doesn't exist and never did. Fix them."

"They will still exist in other archives, though."

"No, I want you to propagate the fix through the mail system."

"That will work in the Commonwealth, but Earth doesn't accept propagated fixes from outside."

"The Earth archives are being handled separately."

"You're really serious."

"Yes. I already said that."

"But you don't have the authority to order that under the Charter."

"Yes, I do. It's the one exception. Military necessity, as long as it's confirmed by the Council in private session, as it has been. Check with your attorneys if you want. And then do it."

Westlake met with Ann Lowenstein at her project headquarters, a temporary building on the construction site of Commonwealth Center.

"It's a change order, I'm afraid," Westlake said.

Lowenstein rolled her eyes.

"I know, I know. But we've been pretty good about limiting change orders. And this one is a requirement we didn't know about before."

"All right. What is it?"

"Ninety-six desks in the Council Chamber, not ninety-nine."

"Oh, thank God. For a minute there, I thought it was going to be something big."

"So, no problem?"

"No problem at all. I think it'll probably be easier. Ninety-nine is a bugger of a number. All odd factors. Makes it hard to lay out. Ninety-six will be easier."

"Let's see it," Westlake said.

The curator of the University of Jablonka Museum, Yvonne Jacobs, opened the cabinet and brought out the glass case containing the original Charter of the Commonwealth. She set it on the table in the center of the room. Ultimately it would be hung in the Council Chamber above and behind the Chairman's desk on the dais, but it was being kept here in the meantime.

Westlake looked at the document critically. The text was printed in small type so it would all fit on one large sheet. There at the bottom were the signatures, arranged in eight columns of eight signatures each, with 'For Doma' and the signatures of the Doma representatives centered below the rest on the bottom. Arranging sixty-four signatures in a straightforward way was easy. The extra two had been centered on the bottom, and those of Doma had been picked for that treatment because they were the host planet.

"I want you to cut it off right above 'For Doma', straight across."

Jacobs gasped. "But you can't. This is an heirloom."

"It's four years old. It's not an heirloom yet."

"But, but you *can't*."

"You don't understand. I have to."

Jacobs looked at the treasured document in its case, and her eyes were bright with unshed tears.

"It won't match the case. It'll be at least two inches short."

"Professor Ansen was never good with dimensions. Do it. Or I'll do it with a scissors."

Jacobs shuddered.

"Yes, sir. I'll do it. But I'll have nightmares about it."

"One more change order," Westlake said.

"Oh, God. Now what," Lowenstein said.

"In the center of the circular drive in front of the Council Center, we want to put up a monument to the signing of the Charter. Right in the center."

"In the center of that circular lawn there? No problem. I just need the design spec for the footings, so it'll fit your monument. Otherwise it'll settle funny."

"I'll get that to you."

Fifteen Years On

They were sitting out on the patio behind the Commonwealth Chairman's residence, looking out over the beach to the Voda Ocean, smoking cigars. The Earth-import cigars, without all the extra duties and taxes, had become much less expensive as trade with the Earth had actually doubled from its level before the Commonwealth.

"Happy anniversary. Again," Orlov said.

"Which one? Thirty-three years since coming to Jablonka, or nineteen years since the signing of the Charter, or twelve years since moving the government into Commonwealth Center?"

"All the above, I guess. They all turned out. Our plans."

"Yes, they did. They truly did. Amazingly enough."

Westlake and Orlov had been planning the independence of the colonies for decades, first as a lark in school, then in earnest when Westlake was posted to Jablonka by his father, joining Orlov in Jezgra. And, unbelievably, they had pulled it off.

"That was a nice gesture, renaming Jablonka Fleet Base."

"He deserved it. He planned and built the original Navy. Won the battle of Earth and secured the treaty. Spent fifteen years as Chief of Naval Operations. Built up the CSF and gave it the sort of traditions and culture that will carry it into the future. We owed him a lot."

"Sigurdsen Fleet Base. Has a nice ring to it."

"Sigurdsen Military Hospital, too.

"Also has a nice ring to it," Orlov said with a smile.

"And the new Navy he designed has been coming out of The Yards for five years now. I'm glad he was alive to see it."

"And all beam weapons. No more of those rock-throwing mines."

"Admiral Sigurdsen said the battles with the Earth ships proved the inefficacy of any weapon that wasn't speed-of-light. Waste of money, according to him."

"I miss him," Orlov said. "What's it been now. Couple years?"

"Yes. He didn't last two years once he retired. I think building the CSF kept him going."

"There's a lesson for you. Never retire. It's bad for your health."

"Well, he was almost ninety years old."

"Yeah, he had a good run."

The sun was angling down toward what promised to be a beautiful sunset. It was a beautiful day, at a beautiful spot.

"Oh, I meant to tell you," Westlake said. "I ran into Mineko Kusunoki at the rededication ceremony at the base. She's finally given me permission to put a statue of Ansen on the monument to the signing of the Charter in front of the Council Chamber."

"She finally gave in?"

"Well, I had given up on it. But she stepped down from the Council two years ago – the Jablonka planetary government would have let her serve as long as she wanted – and she's OK with it now."

"She probably just didn't want to look at it all the time, going to Council."

"That may be it. Anyway, she gave her permission. And we're agreed on the pose for the sculptor."

"That's good. A nation needs its heroes."

A Charter For The Commonwealth

Appendix

Inhabited systems (capital city)

Earth (New York City)

Members of the Commonwealth of Free Planets:
Anders
Bahay (Kabisera)
Bliss
Boomgaard
Calumet
Courtney
Hutan
Jablonka (Jezgra)
Kodu (Linn)
Meili
Mountainhome
Natchez
Pahaadon
Parchman
Saarestik
Shaanti
The Yards [Doma] (Phoenix [Nadezhda])
Valore
Waldheim

A Charter For The Commonwealth

Some of the Drafters and Signers of the Charter of the Commonwealth of Free Planets

Gerald Ansen - Jablonka

Roman Chrzanowski - Saarestik

Jacques Cotillard - Valore

Willard Dempsey - Mountainhome

Nils Isacsson - Boomgaard

Ikaika Kalani - Hutan

Aluna Kamau - Courtney

Manfred Koch - Waldheim

Mineko Kusunoki - Jablonka

Anderson Lail - Bahay

Donal McNee - Bliss

Patryk Mazur - Kodu

Sania Mehta - Calumet

Hu Mingli - Meili

Matheus Oliveira - Calumet

Jane Paxton - Bahay

Guadalupe Rivera - Parchman

Notes on Navigational Notation

The Commonwealth Space Force uses the following standards with respect to navigational bearings and distances.

Navigational bearing and distance are specified as:

rotation mark/minus elevation (on point) (at distance)

All such references are with respect to a point, a baseline, and a plane.

- If no point is specified, the point is the ship, the baseline is the long axis of the ship projected through the bows, and the plane is defined by the plane of the ship with the command cylinder(s) considered to be 'up'.

- If another ship is specified as the point, such as 'on the enemy', the point is the enemy ship, the baseline is the vector of the enemy ship's velocity, and the plane is the plane of the ecliptic.

- If a planet is specified as the point, the point is the planet, the baseline is a line from the planet to the sun, and the plane is the plane of the ecliptic.

- If a sun is specified as the point, the point is the sun, the baseline is a line from the sun to the primary inhabited planet, and the plane is the ecliptic.

- If the galactic center is specified as the point, the point is the galactic center, the line is the line from the galactic center to the ship, and the plane is the plane of the galactic lens.

Bearing angles are always specified as 'number-number-number'. Designations such as 'ninety-three' and 'one-eighty' are not permitted. These are correctly specified as 'zero-nine-three' and 'one-eight-zero'.

A Charter For The Commonwealth

An exception occurs for 'zero-zero-zero', which may be stated simply as 'zero', such as in 'zero mark zero' or 'zero mark one-eight-zero'.

These rules were standardized by the CSF after the War Of Independence. Prior to that time, the less formal designations were often used.

rotation is specified as 'number-number-number' in degrees clockwise from the projection of the baseline onto the plane when viewed from above. Leading zeroes are included, not dropped. number-number-number runs from zero-zero-zero to three-six-zero.

- If the point is the ship, 'above' means from above the ship with the command cylinder(s) considered to be 'up'.

- If the point is an enemy ship, a planet, or the sun, 'above' means from the north side of the solar system as determined by the right-hand rule: with the fingers of the right hand in the direction of orbit of the planets, the thumb points north.

- If the point is the galactic center, 'above' means from the north side of the galaxy, as determined by the right hand rule applied to the rotation of the stars about the galactic center.

elevation is specified as 'mark/minus number-number-number' in degrees up/down from the plane. 'mark' is used for bearings above the plane, and 'minus' is used for bearings below the plane. 'Above' is defined as for rotation. Leading zeroes are included, not dropped. number-number-number runs from zero-zero-zero to one-eight-zero.

distance is specified in light-units, most frequently in light-seconds.

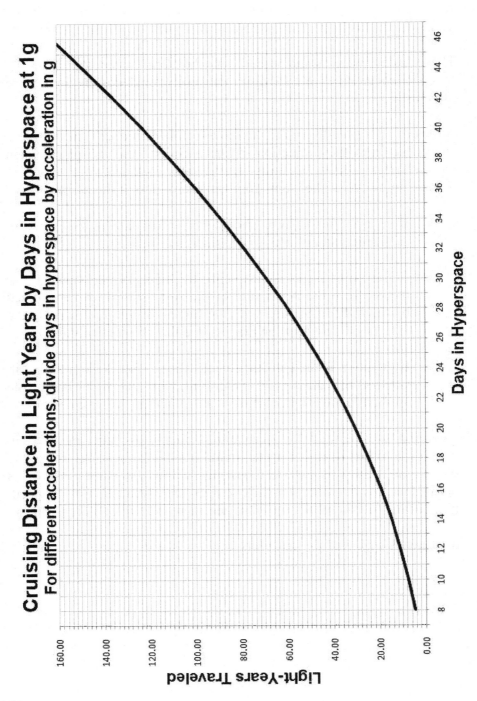

Cruising Distance in Light Years by Days in Hyperspace at 1g
For different accelerations, divide days in hyperspace by acceleration in g

Days in Hyperspace

Light-Years Traveled

Acronyms and Terms

AAR – After Action Report.

below decks – cylinders on a ship containing enlisted quarters and mechanical areas such as propulsion, weapons control, etc.

bogey – an unidentified contact, such as on radar.

bulkhead – wall on a spaceship.

CFP – Commonwealth of Free Planets.

CNO – Chief of Naval Operations.

Commonwealth – Commonwealth of Free Planets.

CPS – ship prefix, Commonwealth Passenger Ship.

CSF – Commonwealth Space Force.

CSS – ship prefix, Commonwealth Space Ship.

deadhead – make a trip aboard ship while not serving; guest; ferry.

deck – floor in a spaceship.

deckhead – ceiling in a spaceship, with a room directly above.

division – half of a squadron; in CSF, four ships.

door – physical closure on a doorway; may not be airtight.

doorway – opening in a bulkhead.

ENS – ship prefix, Earth Navy Ship.

ESN – Earth Space Navy.

EVA – Extra-Vehicular Activity. Working outside the ship, in space.

Exam – Citizenship Exam of the Commonwealth of Free Planets.

g – one gravity, the amount of gravity one feels on Earth.

Goat Locker – Chief's Mess on a ship.

hatch – airtight cover on a hatchway in a deckhead or overhead.

hatchway – opening in a deckhead or overhead, with a hatch.

HQ – Headquarters.

IS – interstellar.

ladderway – opening in a deckhead or overhead, without a hatch.

light-second – distance light travels in one second; 186,282 miles.

light-year – distance light travels in one year; 5.88 trillion miles.

low-g – low gravity; gravity under 0.2 g.

MP – Military Police.

OGS – ship prefix, Orlov Group Ship.

overhead – ceiling in a spaceship, without a room directly above.

PhD – Doctor of Philosophy; the most advanced degree in a field.

R&R – Rest and Recuperation.

section – half of a division; in CSF, two ships.

squadron – group of ships under one command; in CSF, eight ships.

system periphery – published boundary inside which hyperspace cruise and transition are dangerous to the ship.

topside – cylinder(s) on a ship containing officer's quarters and command & control areas like the bridge, CIC, etc.

UJ – University of Jablonka.

XO – Executive Officer, First Officer.

zero-g – completely weightless; in free fall.

Made in the USA
Middletown, DE
21 December 2021

56839933R00146